IN NEED OF CLOSURE

P.F. FORD

Cover design by Bespoke Book Covers

For Suzanne

CHAPTER 1

'RIGHT THEN, FLUTTER.' The prison officer pointed to the paperwork. 'Just sign here and then you can be on your way.'

The man called Flutter signed his name, and the officer slid an envelope across the counter.

'These are your train tickets. Make sure you go straight to Paddington and make sure you catch the right train. We'll know if you don't.'

'Yeah, yeah, yeah,' said Flutter, impatiently.

'It's all part of the release conditions,' said the officer patiently.

'Don't worry, mate, I'll get there,' said Flutter.

'You'd better make sure you do. Come on, let's go.'

Flutter picked up his rucksack and followed the prison officer down the corridor to the gate. As he unlocked the gate, the officer spoke over his shoulder.

'And make sure you don't come back.'

'No chance,' said Flutter. 'I should never have been sent here in the first place. I didn't do it, you know.'

The officer grinned ruefully and shook his head as he walked.

'Of course, you didn't do it, Flutter, that's why you were found guilty.'

'They set me up. Even the judge could see it, that's why I only got twelve months.'

'Is that right? Well, perhaps you should be more careful about the company you keep.'

'Don't worry, I've learnt my lesson. I'm making a new start.'

The prison officer raised an eyebrow.

'Making a new start doing what?'

'Keeping my nose clean, of course.'

'You think it's going to be that easy do you?'

'What's that supposed to mean? Don't you want me to go straight?'

'Of course, I want you to go straight, but it's not that easy or everyone would do it, wouldn't they? Trust me, I've seen it hundreds of times. Unless you've got a plan with some sort of purpose in your life, you'll drift straight back into your old life.'

'Not me, mate. From now on, I'll be keeping my nose clean.'

The prison officer offered another wry smile.

'If I had a pound for every man whose told me that, I would have retired years ago. People like you never learn, and you never change. Trust me, if you haven't got a plan and a purpose, I'll give you six months at best, and then you'll be back here. You mark my words.'

Flutter looked at the prison officer with something bordering on amusement.

'You'll miss me, you know.'

'Sure, I will,' said the officer sarcastically. 'Because I need people like you in my life, just like I need herpes. Now, go on, be on your way.'

He opened the pedestrian gate, and Flutter took a pace forward. He looked nervously out at the world before finally stepping through into daylight and freedom. The door slammed closed behind him, and he walked forward a few paces, then turned and looked back at the huge gate and the massive walls. The old Victorian building looked tired, and he stopped for a second as he searched his mind for the right word. Then a smile creased his face.

'Jaded, yeah, that's the word. And I know exactly how you feel,' he muttered to the dirty grey building.

After spending a year in this Godforsaken place, all he wanted to do now was get away as fast as he could. He turned, lifted the rucksack onto his shoulder and began to walk away, all the time looking left and right.

He had been warned inside that people would be waiting for him when he came out. He had no idea if this was a genuine threat, or if someone had started a rumour to try and scare him but, either way, Flutter had decided he was taking no chances.

As he reached the road, he looked to his left and right. A man seemed to glance his way as he disappeared into a small shop about fifty yards off to his left, but apart from this, no one seemed to be paying particular attention to him.

Satisfied he was safe for the moment he waited for an oncoming car to pass before he crossed the road. The car suddenly slowed and, for a moment, he held his breath as he envisioned it stopping, the back door opening, and a voice calling his name. Then the car accelerated again, and as it passed by he could see a woman driving with two children in the back. He sighed in relief as he realised he had nothing to fear there.

Now the road was clear he put his head down and walked across, turning right as he reached the other side. His immediate destination was the nearest tube station which was just around the corner, about a hundred yards down the road. He was confident that, if he could make his way inside unseen, he should be safe enough. And then he heard the shout.

'Oi, mate!'

Flutter turned and looked back down the road. The man he'd seen going into the small shop had just emerged and was pointing in his direction. Now he called out again.

'Hold on a minute. I need to speak to you.'

'No chance, mate,' muttered Flutter as he spun on his heel and sprinted for the tube station. Unseen, and unheard, the other man was now holding an envelope aloft and waving it in Flutter's direction.

'Come back, you idiot,' he called. 'I've got something for you.'

But it was obvious Flutter wasn't listening.

'Moron,' muttered the man as he watched Flutter tearing towards the tube station. 'Now I'm going to have to waste more of my precious time.'

A few minutes later Flutter was standing on a platform deep underground. He was sure the man hadn't followed him into the tube station, but even so, he could feel his heart pounding and he couldn't relax.

He had a ticket to Paddington station clutched in his hand. Once there, he would get the first train heading west and leave the City behind forever. It wasn't quite the life he had in mind a few years ago, but then, his original plan hadn't included serving time for a crime he hadn't committed. When something like that happens, it tends to ruin up whatever plans you might have had.

On the plus side, he was alive, and he was healthy. So, now he was free, he just wanted to put it all behind him and start again. Conveniently for Flutter fate had determined he would make that fresh start in Waterbury.

CHAPTER 2

AFTER LIVING in a tiny cell for months Flutter had forgotten how huge Paddington station was, and it was only after wandering around for a few minutes that he began to adjust to the hustle and bustle surrounding him. But the wandering had also served to convince him he wasn't being followed and he finally began to relax.

He had twenty minutes to kill before his train was due to leave so he bought himself a small bottle of water and a newspaper, then looked around for somewhere to sit. He settled for an empty bench that gave him a good view of the clock and the platform his train would be leaving from.

The train had just arrived and was now disgorging its passengers onto the platform. Absently, he watched as they swarmed through the gate and onto the main concourse and wondered if twenty minutes was enough time for the train to be made ready to head back down the line.

He became aware someone else was now sitting on the other end of the bench and he cast a sideways glance at the newcomer. He felt he should know the man but he could only see him in profile so he couldn't be sure. The man began to turn towards him and Flutter quickly looked away.

'I hope you're not going to run off again,' said the man.

Flutter turned and now he could see exactly who it was. His face must have shown his alarm.

'Why are you following me?' asked Flutter.

'I'm not here to hurt you, if that's what you think,' said the man, hastily.

'I dunno what to think right now. First you're outside the prison and now you've followed me here. I was warned someone would be waiting for me, so what do you expect me to think?'

'You've got nothing to fear from me.'

'How do I know that? I don't know you from Adam.'

'You don't need to know who I am. I've got something for you.'

'Yeah, that's what I'm worried about,' said Flutter.

The man moved to reach for his pocket but Flutter's eyes nearly popped out of his head, so he stopped, his hand in mid-air.

'Blimey, what's up? D'you think I've got a shooter in my pocket?' he asked.

Flutter licked his lips.

'Like I said, I dunno what to think, do I?'

'Jesus, man, pull yourself together. Do I look stupid enough to pull a gun in a crowded place like this? I'm a messenger with an envelope not a gangster with a gun.'

'An envelope?'

'Yes, an envelope. It's not your average deadly weapon, is it?'

'Why have you got an envelope for me?'

'Because I was asked to make sure you got it.'

'What's in it?'

'My guess is it's a letter. What do you think?'

'Is it important?'

'Gawd, I don't know, do I? I didn't write the damned thing. I was just asked to deliver it.'

'Who asked you to deliver it to me?'

'A guy who calls himself Shifty. You do know him, right?'

'Yes, I know him. We shared a flat together.'

'Right, well, he said the letter was delivered to the flat, but you didn't live there anymore. So he asked me to find you and make sure you got it.'

'Is it important?'

'I've no idea; he didn't say, but I'm guessing he thought so, or he wouldn't have paid me to find you and give it to you.'

'He paid you?'

'Of course he paid me. You don't think I spend my time chasing people like you for fun, do you?'

'Why didn't he bring it himself? Come to that, why hasn't he been to visit me? I've been inside for twelve months and I've not had a single visitor.'

'Search me. Maybe he didn't think you'd want to see him.'

'Why wouldn't I want to see him?'

'How would I know what he's thinking? I'm not his psychiatrist. I'm a messenger, and he's just a bloke who asked me to deliver a letter.'

'He's my best mate, or at least I thought he was.'

The man sighed.

'Look, much as I'd love to sit here and sort your life out, I've got a lot on today, and you're starting to make my head ache. Now, do you want this letter, or not?'

'Well, yes, I suppose so,' said Flutter.

The man reached slowly for his pocket, carefully withdrew a white envelope and handed it to Flutter who took the envelope and looked at it curiously.

'Right, I'll be off, then,' said the man getting to his feet.

Flutter looked up at him.

'Why didn't Shifty visit me in prison?'

'Why don't you ask him yourself?'

'You know, though, don't you?'

The man gave Flutter a sad little smile.

'I make it my policy never to speak for other people.' He nodded towards the platform where Flutter's train was waiting. 'It looks as if your train's just about to leave.'

Flutter looked towards the platform and realised the man was right. He grabbed the rucksack and galloped towards the train.

The man watched Flutter stuff the envelope into his coat pocket as he ran, and watched him climb onto the train. As Flutter disappeared from view the messenger offered an unseen wave of his hand then turned and headed for the exit.

As the train set off Flutter gazed through the window at nothing in particular and contemplated his future. Up until the time he'd been arrested, the ethics of the lifestyle he had fallen into had never bothered him. He felt his philosophy was justified because he only took advantage of what he regarded as other people's carelessness. Anyway, as long as he could eat, pay the rent, and have a laugh, did it really matter how he came by his money?

He was proud of the fact he had never committed anything he considered to be a serious crime and had never physically hurt anyone. In a weird way he thought this made him the acceptable sort of criminal, tolerated, and accepted by society, so he had felt it was the ultimate injustice when he had been found guilty and locked up for a crime he hadn't committed.

The irony of the situation completely escaped him, but being locked away had given him plenty of time to think. At first all he could focus on was the injustice of it all and how he was going to find out who had done this to him and how he would exact his revenge.

But then a chance encounter with the prison padre had led to a series of conversations which finally made him face up to the reality of his existence. On one occasion the padre's words had painted vivid pictures in Flutter's head of a young woman with hungry kids and no money to buy food or even pay the rent because a thief like him had scooped up her purse and run off with it.

As a child he had known times when he, too, had gone without food, and the padre's story reminded him of the misery that went with such hunger and, for the first time, he began to understand what it must be like for the parents who'd done their best to find the money to feed their kids and then had it snatched away by people like him.

By the time his sentence was nearing its end, fate intervened in the form of a letter telling him his uncle William, who had acted like a father and raised him, had died and left him a house in Waterbury. To Flutter this was a sign that was pointing him away from his troubled past in London and offering him the chance to make a new life in the town where he grew up. He knew it was too late to put right what he'd done wrong in the past, but maybe in the future he could make amends in some way.

It was a pretty vague plan as Flutter had absolutely no idea how he was going to achieve this aim, but then he had never been one for details. He would think of something. He always did.

As he settled into the journey he remembered the envelope the messenger had handed him at Paddington station. He fumbled in his coat pocket, withdrew the letter and studied the envelope, then he carefully flipped it over and studied the back looking for any tell-tale marks that would prove it had been opened, but as far as he could tell it had not been tampered with. To his surprise the return address on the back indicated it had been sent from Henry Roebuck, Solicitor, whose office was in Waterbury.

This presented him with a dilemma. In Flutter's rather limited experience, anything that sounded remotely official was unlikely to be good news and he wondered if perhaps he could get away with throwing the letter out of the window and pretend he'd never received it.

He was about to stand up and reach for the window when his curiosity got the better of him, and a better idea popped into his head; why not open the letter and read it? If it was bad news he could still get rid of the evidence and plead ignorance.

It took him the best part of twenty minutes to read the three page document. This was in part because of what Flutter called the "legal-speak" language which he struggled to make sense of. Once again it was telling him he had been left a house in Waterbury only this time it was a little confusing as it mentioned the death of his father, Walter.

Flutter's parents Wesley and Julie, had died in a traffic accident when he was very small, and he had been raised by his Uncle William and Aunt Sylvie. So, who was Walter?

This worried Flutter for a few minutes, but he finally decided this was merely a technicality as his uncle had raised him like a father and had often called him "son". Calling his father Walter was obviously an error which could easily be resolved when he met the solicitor.

He didn't recognise the address of the house either, but then he'd been away for years and they'd lost contact. Uncle Billy could easily have moved house in that time.

Two hours later, Flutter was standing on the platform at Waterbury railway station studying the giant street map on the wall. Although he had spent his childhood in Waterbury, he had left fifteen years ago and the address he was heading for was unfamiliar. Carefully he made a mental note of the directions to his destination before he set off.

As he made his way through the exit, Flutter looked up at the sky. Large, dark clouds were gathering from the West. He estimated it would be roughly a ten minute walk and as he set off he wondered if he would reach his destination before the heavens opened.

Walking through the town, Flutter was keen to take in his surroundings. Waterbury didn't seem to have changed that much and remained a pleasant enough little town. It was going to be a bit quiet after London, but that was then and this was now. Now he wanted small and quiet. Small and quiet would be good. Perhaps this would be the place where he could find a proper job, keep his head down and become part of the furniture. Perhaps...

· · ·

Had he been wearing a wristwatch, he would have been pleased to know he had been spot on with his estimated journey time to Willow Grove. Sadly, several months ago, he had found it prudent to donate his watch to a fellow inmate in return for not getting smacked around.

Flutter had no idea what Willow Grove was going to be like but he remembered the house he had grown up in. With this in mind he was expecting to find a row of tiny, two-up, two-down, terraced houses. So, when he finally found the sign saying Willow Grove, he stopped, mouth open. He looked again at the street name, to be sure, but there was no mistake.

The road before him swept away in a long graceful curve to the left. From what he could see, many of the houses were hidden behind neat, tidy hedges, and they were much more extensive than he had expected, and detached, too. He squinted at the house opposite and made out the number 2. He was looking for number 54, so he crossed the road and began to walk.

He shifted the bag onto his other shoulder as he walked and realised he must look out of place in these surroundings. He only possessed the clothes he was wearing, and much as he loved his old duffel coat, it hadn't exactly been fashionable when he bought it ten years ago, and his tatty jeans had definitely seen better days.

He looked across the road at a house with large imposing windows. A disapproving face stared back from an upstairs window. Flutter instinctively looked away, and for a few seconds, he faltered. The desire to turn and run was almost overwhelming, but he had learned all about self-control in prison. After a few deep breaths, he regained his composure, and now he looked up at the face.

'Nuts to you, mate,' he said, as he waved and smiled at the face in the window. 'I know what you're thinking, but I own one of these houses, so I'm as entitled to be here as you are.'

The owner of the face at the window seemed shocked at the audacity of the stranger and slunk back guiltily. Head held high, Flutter continued proudly down the road in search of his house.

. . .

A tall red brick wall surrounded number 54, and a pair of ornate iron gates guarded the driveway. Flutter walked up to the gates and peered through at the house.

'Bloody hell, this can't be right, can it?' he muttered.

He pulled the letter from his pocket and unfolded it again. He knew the contents by heart, but even so, he quickly read through it again. He looked at the house and read the address out loud.

'Number 54 Willow Grove, Waterbury. This has to be the one. Uncle Billy must have won the lottery!'

Ornate trees surrounded the large courtyard on the other side of the gate. They created the perfect setting for the elegant, imposing house. There was a large double garage off to one side, and he wondered if there were any cars inside. They weren't mentioned in the letter, but then there had been no mention of a mansion, had there?

He pushed at the gates, but they didn't budge so he turned his attention to the wall. He guessed it was about eight feet high, and when he raised his arms his fingertips were a few inches below the top. He knew if he could get a good run-up, he would comfortably be able to reach the top and scramble over, but it would be in full view of anyone who might be watching. The last thing he wanted was some nosey neighbour calling the police.

He stepped back and scratched his head, and that was when he noticed the keypad. He looked down at the letter again and then smiled as things fell into place.

'So that's what that number's for. Why didn't they just say there's a keypad outside? What am I supposed to be, a mind reader?'

Carefully he tapped each number into the keypad, double-checking each one against the letter to make sure. As he pressed the green "enter" button, he held his breath. For a second, nothing happened, then there was the low, whirring sound of an electric motor, and the gates slowly opened.

Flutter watched in fascinated delight as the gates opened. Things like this didn't happen to him, and he wondered if perhaps this was a dream and at any minute he would wake up and find he was still in that pokey cell...

As the gates reached their fully open position, there was a satisfying "clang". There was another keypad a few yards through the gate. Flutter walked over to it and pressed the "close" button. Then he stood and enjoyed watching the gates again, until another "clang" told him they were closed.

He was sorely tempted to open and close the gates again just for the fun of it, but the first few drops of what looked a potentially heavy shower were beginning to fall. Now a more powerful urge took over. There was something he had been unable to do for what had been a very long year.

A broad canopy covered the front door of the house. He hurried across the courtyard to it, placed his bag on the floor, slipped off his duffel coat and dropped it alongside. Then he walked back into the centre of the courtyard and stopped. As big, round, fat drops of fresh rain splattered to the ground he raised his face to the sky and spread his arms.

Oh, that felt so good...

Once his hair and tee-shirt, were suitably soaked, Flutter walked back to the front door. There was another keypad here, but they had told him about this one. He didn't need the letter to recall the code. This was an easy one to remember; it was four zeros.

'That'll have to change,' he muttered as he tapped the number in. There was a loud click as the locks opened, and the door swung open. He was in!

CHAPTER 3

HE STEPPED INSIDE and pushed the door closed. Hardly daring to breathe, he dropped his coat on the floor, slipped the bag from his shoulder, leaned back against the door and closed his eyes. It took a few minutes of deep breathing before he dared to open his eyes and look around.

Thick piled, white carpet covered the hallway floor, and as Flutter stared at it, his first thought was that this wasn't the most practical colour anyone could have chosen. For a moment, he wondered where such a thought had come from, and then he remembered.

When he was about eight years old, his uncle had given his aunt the money to buy a cheap carpet for the hall in their tiny terraced house. Flutter had the misfortune to come home from school with dog shit on his shoe that day and unwittingly christened the new carpet. He hadn't realised until he felt the slap around the back of his head. The blow had knocked him clean off his feet, and he could still recall how his ears were ringing for the rest of that day.

The memory vivid in his mind, he slipped his shoes off, unable to resist the urge to check the soles, just in case. Then he set off to explore the house. There was an enormous kitchen at the end of the hall, finished in stainless steel and white, but there wasn't a single gadget to be found on any of the worktops.

'Very nice, if perhaps a tad clinical,' he thought. 'But then a splash of colour here and there will soon fix that.'

Just to be nosey, he opened one or two of the drawers and cupboards. Now he knew why there was nothing on the worktops. The kitchen was fully equipped, but everything had its own place in the cupboards. He took another look around the neat, tidy kitchen. He wasn't very good at putting things away so he knew it was unlikely it would ever be this tidy again.

Double doors at the far end of the kitchen opened into a large dining room. It was dark inside, but there was enough light from the open door to reveal a long table surrounded by chairs. The whole thing was covered in dust sheets, but Flutter guessed the table could easily seat at least eight people. He tried to think of seven people he would like to invite to dinner but soon gave up when he realised he couldn't actually think of any.

'Maybe I can sit in a different seat every night to make sure they wear evenly.'

The far wall was hidden behind curtains. He walked around the table and peered through the curtains to discover they covered full-length folding glass doors. He opened the curtains to let the light in and for the first time he saw the back garden which he guessed was at least the size of a football pitch. The same high, brick wall surrounded it.

'Bloody hell. I always wanted a garden, but this is like a park!'

He resisted the temptation to go out in the garden and instead made his way through another doorway out into the hall. He checked out the rest of the rooms downstairs and then ran up the stairs to explore the bedrooms. Again they were all furnished, but everything was covered in dust sheets. Thoughtfully, he made his way back down to the dining room and gazed through the doors at the garden.

'This can't be true,' he said out loud. 'Things like this just don't happen to me. There's got to be a catch.'

A furious buzzing from the hallway rudely interrupted his thoughts. Curious, he wandered out to the hall, then realised it was the buzzer on the intercom behind the door. A small screen showed him who was at the gate. His immediate instinct was to ignore the visitor, but when the buzzer sounded again he knew that wasn't going to work so he pressed a button alongside the screen, which said: "speak."

'Hallo.'

'This is the police,' said a distorted voice. 'We had a call to say someone had been acting suspiciously outside your gates.'

'I'm afraid you've wasted your time, mate. Everything's fine here.'

'I'm outside the gates now, sir, so if you could just open them, I'll check the grounds for you, just in case,' insisted the police officer.

Flutter's heart sank. He was tempted to tell the guy to clear off, but that would be stupid. He realised he had no choice, and with a sigh, he pressed the button to open the gates.

'Thank you, sir.'

Flutter knew he had every right to be here, but the urge to run from the police was a hard habit to break. Once again, he had to call on his self-discipline, and once again, it didn't let him down. Tapping his pocket to make sure he had the solicitor's letter, he opened the front door and waited as the police car pulled through the gates, drove up to the house and stopped. A lone, uniformed police officer climbed from the vehicle. Automatically Flutter sized him up, and decided he might lose a fight against the overweight policeman but he could easily outrun him.

'I'm PC Blackwell,' announced the approaching policeman. 'Is this your house?'

'That's right.'

Flutter watched the man's face and decided PC Blackwell would make a rubbish poker player.

'It's just that we had a call about someone acting suspiciously,' said Blackwell.

'Yeah, so you said.'

'The thing is, you match the description we were given,' said Blackwell. 'It seems the person appeared to be sizing up the gates as if they were trying to figure out how to get in. I reckon the owner of the house would know how to get in, don't you?'

He finished with a self-satisfied smirk. Flutter had initially been prepared to co-operate, but he knew he had been judged already and now he couldn't help but smile back.

'And d'you think, if I were a burglar, I would answer the buzzer and let you in, just like that?'

Blackwell crossed his arms.

'That would depend on how confident you were that you could pull the wool over my eyes. I'm just doing my job and, like I said, you match the description we were given.'

Flutter could see Blackwell had no intention of making life easy for him.

'The thing is, officer, I've never been here before,' he explained. 'They didn't tell me about the keypad at the gate, and I didn't see it at first. For a minute, I thought I might have to climb over the wall.'

'I thought you said you owned the house.'

'I do. I'm moving in today. Right now, in fact.'

PC Blackwell looked around.

'You don't seem to have much in the way of possessions.'

'I travel light.'

Blackwell frowned.

'The house comes fully furnished,' said Flutter.

'D'you mind if I ask how much you paid for this house?'

'I don't think that's any of your business.'

PC Blackwell considered the younger man standing before him. He didn't fancy getting into a fight with him, but if it came to it, he figured a face full of pepper spray would stack the odds nicely in his favour.

There again, the young guy looked pretty fit. If he made a run for it before the spray could be deployed, there was no doubt which of them would win a foot race. He moved a little closer to Flutter to block his escape route. Flutter had no intention of getting into a fight with anyone, but as he saw what Blackwell was doing his smile widened into a grin.

The standoff didn't last long.

'Can you prove who you are?' asked Blackwell. 'Have you got a passport perhaps, or a driving licence?'

'I don't have either of those,' said Flutter.

'You expect me to believe you can afford to buy a house like this, but you don't have a driving licence or a passport?'

'I didn't say I bought the house.'

'Ah. So, I was right, it's not yours.'

'Sure, it is.' Flutter produced the letter with a flourish and handed it over. 'Here you go. It says so on here.'

Blackwell read the letter, then looked doubtfully at Flutter.

'What?' said Flutter. 'You think I'm making it up? Go on, the phone number's in the letter. Call 'em if you don't believe me.'

'This letter might prove someone called Harvey Gamble owns this house, but how do I know you're him if you've got no ID?'

'I've got another letter inside the house that'll prove who I am.'

As Flutter made to turn round and go into the house, he noticed Blackwell reaching for his belt.

Flutter, stopped and raised his hands.

'Look, there's no need for the spray,' he said. 'I'm not going to run for it. Why would I? Like I said, it's my house. I've every right to be here.'

Blackwell studied Flutter's face again.

'You know about the spray, then?' he asked. 'Had experience, have you?'

'I've got a letter,' said Flutter, ignoring the question, 'but it's in my bag behind the door.'

Blackwell didn't look convinced, and now the spray was in his hand.

'One wrong move, and you'll get this right in the face,' he threatened.

'Yeah, I think everyone knows how it works, mate. Trust me, I'm not moving anywhere, but that letter won't make its own way out here.'

'I'm going to cuff you,' said Blackwell.

'Really?'

'Yeah, really.'

Flutter sighed.

'There's no need for that.'

'I think you'll find that's for me to decide,' said Blackwell.

'Yeah, of course it is,' said Flutter, resignedly. 'It's really not necessary, but I suppose, if it makes you happy.'

'Yes it does make me happy. Now turn around and put your hands behind your back.'

Flutter turned obediently and Blackwell snapped on the handcuffs.

'And now I'm going to put you in the car and call for backup.'

'Backup? What d'you want backup for?'

'Because there's something funny going on here.'

'No, there isn't,' argued Flutter. 'I told you, th—'

'There's a letter in the house,' finished Blackwell. 'Yes, you already said that.'

He grabbed the handcuffs and dragged the protesting Flutter unceremoniously, backwards, to his car, opened the door and shoved him into the back seat. Flutter winced and stifled a cry as he landed on his hands and the cuffs bit into his wrists. He knew better than to give a bully like Blackwell the satisfaction of knowing how much it had hurt.

'Right,' said Blackwell, staring down at Flutter. 'You sit there and behave yourself until the troops arrive. Got it?'

'Got it,' said Flutter.

Blackwell reached for his radio, clicked the button, and began to speak. 'Control, this is—'

'You'll look a right tit when your mates arrive and find they wasted their time because you couldn't be arsed to read the letter.'

Blackwell released the button on his radio and glared at his prisoner.

'What?'

'I said you'll look a right idiot when they get here and find they've wasted their time. What will there be? Two men, three, four? And what are they going to do, stand there and watch you read a letter? It's a bit of a waste of resources, don't you think? You could just read it now and save everyone the trouble.'

Blackwell considered this idea for a few seconds. He didn't trust his prisoner, but he had a point. There again, he didn't intend to lose face.

'I tell you what I'm going to do,' he said. 'I'll find the letter and read it, then I'll call for backup.'

Flutter rolled his eyes.

'Now that's a good idea,' he said. 'I mean, you wouldn't want to look an idiot, would you?'

The irony was lost on Blackwell.

'In a bag behind the front door, you said?'

'That's right. You can't miss it. It's the only one there.'

'Right,' said Blackwell, 'and just to make sure you can't run away I'm going to lock the car.'

Flutter sighed.

'Don't you think this is overkill? I mean, have you tried running with your hands cuffed behind your back? How far do you think I could get? Anyway, I already told you I'm not running anywhere. I've got no reason to.'

'Yes, well, we'll see about that.'

Blackwell slammed the door, locked the car, and strode towards the house. The front door was still open and, just as Flutter had said, he could see a small bag on the floor. Gingerly he picked it up, carried it back to the car and unlocked and opened the back door.

'Right,' he said, offering the bag towards Flutter. 'Where's this letter?'

'That pocket on the front. Just undo the zip, and you'll see it.'

Blackwell opened the pocket and fished the letter from inside. As he opened it, he couldn't hide his surprise.

'Well, well, well,' he said. 'Been a naughty boy have you?'

Flutter sighed and thought about arguing his case for innocence, but realised Blackwell wasn't the sort to listen.

'Yes, I've been inside,' he said patiently. 'I've done my time, learned my lesson, and now I'm a changed man making a new start.'

Blackwell guffawed.

'Yeah, right, of course you are,' he said. 'The trouble is people like you never change.'

'You're the second person to say that today,' said Flutter.

'That should tell you something.'

'I have to say it's really inspiring to know you people in authority are so keen to offer me support and encouragement.'

'That's because we know the reality.'

'And that's exactly why so many people don't even try,' said Flutter. 'Can't you see you just perpetuate a vicious circle by your attitude?'

Blackwell ignored Flutter and focused on the letter.

'So it looks like you might really be Harvey Gamble,' he said when he finished reading.

'There's no "might be" about it. I am Harvey Gamble, so how about you take these handcuffs off and let me go about my lawful business?"

'Don't get cocky sunshine. I'm not sure I'm convinced yet.'

'So, why don't you make some enquiries and prove it?' suggested Flutter. 'That's what you coppers are supposed to do, isn't it?'

'Just sit there and keep quiet,' said Blackwell. 'If I'm not happy, we'll be taking a little ride down to the station.'

He left Flutter in the car, wandered a few yards away and began to speak into his radio.

'Arsehole,' muttered Flutter as he watched Blackwell's face.

It took about ten minutes, but Flutter could tell by the gradual darkening of the expression on Blackwell's face that he couldn't prove that Flutter wasn't who he said he was. Now he was trudging reluctantly back to the car.

'Happy now?' asked Flutter.

'Unbelievable as it seems, I am advised you are Harvey Gamble, and you are the legitimate owner of this house.'

Flutter grinned.

'Which is exactly what I told you about half an hour ago.'

Blackwell stared blankly.

'I also seem to recall you addressed me as "sir" before you thought I was a crook,' continued Flutter. 'Shouldn't you be doing that now?'

Blackwell leaned into the car and dragged Flutter out.

'Don't be a smart-arse,' he said, unlocking the handcuffs. 'For your information, I was right, you are a crook. That second letter proves it.'

Flutter flexed his hands now the cuffs were off. He decided it was time to get Blackwell off his property.

'Well, thank you so much for your help, officer,' he said. 'It's been an absolute pleasure meeting such a pleasant, helpful, and understanding individual. You're a credit to the force.'

Blackwell looked daggers, but Flutter merely offered a pleasant smile in return.

'I'll be watching you,' warned Blackwell.

'I'm sure you will,' said Flutter, 'but unless you come armed with a search warrant, I'm afraid you'll have to do it from the other side of that gate. Now, clear off, and leave me alone.'

Blackwell scowled at Flutter as he climbed into his car. Undaunted, Flutter smiled and waved cheerily as he watched him turn the car around and drive down to the gate, which opened automatically as he approached.

'Goodbye. Don't bother coming back,' muttered Flutter, as Blackwell drove through the gate, turned left, and disappeared from view.

He watched as the gates began to close and let out a sigh of relief when they finally clanged shut. Then he turned back inside the house and closed the front door. He would have been happy to spend the rest of the day relaxing, but as the house appeared to be devoid of food, he would have to go shopping, and he might as well call in at the solicitors on the way.

CHAPTER 4

FIVE MINUTES LATER, Flutter walked back down the road towards town. As he reached number 33, he saw the nosey neighbour was watching him again, so he crossed the street, walked up to the front door and knocked loudly. After a few seconds, the door opened just enough for a beady eye to appear above the security chain.

'Hello there,' said Flutter, cheerily.

The eye blinked twice.

'I figure it must have been you who called the police, so I thought I'd come and introduce myself. Hard as it may be for you to believe, I actually do own the house you thought I was trying to break into. I just wanted to thank you for being so neighbourly. Where would we be without such public spirited people like you, eh?'

The eye seemed to widen so much Flutter felt tempted to poke it with his finger. He thought it would probably pop right out, and for a bizarre moment, he imagined himself trying to catch it.

'I must get on now,' he said, 'I'm hoping to meet some decent human beings this afternoon.'

He smiled and waved to the eye, then turned and walked away, whistling to himself as he went.

. . .

The office of Henry Roebuck, Solicitor, was on Queen Street, which Flutter remembered was considered the posher part of town when he was a kid. As he rounded the corner from Kings Road, he could see nothing much had changed.

A terrace of tall, white-painted, four-storey, Georgian style houses ran the length of both sides of the street, their huge, elegant, front doors finished in gleaming gloss paint with perfectly polished brass door furniture.

The office he sought was at number 16 which was half-way down the street. A large button at the side of the front door invited him to "press to gain access" which he did. A click and a buzz signified he had access, so he pushed the door and walked in.

A staircase led upstairs, and a single door to the left of the staircase said "Roebuck's" suggesting the solicitor occupied the entire ground floor. Flutter pressed the buzzer on the door and waited. After a couple of minutes he pressed again. He could hear the buzzer sounding inside but when he pressed his ear to the door there was no other sound.

'Come on, come on,' he muttered, pressing the buzzer again. 'You can't be closed yet, it's mid-afternoon.'

He hammered on the door with his fist.

'Can I help you?' asked a voice from behind him.

Flutter spun around. A sour-faced, bespectacled woman in a smart business suit stood before him.

'Er, I need to speak to Mr Roebuck, the solicitor,' he said.

The woman looked him up an down suspiciously, slowly taking in the jeans and the tatty duffel coat.

'I'm afraid you'll find that rather difficult,' she said.

'Why's that?' he asked.

'They're closed.'

'Well, yeah, I kinda figured that one out when no-one answered the door,' said Flutter. 'D'you know when they'll be open?'

'Well, that's the problem, you see. They're closed until further notice.'

'But Mr Roebuck sent me a letter,' said Flutter. 'I need to speak to him.'

'I'm afraid you'll need the assistance of a medium if you want to do that.'

Flutter frowned.

'A medium? I don't understand.'

'Mr Roebuck died a few weeks ago.'

'You're joking.'

'Do I look as though I find death amusing?'

Flutter thought it unlikely she would find anything amusing.

'How did he die?'

'I heard it was a heart attack.'

'But he had associates, right?'

'No associates, just a secretary.'

'Maybe she can help me.'

'As I said, the offices are closed until further notice. There are no partners, and no-one seems to be in any hurry to re-open, or take over his business.'

'Why's that?'

'I have no idea.'

'What am I going to do now?' said Flutter, of no-one in particular.

'I don't know,' said the woman, 'but standing there making the place look untidy isn't going to help any of us. There's no-one here who can help you so I suggest you try the police. Maybe they can help.'

Flutter had a retort on the tip of his tongue but he knew better than to waste his breath. People like her just weren't worth the effort, and if he let this develop into an argument she might even report him to the police.

Silently he adjusted the rucksack on his shoulder, made his way from the building and headed back down the street. As he walked he considered his options. Okay, so he hadn't got any answers, but he still had the letter, and that proved he owned the house. And there was the matter of a bank account too.

. . .

As Waterbury was an old market town, there was a wide street running through the middle. A bank stood almost exactly in the centre of town, just as he remembered, with an ancient pub adjoining on one side.

On the other side of the bank stood a coffee shop which definitely hadn't been there when he had lived here. He could see a sign bearing a supermarket logo in the distance, and he could certainly do with buying a few bits and pieces, but there was something he needed to do before that. Once again he pulled the solicitor's letter from his pocket and walked into the bank.

A cheery receptionist smiled at him.

'How can I help you, sir?'

'I'd like to see the manager.'

'Can I have your name, sir?'

'Gamble. Harvey Gamble.'

The receptionist looked at her computer monitor.

'I can't see your name, sir. Are you sure you have an appointment?'

'No, I don't have an appointment, but I do have this.'

Flutter handed her the solicitor's letter. She scanned it, glancing up once or twice as she did.

'This seems to be in order,' she said at last. 'If you could just wait a moment, I'll see if the manager's free.'

Ten minutes later, Flutter re-emerged from the bank. Just as he had been informed in the letter, a bank account had been created for him. He was disappointed he could only get his hands on two hundred quid in cash when there was several thousand in the account. But, according to the bank manager, his father had set it up this way so he couldn't go mad and spend it all in one go.

'After all, Mr Gamble, you've been somewhat deprived recently, and your father thought it might tempt you to make up for lost time. I'm sure he had your best interests at heart, and you will have full access in due course.'

'Did you know my father?' asked Flutter.

'I'm afraid not. Everything was set up through your father's solicitor so I never had the pleasure.'

'And you're sure his name was Walter, and not William?'

'Any irregularities such as a wrong name would have come to
light when we did our checks.'

Flutter scratched his head. He wanted to ask so many more questions he couldn't think where to start, but it was apparent the bank
manager wanted him away.

'I hate to appear rude, Mr. Gamble, but I'm afraid I have an
appointment waiting,'

Flutter said his goodbyes and walked back out onto the street. He
took a quick look up and down as if to decide which way to go, but he
already knew where he was going next. He needed to think, and he
hadn't had a decent cup of coffee for at least a year!

CHAPTER 5

WHILE FLUTTER WAITED at the counter for his coffee to be prepared, he was deep in thought. If this guy Walter was really his father why had Uncle Billy told him his father was called Wesley? And if Walter had been alive all this time why didn't he make himself known? Of course, the solicitor would have known all the answers, but he's not going to be much use now, is he?

His thoughts were interrupted by the arrival of his coffee and he looked around for somewhere to sit. There were plenty of seats to choose from, but he was having difficulty deciding. As he looked around the room, his eyes settled on an attractive young mum. She was enjoying a peaceful cup of coffee while her toddler slept in a buggy next to her.

Attractive young women hadn't featured in Flutter's world recently, and he couldn't resist letting his eyes linger. Then she suddenly looked up and smiled. Guiltily Flutter smiled back then, feigning innocence, carried on looking around the room.

Almost immediately, his eyes were drawn back to the young mum as he heard a chair scrape across the floor. The toddler was stirring, and this was obviously the signal for her to gather her things and prepare to leave. She got to her feet, released the brake on the buggy and began to manoeuvre it towards the door. He caught her eye again, and shyly, she smiled back. Flutter smiled and nodded towards the toddler as if he understood exactly what it was like to have a small child.

In reality, of course, he had no idea what it was like, but that didn't matter. This was all a bluff to hide the fact he had noticed the purse she had left on the table. Old habits die hard, and as the door closed behind the young mum, he grabbed his coffee and hurried across to the table she had vacated. Quickly he looked around, but no-one seemed to have noticed him, so he placed his coffee next to the purse and sat down.

He looked around again. A young woman was sitting at a table across the room tapping away at a laptop and, as he looked in her direction, Flutter thought she might have looked away as if she had been watching him, but he couldn't be sure.

He sipped at his coffee for a minute, looked around the room again, and then slipped the purse into his pocket. He had been doing things like this for so long it was almost second nature, and yet this time it felt different. He considered why this should be. Okay, he hadn't done it for months, but even so...

The frantic return of the young mum, still pushing the buggy but now in tears, interrupted his thoughts. Keen to make this a shared family experience, the toddler was now enthusiastically bawling his head off. Distraught, the young woman ran up to the counter.

'Has anyone handed in a purse?' she cried, pointing vaguely in Flutter's direction. 'I was sitting over there. I think I must have left it on the table.'

Now, as all eyes turned in Flutter's direction, he ducked under the table.

'Here you are, luv,' he called, holding the purse aloft as he emerged from under the table. 'It was on the floor. You must have dropped it.'

'Oh, thank God,' she said. 'All my housekeeping's in there. My husband would kill me if I lost it.'

Flutter felt himself redden as he carried the purse across to her and handed it over.

'You need to be more careful,' he said, over the sound of the bawling child. 'Someone else might have put that in their pocket and walked off with it.'

'Yes, you're right,' agreed the young mum. 'You're very kind. Thank you.'

She gave him a grateful smile, then turned towards the door. Flutter scuttled after her, opened the door, and held it for her. She smiled again, then left the shop pushing the buggy with one hand and clutching her purse in the other.

Flutter admired the fit of her jeans on her backside as he slowly closed the door, then returned to his seat. He stared through the window at nothing in particular and considered what had just happened.

His intention was to turn over a new leaf, and yet he'd reverted to type at the first opportunity. It's true he had stayed alive over the past fifteen years by profiting from other people's misfortune, but was it really going to be such a hard habit to break?

On the other hand, when the young mum had appeared he'd handed the purse back without a moment's hesitation. So, did this mean he had successfully turned over a new leaf?

There again, there could be no denying his first instinct had been to pocket the purse. So, did that mean he had failed?

Flutter sighed as he considered his confusion and then a female voice interrupted his thoughts.

'Mind if I join you?'

It was the young woman he thought might have been watching him earlier. She was already settling into a chair opposite him, the laptop set down on the table before her. She had long brown hair and piercing green eyes that dared him to object.

'You had that purse in your pocket. You were going to steal it,' she said.

Flutter stared expressionlessly at the woman. Twelve months

cooped up in an environment where some inmates were permanently at flashpoint had taught him that, if the situation allowed, he should always think before he reacted.

'It was on the floor,' he said. 'Everyone saw me pick it up off the floor.'

'Everyone saw you emerge from under the table with it in your hand, but we both know that's not where it was,' she said. 'You got away with it because I was the only one who saw you slip it into your pocket before the owner returned.'

'You must be mistaken,' he said.

'What happened? Did your conscience get the better of you?'

'I dunno what you're talking about. It was on the floor.'

'It's all right, I won't tell anyone,' said the woman. 'She's still got her housekeeping, so I guess there's no real harm done. I'm just curious why you changed your mind.'

Flutter studied the face opposite him. Her bright green eyes stared straight back at him and seemed to bore deep into his head. He thought he would best describe her expression as disapproving.

To be honest, he could do without the interrogation, but beneath the disapproving frown he thought she was quite good looking. His eyes carried on downwards, taking in a graceful neck, and then sweeping down towards the open collar of her blouse...

She coughed, and his eyes snapped back up to her face.

'I saw the way you were looking at her, too,' she said.

'What's that supposed to mean?'

'You were staring at her, and you looked her up and down. You just did it to me, too.'

'Blimey, when did it become against the law to look at people?' asked Flutter.

'It's just not very polite.'

'Not polite? Gawd, you've got some nerve,' he said. 'So, it's not polite for me to admire someone of the opposite sex, but it's okay for you to plonk yourself down at my table, uninvited, and accuse me of stealing a purse when you've just seen me give it back to the owner? How is that polite?'

'Far too many men treat women as sex objects.'

'Sex objects? How do you work that one out? I'm not treating anyone as a sex object. I like sports cars, but if I stop to admire a Ferrari it doesn't mean I'm expecting to jump in and drive it away.'

The woman tried hard not to smile at the analogy and looked away to hide it. Despite his irritation, Flutter was immediately won over.

'You've got a nice smile.'

She looked doubtful.

'And you need to learn how to take a compliment,' he continued. 'I give 'em away free, and there are no conditions attached.'

She looked puzzled

'Conditions?'

'I expect nothing in return. No, hang on, let me change that. In this case there is one condition; can you please stop the interrogation.'

Now she seemed to relax.

'I'm sorry,' she said. 'I didn't mean it to be like that. Can I start again?'

Flutter pretended to be thinking about it. He wasn't sure he wanted company, but then the situation could have been much worse. She could have blown the whistle, and then he'd have been in big trouble. And he'd had no female company for a long time.

'Go on, then,' he said.

'My name's Katie Donald. I'm a journalist, but I'm also writing a book about the psychology of crime.'

'Oh, I see. So, because I like to admire a good looking woman, you think I'm Jack the Ripper reincarnated, is that it?'

'Now you're being silly. I'm just interested in what makes people grab something and slip it into their pocket when they know it's not theirs.'

'Well, I wish you good luck with your book, Katie Donald, but I'm not a good subject for your research. I'm afraid you won't learn anything from me.'

She looked disbelievingly at him but didn't push it.

'And who are you?' she asked. 'You're not local, are you?'

'People who know me call me Flutter.'

'Flutter? What sort of name is that?'

'What's it matter? A name is just an identifier. I mean, we could just as easily use numbers, couldn't we?'

She pulled a face, but again she didn't argue.

'If you must know,' he said, 'my real name's Harvey, but I've been called Flutter for as long as I can remember, and I much prefer Flutter.'

'Okay then, Flutter, so what are you doing here? Just passing through?'

'I might be.'

'Oh, a man of mystery, are we?'

'I'll tell you one thing, Katie. You ask a lot of questions.'

'I told you, I'm a journalist. It's what we do.'

'It must put people off.'

Now she laughed.

'Yes, sometimes,' she admitted. 'Especially when they have something to hide.'

'Maybe it's got nothing to do with having something to hide. Perhaps it's just that they like a bit of privacy.'

She nodded her head in acknowledgement.

'Is that what you want?'

'I don't want an interrogation.'

'I think that's harsh,' she said. 'I'd hardly call it an interrogation. I was just trying to be friendly.'

'Where I come from you don't make friends by accusing people of doing something they haven't done.'

'Can't we forget about that? I did apologise.'

Flutter considered briefly, then nodded.

'All right then, I suppose that's fair enough,' he said.

'So, why is a man called Flutter passing through a little town like Waterbury? It's not as if it's on the way to anywhere, is it?'

'Actually, I'm not passing through. I was born here, I've been away for a few years, and now I'm back. So, you could say I'm an actual, genuine, local. At least I will be if I stay.'

'Oh, really? Where do you live? Do I know your family?'

Flutter held his hands up.

'There you go again with the questions again,' he said.

'What was your father called?'

'I suppose if I'd ever met him, I would have called him Dad.'

She shared a grin with him.

'You know what I mean.'

'I never knew him. I was told he died when I was little.'

Her smile had vanished.

'Oh, I'm so sorry.'

'No, it's okay,' said Flutter. 'It was a long time ago. I was told my mum and dad had both died. So, I never knew either of them. I was raised by my dad's brother, my uncle Billy.'

'What was your father's name?'

'His name was Wesley Gamble, and my mum was Julie.'

'So, does this mean you're Mr Gamble, too?'

Flutter nodded and winked.

'Well done, Sherlock,' he said.

She thought for a moment.

'Is that why you're called Flutter?'

He grinned again.

'Wow! You are a sharp one, aren't you?'

'Everyone likes a flutter, right?'

'My, you are good. I usually have to explain it. That's how it started when I was a kid.'

'And is it right? Does everyone like you?' she asked.

Flutter's smile vanished.

'If my recent experiences are anything to go by, not everyone, no.'

'Oh, sorry,' she said. 'I didn't mean to...'

There was a brief, awkward, embarrassed silence, but Flutter didn't let it last. It had occurred to him that a local journalist could prove to be a useful ally. Perhaps she could help him figure out some of his current confusion.

'Anyway,' he said. 'You were asking about my dad. Did you recognise his name?'

'No, I don't think so.' She thought for a moment, then spoke again. 'But if he died years ago I wouldn't have, would I?'

'Ah, well, there's the thing. Earlier today I discovered I'd been named in a will and left a house by someone called Walter Gamble whose supposed to have been my real father. The thing is, he only died a couple of months ago. So, as you can imagine, it's all got a bit confusing and now I'm not really sure about any of my past.'

'Oh, really?' said Katie, not quite sure how to respond. 'That is confusing.'

'Yeah, well, it is what it is,' said Flutter, casually. 'You just have to move on with life don't you?'

But, just as Flutter had hoped, Katie's journalistic radar had been triggered. There was no way she was going to move on just yet.

'Walter Gamble, did you say? No, it doesn't ring a bell. I'm sure I've never met him.'

'Now, there's a coincidence,' said Flutter. 'You probably didn't miss much, though.'

'That's not a very nice thing to say about your father.'

'I don't think he was a very nice bloke if he's been alive all this time and never told me.'

'But he can't have been all bad.'

'I suppose he could have been a saint, but I wouldn't know because I never met him.'

'But, even so. He did name you in his will.'

Flutter pursed his lips, thoughtfully.

'Maybe he had a guilty conscience.'

'You can't know that.'

'All right, let me put it this way; if you had spent 30 years being told your father had died when you were small and then you suddenly got a letter telling you he'd actually been alive all the time, how would you feel?'

'When you put it like that, I suppose you have a point,' she said. 'Hang on a minute; if you were named in a will there must be a solicitor. Can't he help you?'

'Not really. He's dead. You might know him. His name was Henry Roebuck. He had an office on Queen's Street.'

'I didn't know him, but I know of him. He died a few weeks ago.'

'In suspicious circumstances, I'm told,' said Flutter.

Her eyes widened and Flutter could see he'd really triggered her radar now, but before she ask any more questions there was a shrill bleating from her handbag.

'I'm sorry,' she said. 'It's my phone. I hate the damned thing, but I have to have it because of my job. I've got to answer it.'

'Carry on,' said Flutter, 'Don't mind me.'

She took her phone and retreated from the table to take the call.

He reached for his coffee but realised it was cold now. To tell the truth, he was rather enjoying her company.

'Fancy another coffee?' he asked when she finished her call.

'I'm sorry, but I've got to go,' she said. 'Work.'

Flutter thought this was typical of his luck.

'Oh, right,' he said, as she grabbed her bag ready to rush off. 'Maybe I'll see you around.'

She gave him a smile. 'Yes. You never know.'

She left the shop like a small tornado, and as Flutter watched her go, he half expected to see tables rocking in her wake, and pieces of debris drifting to the floor.

Half an hour later, as he walked back to the house, Flutter was thinking just how stupid he was. The prison officer had told him he wouldn't change, and he had assured the man he was wrong to write him off so soon. Then a cynical police officer had told him the same thing.

'And what did I do at the first opportunity? I tried to steal a purse. Even worse, I allowed someone to see me do it.'

His instincts had been correct when he thought the woman had been watching him, and he had ignored those instincts, and it could have cost him dearly.

'This isn't exactly the perfect start to my new life, is it?' he thought. 'I can see it's not going be as easy as I thought. I'm going to have to try much harder.'

Having made the resolution, it was natural for his thoughts to turn to the woman who had caught him out. Katie Donald. It was a name with a nice ring to it. She had a cute smile, too. In fact, despite the rocky start to the conversation, everything about her had been engaging.

The problem was she already knew he was a thief, so he would have no chance there, would he? He had probably blown it before he had even met her!

But Flutter was nothing if not an optimist. He thought maybe, in time, if he kept in touch with her, he might just be able to engineer an opportunity to make the right impression.

CHAPTER 6

FLUTTER ENTERED the code number into the keypad and experienced that small thrill all over again as the gates opened for him. Then he walked through and did the same thing as the gates closed. He felt slightly foolish, getting excited by a pair of gates opening and closing, but what the hell. After spending a year locked up, he felt entitled to a little pleasure here and there, however simple. Besides, he knew the novelty would wear off soon enough.

He ambled up to the front door, punched in the code and enjoyed another simple pleasure. He walked into the hall, turned to close the door, and slipped off his shoes. What he really fancied right now was a cup of tea, but there was just one problem. He had gone all the way into town, allowed Katie Donald to distract him, and then forgotten all about the shopping.

'Oh, bugger,' he muttered quietly, as he mimed banging his head against the door.

He turned and began to walk down the hall to the kitchen, but he only took two steps before he stopped. He hadn't been in the house long enough to be sure where everything had been before, but he was convinced something was different. He stared at the bookcase to his left. Had it been there when he went out? And that small table with the telephone on it? Where had that come from?

He scratched his head. Now he remembered. There were definitely bits of furniture in the hall, but they had been covered in dust sheets, hadn't they?

He trotted past the kitchen and turned into the dining room. Again the dust sheets had gone, and now he could see he had been correct when he guessed the table seated eight diners. He scratched his head again. Then there was the faintest of creaks from the ceiling above him, and his senses were suddenly on full alert.

Stealthily, he crept up the stairs. He knew he had closed all the bedroom doors earlier, but now three of them were ajar, and there was a weird, unfamiliar noise coming from the furthest one. He listened hard, but couldn't quite make out what the sound was. He thought perhaps someone was strangling a cat. He would have liked to have a weapon to hand, but there wasn't time to find one. He would have to deal with this as best he could.

In the bedroom, Mrs Walker, the sixty-year-old housekeeper, was getting the house ready for its new owner. As she worked, she practised her best Adele impression, blissfully unaware the singer had nothing to worry about.

Carefully, Flutter crept up to the door. There was that weird sound again, and he wondered how many cats could there be in this house? He took a deep breath, pushed the door open and stepped inside.

In the room, Mrs Walker was removing the dust sheet from the bed. At the precise moment Flutter entered, she had just pulled the cover from the bed and was holding it as high as she could, ready to fold it.

'Right!' he roared. 'Whoever you are, you'd better have a bloody good reason for being in my house!'

'Aaahhhh!' she screamed, from behind the dust sheet, as she turned to face the voice.

'Jesus, it's a ghost!' yelled Flutter, taking several steps back.

Almost in slow motion, Mrs Walker lowered the dust sheet to reveal an ashen face with wild eyes. Her hair appeared to be defying gravity and was standing on end. They stared at each other in silence for what seemed like an eternity.

'Who the hell are you?' he asked finally.

She looked him up and down.

'I take it you must be Harvey.'

'Never mind who I am, who are you?'

'I'm Mrs Walker. I look after this house and cook. I suppose you could call me the housekeeper.'

'Housekeeper? No-one mentioned a housekeeper. I didn't know what to think when I heard you creeping about up here. You scared the crap out of me!"

'I scared you? How d'you think I feel? I'm minding my own business, doing my job, and then you run into the room screaming your head off. Honestly, I nearly wet my knickers!'

Flutter closed his eyes and shook his head.

'I think that's probably more information than I really need to know,' he said.

'Well, I'm sorry, but I'm not as young as I used to be.'

'Yeah, okay, I think I've got the picture. I'm sorry, honestly, but I had no idea anyone else would be in the house.'

She had been staring at him, and now her tone changed.

'You look like him, you know.'

'Look like who?'

'Your father.'

'I'm not sure if I find that comforting or worrying.'

'You didn't get on, did you?'

'It would be fair to say we weren't exactly best mates,' he admitted. 'But then we didn't have much chance to be friends because I never met him. When I grew up I was told my father, Wesley, had died when I was a baby. It was only earlier today I found out my dad was actually called Walter, and had been alive until very recently.'

'I'm told he thought the world of you, you know.'

'Are you sure we're talking about the same bloke? He never clapped eyes on me!'

'As I understand it, he was only trying to keep you on the straight and narrow.'

'Well that didn't exactly go to plan, did it?' said Flutter. 'And what d'you mean "as I understand it"? What did he tell you?'

'He didn't tell me anything. I've never met him. The solicitors employed me to look after the house after he died.'

'So you only know what they told you?'

'That's right. Apparently, he was sad that he'd lost you.'

'Lost me? You can't lose something you never had in the first place! I didn't even know he existed.'

'They told me he had always hoped you'd try to get in touch.'

'Why would I try to get in touch with someone I didn't even know existed? And if he was so concerned, why didn't he get in touch with me?'

'Did he know where to look?'

Flutter could feel himself filling with guilt, although he did not understand why he felt that way.

'Don't put this on me,' he said. 'I think the onus would have been on him being as how he knew I was his son, and I didn't even know he existed.'

She studied his face for a moment, then came to a decision.

'We have things to talk about,' she said. 'Let's go down to the kitchen, and I'll put the kettle on.'

CHAPTER 7

'GAWD, WHAT'S THAT NOISE?' asked Flutter as he followed her into the kitchen.

'That'll be Winston,' she said. 'His snoring gets worse as he gets older.'

'Winston?'

She pointed to what looked like a heap of blankets in the far corner.

'The dog.'

'What's he doing here?'

'He lives here.'

'He wasn't here earlier.'

'Of course not, he was with me.'

'So he's yours, then?'

'He was your father's, but I can't leave him here on his own, now can I?'

'He's not much of a guard dog is he? Shouldn't he be barking at me or something?'

'Oh, he doesn't bark,' she assured him. 'He's going deaf, and he sleeps like the dead. He'll know you're here when he wakes up.'

'Then what?'

'He'll probably mope around like he always does. Poor thing. I reckon he's been depressed ever since your father died.'

'Winston, did you say? What is he, a bulldog?'

'No, he's just some old mongrel. He was lost, so your father brought him home and adopted him. I think your dad used to spoil him something rotten. He even built him a special bed in the garden, with a shade so he could sit in the sun and not get too hot. He spends hours out there if it's a nice day.'

As Mrs Walker made the tea, Flutter wandered over to inspect the dog. He was curled up in a bed that was such tight accommodation a large ear flopped over the side.

'Blimey, he's got some massive ears, hasn't he?' said Flutter.

He bent down and gently scratched behind the protruding ear.

'There's a bit of Basset hound in him if you ask me,' said Mrs Walker. 'He's got those great big ears, and a long body, and legs that are a bit on the short side. You'll see what I mean when he gets out of bed.'

The dog was stirring now, and he suddenly opened a bloodshot eye and stared at Flutter who hastily drew his hand away.

'Does he bite?' he asked, taking a step back.

Mrs Walker chuckled.

'He might, if you were a biscuit, but he likes people. You'll be fine.'

The dog stiffly eased his body from the bed, shook himself, then began sniffing around Flutter's feet. His coat was a wiry grey, and just as Mrs Walker had said, his legs were a little on the short side. His body was also slightly too long, and the massive ears framed a face that seemed to be filled by a pair of huge, sad, saggy eyes which he now raised in Flutter's direction.

'He doesn't look this sad all the time, does he?' asked Flutter. 'He'll break my heart every time I look at him.'

'I'm afraid he's always looked like that, but I think he looks even sadder since your father passed away.'

'He's a Friday afternoon dog,' said Flutter.

'What does that mean?'

'They must've made him from all the leftover bits,' said Flutter, as he sank to his knees and began to fuss the dog who responded by vigorously wagging his tail.

'Oh look, he likes you,' said Mrs Walker.

Flutter was more than happy to fuss Winston, but there was no avoiding the odour that emanated from him.

'Jesus, Winston, you stink, mate,' he said.

'You're right there. He needs a bath, but I find it a struggle on my own.'

She sat down and watched as Flutter and Winston made friends.

'D'you know that's the happiest I've seen him.'

'So, where does he live when he's not here?' asked Flutter.

'I've got a flat above the garage. He lives there with me.'

'Oh, I see.'

Flutter was beginning to realise the letter the solicitors had sent him had been a tad scarce on details. It had suggested there was a condition to fulfil to enable him to keep the house, but there had been no mention of a housekeeper, or a stinky old dog.

'In the letter, it mentioned conditions I had to meet,' he said. 'I suppose you know about those?'

She shifted in her chair.

'Yes, that's what we need to talk about. Your father's will stipulated that I should be the one who told you.'

'Can I ask a question before you start?'

She nodded.

'Why did he stipulate you had to do it when he didn't even know you were going to be here?'

'Your father knew he was dying, and he knew he was going to be dead before you were released, so he made me the executor, or whatever you call it.'

'What does that mean?'

'It means I have to make sure you are aware of all the conditions.'

'Isn't that the solicitor's job?'

'Do I look like a legal expert? All I was told is that it was my job to make you aware of the conditions.'

'And what if I don't like the conditions?'

'I don't know. They never told me what I had to do if that happened. I suppose your father thought the conditions were reasonable and that you would be reasonable, too. Anyway, he's dead now so we can't ask him, can we? I suppose I should have asked the question but, to be honest, I was just grateful they employed me, especially as I got the flat as part of the arrangement.'

'And from what I understand we can't ask the solicitor now, either.'

'Yes, that's right, but you don't need to worry about paperwork. I've got copies of all the documents for you. They're locked in my safe.'

'You have a safe?'

'There's one in my flat. You can't be too careful you know.'

'About the flat,' said Flutter. 'I assume that's part of the conditions, right? You and the dog.'

'Yes, it is, but I would understand if you didn't want to honour it.'

'What does that mean?'

'It means you can kick me out, but if you intend to, I hope you'll give me some time to find somewhere else.'

He stared at her, not sure if he was doing the right thing, but then, what did he have to lose?

'Leave? Why would I ask you to leave? This is your home, isn't it?'

'Well, yes, but—'

'What sort of bloke do you think I am? Do I really look the sort who would kick an old lady and her dog out on the street? Besides, I'm not sure I can look after a big house like this on my own. I've only ever had a tiny flat, and that was shared.'

'I'm not sure I agree with your idea that being sixty-two qualifies me as an old lady, but if you're sure...'

Now he'd made the first step, Flutter thought he might as well get all the baggage out in the open and get it over with.

'Look, I know you're being polite and avoiding the elephant in the room,' he said, 'but I'd rather be honest with you and lay my cards on the table. We both know I've just come out of prison, right?'

Now she seemed flustered by the change of conversation, and didn't know what to say, but he didn't give her a chance to speak.

'What I'm trying to say is, it happened, and even though I was innocent I've got a criminal record now and there's no point in trying to pretend I haven't. The good thing is, being in prison has taught me a lesson I will never forget. While I was in there, I resolved to make a new start.'

'I've heard being in prison can do that,' she said.

'Then I got this letter telling me my dad was dead,' continued Flutter, his voice faltering, 'and that I'd inherited a house.'

He paused for a moment to regain his composure.

'It must have been a bit of a shock for you.'

'That's an understatement,' said Flutter. 'I mean, what a way to find out my dad wasn't who I thought he was and that my real dad had been alive all this time! I'm not sure I would have wanted to meet him, but now I won't ever get the chance. I even missed his funeral.'

'No-one can blame you for that if he never came forward, and you didn't even know him.'

'I had no idea he was alive until the solicitor wrote to me, and that was to let me know he was dead!'

Flutter stopped speaking and stared down at his hands. Mrs Walker patted his shoulder.

'Now listen, son,' she said. 'You can't live your life thinking maybe this, or maybe that. None of us can change the past. You can only accept what's happened and move on with your life.'

A deathly silence seemed to fill the room until, after what seemed an eternity, a loud snore punctuated it. Flutter looked around. The dog had climbed back into bed and was comatose once again.

'That dog goes a long time between breaths,' he said.

'I told you, he sleeps like the dead.'

Flutter smiled at the dog, then looked at Mrs Walker.

'I know the dog's name, but I don't know yours,' he said. 'Or do I have to be formal and call you Mrs Walker? I won't be comfortable with any of that Upstairs Downstairs nonsense.'

'You can call me Doris.'

'Right then, Doris, I want you to know I'm on a mission. I realised I messed up my life, but I made myself a promise before I left prison that I would make a new start. I'm here now, and I've got this house, so I've got no excuse for not giving it a go.'

'Well, good for you,' she said. 'I hope you succeed.'

'The thing is, I found out this afternoon that it won't be as easy as I thought.' He hung his head. 'A young woman left her purse on a table in the coffee shop, and I sort of nicked it.'

She sucked in a breath and gave him a disapproving look.

'I'm not proud of myself,' he said.

'Sort of nicked it?' she said. 'What do you mean "sort of"? What exactly happened?'

'She came running back into the shop looking for it.'

'And you kept it?'

'No, I couldn't. I pretended I'd found it under the table and gave it back.'

'And how did you feel?'

'At first, I felt terrible. Guilty, you know. Then, when I saw how grateful she was that I'd found her purse, I felt like a fraud. But then later, when I remembered how relieved she was, I felt good that I'd been able to help her, even though I manufactured the situation. It was all a bit weird, to be honest.'

'So, you stole the purse, but then you gave it back?'

'Yeah, that's right.'

'Did you say you weren't proud of yourself?'

'I'm not.'

'I think perhaps you should be. Yes, you gave in to the temptation, but then you did the right thing and gave the purse back. I think we can call that progress.'

'Really?'

'I take it you've been doing this sort of thing for years?'

'Er, yeah,' he said, guiltily. 'You could say it's more or less second nature.'

'So, it's a habit. Anyone will tell you habits are hard things to break.'

'The thing is, I was confident I could do it when I was inside. I even told the prison officers I would do it, but now I'm not so sure I can do it on my own. I think I need some help.'

He gave her his best puppy dog eyes.

'You mean me?' she asked. 'But we've only just met.'

'I admit I might not always have been the best judge of character,' he said, 'but something tells me you wouldn't be frightened to tell me what you think, or even give me a kick up the backside when it's needed.'

'I was never frightened to tell your dad when he was grumpy.'

'Well, there you are, then. I think that's exactly what I need.'

'I don't know,' she said. 'I mean, I'm just the housekeeper, and now I'm suddenly supposed to tell you what to do? I'm not sure I can do that.'

'Then think of me as a lost soul who needs your help, like Winston, there.'

'I don't know.'

'Please?'

'But what do you want me to do, exactly? You're not asking me to follow you around all day, are you?'

'No, no, that would be crazy. But you will be here looking after the house, won't you? All I want you to do is make sure I remember what I'm trying to achieve, and if you think I'm doing anything even slightly dodgy, you tell me, right?'

'I'll soon get on your nerves, and you won't like that, will you?'

'I might surprise you and have a bit more patience than you think but, if that happens, all you have to do is remind me it was my idea.'

She still looked doubtful.

'At least try it,' he suggested. Then, with a smile, 'How about if I make it a condition for you staying.'

She considered for a moment.

'I read somewhere that you can tell a lot about a person from the way they treat animals.'

Flutter looked puzzled.

'I'm not with you,' he said.

'If you're prepared to accept Winston and me so readily, I think it would be churlish of me to refuse to help you. So I'm willing to have a go.'

Flutter grinned.

'That's all I ask,' he said. 'Just don't be frightened to give me a slap if I need it.'

'Are they the only clothes you have?'

'I've got a change in my bag.'

'You'd better let me run an iron over them.'

Flutter wasn't sure.

'It doesn't feel right, you doing stuff for me,' he said.

'I'm the housekeeper, it's my job,' she assured him. 'If this is going to work, you will have to accept that.'

'I'll try,' he said, 'but it will take a bit of getting used to.'

'Right,' she said decisively. 'I'd better get started with dinner. I've made a cottage pie, it's ready to go in the oven if that's all right?'

'All right?' he said. 'It sounds perfect. I can't remember the last time someone cooked for me.'

'What do you intend to do this evening?'

'Well, I thought it would be great to go out and paint the town red, but realistically I figured it would be more sensible if I stayed in and had an early night. But, first, I will climb in the shower with old Winston and help him with his personal hygiene.'

CHAPTER 8

IT HAD BEEN A LONG, long, time since Flutter had eaten a home-cooked breakfast, and he savoured every mouthful as if it was the last meal he would ever eat.

'That was blinking wonderful, Doris,' he said, placing his knife and fork neatly on his plate.

'You're welcome,' she said. 'It's nice to cook for someone with a healthy appetite.'

Flutter sipped at his cup of tea, then placed the cup down and looked earnestly at her.

'I didn't do what they said I did, you know.'

Doris looked uncomfortable.

'Your father was so upset when he found out,' she said.

'I suppose you're going to tell me he never got so much as a parking ticket.'

'I don't know about that,' she said. 'But I do know he was really upset about you being in prison.'

'Yeah, well,' said Flutter. 'Don't get me wrong, I'm not knocking him. If he was straight, he had the right idea, and I was the fool, I know that. But the thing is, I didn't do what they said I did. It was a set up.'

Doris looked doubtful.

'Look,' he said. 'I admit I used to nick things, but it was small stuff, like when that girl left her purse on the table yesterday. But nicking diamonds? No way. That was way out of my league.'

'In the newspaper, it said you had diamonds from the robbery and—'

'It said that I was one of the guys who raided the jewellers, right? Well, for a start I had an alibi. Second, it wasn't a bag full of diamonds I had on me, it was just one tiny diamond in my rucksack, which anyone could have put there. And third, cheating a gang of crooks like that can see a bloke lose his kneecaps, or even worse. So, you either need to be very brave, which I'm not, or a complete idiot, to do something like that. Now, I might be a fool, but I'm not a complete idiot.'

'All right, if you didn't do it, who did?'

'I don't know,' said Flutter. 'But someone put that diamond in my bag and made sure I took the blame.'

'Now, who would do a thing like that, and why would someone do it to you?'

'Much as I don't want to believe it, I think I might know who, and once I get settled I intend to find out why.'

'You want to be careful you don't end up getting yourself into more trouble.'

'I'll be careful, don't you worry. I also want to find out about my father.'

'Find out what?'

'Well, I'd like to find out what he was like for a start. And why he didn't want to know me.'

'Are you sure that's a good idea?' asked Doris. 'Why not just be grateful for the way things have turned out?'

'That's easy for you to say, Doris, but you're not the one whose just had his life turned upside down, are you?'

'Sometimes it's better to let sleeping dogs lie.'

'Yeah, maybe it is, but right now I have lots of questions, and I need some answers.'

CHAPTER 9

FLUTTER WAS BACK in the town centre, studying each shopfront and doorway until he found the one he was looking for. The entrance to the Waterbury Chronicle's offices was tucked away down a small alley beside the coffee shop he had been in yesterday. Flutter thought if he hadn't been looking for it, he would never have noticed it and wondered if this was a deliberate ploy to make the office hard to find.

He pushed through the door, walked up a flight of stairs, through another door and then suddenly found himself in a big open office space which he figured must be above the coffee shop.

'Well, good morning,' said a familiar voice.

Flutter heard the voice before he saw her, but he recognised her immediately.

'It's Katie, isn't it? I should have known I'd find you here.'

'So I didn't totally put you off yesterday?'

'Sorry?'

'You said I ask too many questions and it must put people off.'

He grinned back at her.

'Oh, yeah, that's right I did, didn't I?'

'So, what can I do for you?'

'I'm looking for some information,' he said.

'What sort of information?'

'As you know, I grew up thinking my parents were dead, but it turns out my father was alive all the time. Only now he's dead too, and suddenly I'm the sole heir to his will. He's left me a house that must have cost a million, and an allowance to live on.

'I want to know exactly who he was, why he didn't want to know me, and where his money came from. I would ask his solicitor, but as you know, that's a bit difficult now he's dead.'

'How do you think I can help?'

'I'm not sure you can. I just don't know where else to start.'

'Does it matter where the money came from?'

'It might matter a lot.'

'Why's that?'

'There you go with the questions again,' said Flutter. 'I just need to know, that's all.'

She studied him for a few moments before she spoke again.

'I did some research on you last night,' she said.

Flutter's heart sank.

'You thought that was necessary, did you?'

'I was curious.'

'Isn't that called invading my privacy?'

'It's called journalism. This might be a tinpot little town in the middle of nowhere, but I'm still a journalist,' she said. 'You said you'd been away. I wanted to know where you'd been.'

'Okay, so now you know, I suppose you think I can't be trusted?'

'That's not what I meant. The way I read the story it was never actually proven that you were part of the gang that robbed the jewellers, and personally I think you would have been a bit young when it happened. My feeling is that the worst you might have been guilty of was handling stolen diamonds.'

'It was one microscopic diamond actually and, just so you know, I wasn't part of any gang who robbed a jewellers and I wasn't handling stolen goods. I've never been part of any gang, and I didn't even know any of the guys involved. I was stitched up, and now I'm out. I'll admit I'd love to know who set me up, and why, but most of all I want to put it behind me and start over. I just wish some of you people could understand how hard it is to do that when everyone makes it so obvious they're convinced I'll fail.'

'Who said you'd fail?'

'You want a list? Well, first there was the prison officer who let me out, then there was some arsehole copper who wanted to arrest me for breaking into my own house—'

'Did this policeman have a name?'

'Blackbeard? Blackwell? Something like that. He's a big roly-poly guy with a bad attitude. He was just itching for an excuse to nick me.'

'Were you breaking in?'

'Of course not. A nosey neighbour thought I looked suspicious, so he called the police.'

'Oh, dear. It doesn't exactly sound like a warm welcome home, does it?'

Flutter had just had a horrible thought.

'Hang on. If you're a journalist and you've been researching me, does this mean I'm going to be one of your stories?'

She giggled.

'Oh, yes,' she said. 'I was going to splash your photo all over the front page with a warning that all residents should beware of the newly arrived gangster whose come to terrorise the town. I can see the headline now. Be afraid, be very afraid.'

'You're not afraid of me, are you?'

'Ooh, yes, terrified!'

'Now you're laughing at me.'

'Well, what do you expect?' she said. 'You were inside for handling stolen goods. It's not much of a story, is it? Now, if you'd been done for mass murder...'

'Sorry,' he said. 'I'll try harder next time. Maybe I could start with that nosey neighbour who called the police yesterday.'

He realised he was feeling sorry for himself.

'I'm sorry. I just feel as though everyone's against me.'

'You've had a bad start, that's all,' she said. 'But, to be fair, I would imagine most prison officers have good reason to be cynical. I also know PC Blackwell rather well, and I can confirm he definitely has an attitude problem.'

'He's not your boyfriend is he?' asked Flutter.

She rolled her eyes.

'You must be joking. Although, if he was, at least I could dump him. Unfortunately, he's my big brother, but if I hide behind my old married name people tend not to make the connection.'

'What about you?' he asked. 'Where do I stand with you?'

'When I said I wanted to find out where you'd been, I meant I wanted to find out for me, not for a story.'

'What does that mean?'

'When I met you yesterday, you weren't very forthcoming, so I wanted to learn more about this mystery man who'd just moved back into town.'

'And now you know what I'm like, I suppose you want to steer well clear, right?'

'You forget I saw what happened in that shop yesterday,' she said.

'You mean when you thought I nicked that girl's purse?'

'No. I meant when you gave it back to her.'

'I don't understand.'

'The fact you gave the purse back tells me you really are trying to change. I think that's a good thing and I, for one, will be happy to support you in that.'

'You will? Why would you do that?'

'Because I think underneath all that front it's just possible you're actually a nice guy who somehow got in with the wrong crowd and now wishes he hadn't.'

Flutter thought she was trying hard to cheer him up, and he had to admit her smile was having the desired effect. She might even be flirting with him. This was probably wishful thinking on his part, but if so, it was the sort of wishful thinking he felt he should do more of.

'Tell me why it's so important to know where your father got his money?'

'I'd like to think he was good guy but, now I've got a record, if there is anything dodgy about him, I need to know because it might count against me.'

'But you said you never met him, so how could anything he did count against you?'

'Everyone I know with this sort of money is dodgy, and you're being naïve if you think it wouldn't count against me if he was the same.'

Katie looked thoughtful.

'I hadn't thought of it like that. Look, I've got a story to write this morning, but once I've done that I'll do some digging and see what I can find out.'

'I'd really appreciate it if you could.'

'I can't make any promises, but I'll do what I can. So, how about if we meet for coffee in the morning?'

'In the shop downstairs?'

'That's the place. I usually stop for my break at about 11.00.'

'I'll be there,' said Flutter.

CHAPTER 10

KATIE TOOK a sip from her coffee and placed her cup down on the table.

'Are you sure you gave me the right name and address?'

'Yes. Why?'

She flipped open a notebook.

'Well I started by checking out the address. No-one called Gamble has ever owned, or lived in, number 54 Willow Grove.'

'That can't be right. He must have owned the house. He left it to me in his will.'

'I can't find a will registered in the name of Walter Gamble either, and according to all the records I've found so far, the person who owned the house, and lived in it, was a man called Walter David, and from what I can see, Walter David lived in that house from the time it was built, about ten years ago.'

Flutter scratched his head.

'That makes no sense.'

'Which is exactly what I thought,' said Katie. 'So I decided to start from a different direction. But I have to warn you, you might not like what I found out.'

'What does that mean?'

'You told me the man you originally thought was your father was called Wesley Gamble, right?'

'That's right, Wesley David Gamble was my father but him, and my mum, Julie, died in a car crash, and his brother, William David, was the guy who raised me. They all had David as their middle name after their grandfather.'

'But Wesley had two brothers, William David Gamble and Walter David Gamble.'

Flutter had been raising his coffee to his lips, but now he stopped.

'Two brothers? No, that can't be right.'

Katie used her finger to find the information in her book, and the read it out loud.

'I found their birth certificates. Walter was the eldest, born in 1956, then Wesley in 1958, and William in 1961.'

'So, how come I've never heard of Walter?'

'I don't know,' said Katie. 'Maybe Walter David was the black sheep of the family.'

Katie watched his face and waited while the penny dropped.

'Hang on, Walter David Gamble was my dad's brother, and the guy living in the house was Walter David? That can't be a coincidence, can it?'

'Hold on to that thought. It'll come in useful later,' said Katie.

'I think my head's going to explode,' said Flutter.

'I hope not,' said Katie. 'We've hardly got started yet. I'm afraid I've uncovered quite a story. Perhaps it would be best if we go back up to my office. It'll be more private.'

Somewhat dazed by what Katie had told him so far, Flutter dutifully followed her from the coffee shop and up the stairs to her office. He had always thought he was part of a small, dull, boring family, and he couldn't begin to guess what else she might have uncovered.

She took him through the main office to a smaller room with a couple of easy chairs and sat him down.

'Can I ask how you found this stuff? Only I wouldn't know where to start.'

'I started with your birth certificate and then worked backwards from there.'

'Oh, right, I see,' he said, not really understanding at all. 'Go on then, let's hear it.'

'The first surprise was on your birth certificate itself. The man listed as your father isn't Wesley, it's Walter.'

'And you're sure about that? Only, Uncle Billy always told me my dad was Wesley,' said Flutter. 'He was married to Julie, my mum.'

'According to their marriage certificate, Wesley was married to Julie, but the birth certificate says he wasn't your father.'

'But why would William and Sylvie lie to me? Why didn't they tell me the truth?'

'Maybe it was a family scandal. Perhaps that's why you've never heard of Walter before.'

'Does that mean you know something about Walter?'

'I'm afraid I didn't have time to get that far, but I did learn something about Wesley and William.'

'I already know about William and Sylvie. They were good people and they worked hard but neither of them was clever enough to make any money. They raised me in a tiny house and when they died they were penniless.'

'D'you want to hear about Wesley?'

'I don't know that it matters now, but yes, why not?'

'He disappeared a month after you were born.'

'No, he was in a car crash. Him and Julie, they were both killed.'

'The thing with a local newspaper is we have an archive that goes back years and years. Wesley was reported missing 30 years ago. Apparently he'd been drinking heavily and was depressed. His body was found floating in the river. No-one knows if he fell in, or jumped.'

'So, that's more lies I was told. It's as if you're rewriting history!'

'I'm sorry, but you did ask me to find out.'

'So, what happened to Julie if she didn't die in a car crash with
Wesley?'

'She died six months after Wesley disappeared. The death certificate is pretty inconclusive, but there was a small, "In Memorium"
piece in the newspaper that said she died of a broken heart after she
lost Wesley.'

'D'you know the ironic thing about all these lies?' said Flutter.
'William and Sylvie really did die in a road accident.'

'Yes, I found out about that, too. I'm sorry.'

'Jeez, what a mess my family is,' said Flutter.

'I can't be sure, of course,' said Katie, 'but if I had to guess, I'd say
Walter charmed Julie into bed, and you were the result.'

'Yeah, but why is his name on the birth certificate? I mean, who
would know apart from Walter and Julie?'

'We'll probably never know that, but I can imagine how hurt
Wesley would have been to learn his own brother was the father of
Julie's baby. No wonder the poor guy went downhill after that.'

'It doesn't say much for Julie, does it?'

'Don't be too harsh on her. We have no idea what really
happened between her and Walter. And if she really died of a broken
heart because of Wesley...'

'Yeah, you're right. As I know only too well, it's easy to judge, but
it's better to know all the facts. If only there was some way of finding
out.'

'To do that you need someone who was there, or someone who
has the inside story.'

'Did you come across a woman called Doris Walker?'

'whose she?'

'My housekeeper.'

'How big is this house that you need a housekeeper?'

'It's big. One day I'll take you there and show you round if you
like. The thing is, in the will it states she has to be employed as the
housekeeper.'

'Well, I haven't come across her anywhere. Why do you think she's important?'

'I could be wrong, but she told me she never met my dad and was employed by the solicitor after he died, but then she's also let slip a couple of things that suggest she's lying. Only this morning she said she knew he was upset I was in prison. How could she know that if she never met him? I'm beginning to think she's been on the scene a lot longer than she says.'

'And you think she might know the story.'

'I think I need to go and ask her what she does know.'

'Can I come? We can take my car.'

Flutter looked at her in surprise.

'I'm sure you've got better things to do than—'

'Not really,' she said. 'I've got a free day. I suppose I could go home and clean my house, but it wouldn't be half as interesting. Unless you'd rather I didn't come?'

'No. Of course you can come.'

CHAPTER 11

As they came through the front door, Doris was just coming out of the kitchen, clutching a pile of ironing. She stopped and peered over the top at them.

'Hello, Harvey, you're back early. I wasn't expecting you until later. Oh, and you've bought a friend with you.'

There was an awkward silence, then Doris spoke again.

'Aren't you going to introduce me?'

Flutter knew she was trying to embarrass him, but he knew he would turn the tables on her shortly, so he feigned a smile and did as she asked.

'Doris, this is Katie.'

Doris nodded to Katie.

'Nice to meet you. I'm sure,' she said. 'Let me just take these bits upstairs, and I'll make us all a nice cup of tea.'

'That sounds like a good idea,' said Flutter.

He watched as Doris made her way upstairs, then led Katie through to the kitchen.

'Wow! This is some house your dad left you,' said Katie.

Flutter pointed to the dog bed where the occupant snored happily under his blanket.

'It even comes with its own dog.'

Katie took a step towards Winston.

'He looks very cosy under that blanket,' she said.

'I wouldn't go too near,' Flutter warned her. 'He's a nice old thing, and he's friendly enough, but he smells disgusting. I even bathed him last night and then first thing this morning he found something disgusting ink the garden and rolled in it. I ought to make him sleep outside.'

'Oh, don't be so horrible. I hope you don't tell him he smells.'

'Trust me, he knows,' said Flutter. 'He doesn't need anyone to tell him. I think he must feel incomplete unless he stinks.'

'But you can't make him sleep outside.'

'According to Doris, he loves it out there. The old man even built him his own sun lounger so he could sit in the sun.'

Katie didn't look convinced, so Flutter took her through to the dining room.

'There, that wooden platform thing,' he said, pointing down the garden through the window.

Katie followed his gaze down the garden. Sure enough, she could see what he meant.

'But you can't make him sleep out there in this weather. It's much too cold.'

'Don't worry, I couldn't do it even if I really wanted to. Winston has the sort of eyes that make him irresistible, and the manipulative little sod knows how to use them.'

'So he's won you over already?'

Flutter laughed.

'Yeah. It took him about thirty seconds.'

'So you are a big softie. I thought I was right about you.'

'Only where dogs are concerned,' said Flutter. 'And I'll tell you why; dogs are honest. If they don't like you, they say so right from the start. You always know where you are with a dog, unlike many people.'

Katie was sure he didn't mean her, but her body language must have said otherwise.

'Present company excepted,' he said hastily. 'I think you're one of the good guys, Katie Donald. You don't know me from Adam, and yet here you are standing by me. I appreciate it more than you know.'

She looked up into his eyes, and for a moment Flutter thought his luck might be in, but then Doris's voice destroyed the moment.

'That cup of tea's ready, now,' she said, from the doorway. 'Oh, sorry. Am I interrupting something?'

Flutter sighed.

'Okay, Doris. Thank you. We're just coming.'

'So what brings you home this early?' asked Doris, as she poured the first mug of tea.

'Katie's a journalist,' continued Flutter. 'She's helping me find out about my father.'

'Find out what about your father?' Doris asked suspiciously. 'I already told you what I know.'

'Ah. Yes, so you did,' said Flutter. 'But the thing is, I'm not sure you told me everything you know. In fact, I'm pretty sure you barely skimmed the surface.'

Doris put the tea pot down and pointed at Katie.

'I don't know what rubbish she's been filling your head with, but I wouldn't listen to her if I were you. You can't trust journalists.'

'Two things you need to know Doris. First, you're not me, and second, Katie hasn't told me anything, and if she did, I'd trust her to tell me the truth, which is more than I can say for you.'

Doris narrowed her eyes.

'What's that supposed to mean?'

'Well, you told me you never knew my father and were employed by the solicitor.'

'Yes, that's right.'

'The thing is, I don't think it is right,' said Flutter.

'Why on earth would you think that?'

'Because there are one or two inconsistencies in your story.'

'What inconsistencies?'

'Well, for a start there's the dog. I'm assuming there was a gap between when the old man died and when you arrived, so where was Winston in the meantime? I mean if he'd been taken to live some-where else, why bring him back here?'

'I can't tell you what went on before I got here.'

'When I said he looked sad, you told me he'd always looked like that but he looked even sadder since my father died.'

Doris stared down at the teapot.

'Did I say that?'

'Yeah, you did, and there's only one way you could know that.'

'It was just a figure of speech.'

'Really? What about when I said you might need to give me a kick up the arse now and then? You told me it wouldn't be a problem because you were never frightened to tell my dad when he was grumpy. Was that another figure of speech?'

Doris licked her lips and then slowly looked up at Flutter.

'You don't miss much do you? I thought you hadn't noticed when I let that slip.'

'Yeah, well, maybe I'm not as stupid as I look,' said Flutter.

Doris sighed, resignedly.

'What is it you think I know?'

'Well, where shall we start? I know, how about you tell me where the money came from?'

'He had it when I met him.'

'Ah, so you admit you met him. That's not what you said before, is it?'

She licked her lips but said nothing as she filled two more mugs with tea. She placed the three mugs on a tray, then she nodded towards the table.

'Can we all sit down?' she asked.

'Sure,' said Flutter.

Doris bought the tray over, placed a mug in front of Katie, another before Flutter, then took her own and sat down.

'Okay,' she said. 'I can see there's no point in pretending. You were honest with me, so now I'll be honest with you. I was your father's girlfriend.'

There was a brief, stunned, silence.

'His girlfriend?' spluttered Flutter.

'All right, his lover, if that's what you want me to say. It's not so hard to believe, is it? I was quite a catch in my day, I can tell you.'

'I'm not disputing what you say,' said Flutter. 'It turns out I've spent thirty years believing in a family fantasy, so everything I hear about it now is news to me.'

'It must be very confusing for you.'

'Confusing? Yeah, you could say that. So, he never married, then?'

'As far as I know, he wanted to marry your mother.'

'Hang on a minute,' he said. 'I though you said you were going to tell the truth.'

'I am—'

'No, Doris, you're not. We already know my mother married Wesley and died less than year after I was born.'

'Ah, so you know about that. What else do you know?'

'Sorry, Doris, but that's not how this is going to work. I'm asking the questions. So, why don't you tell me what happened.'

'I don't know all the details. I wasn't on the scene back then. I only met Walter a few years ago, but I'll tell you this; he was a very sad man.'

'Sad?'

'Yes, sad. He'd lost touch with his family, and lost the woman he loved.'

'You're talking about my mum, Julie, right?'

'That's right.'

'If he loved her so much, why didn't he say so before she married Wesley?'

'I don't know. As I said, this all happened years before I came on the scene. I only know what he told me.'

'So what did he tell you?'

'He'd been in love with Julie before Wesley even met her, but then he got a job up in London. He went to live there and left her behind. That's when Wesley met her and after a year or two they got married. Of course, Walter came back for the wedding, met Julie again and realised what he was missing.'

'So they started an affair? When she'd only just married?'

'No, it didn't happen like that. She told Walter she loved Wesley and didn't want to hurt him, so Walter agreed to stay away. And he did stay away for a while, but in the end he just had to come and see her, and it turned out she felt the same way. That's when the affair started, and it wasn't long before she got pregnant.'

'And then I came along,' finished Flutter. 'But why didn't they just keep quiet about it? Surely no-one would have known.'

'Apparently William knew somehow, and he insisted Walter had to tell Wesley the truth. They got into a fight over it, and then Wesley came across them fighting and wanted to know what the fight was about. So William told him, and once the cat was out of the bag Walter insisted his name had to go on the birth certificate.'

'Jeez, no wonder poor old Wesley ended up depressed and drank himself to death,' said Katie.

'That's what people thought,' said Doris.

'What's that supposed to mean?' asked Flutter.

'According to Walter, Wesley got drunk one night and came looking for him. Walter didn't want to fight his brother but he wouldn't stop, so he pushed him away. Wesley was so drunk he tripped and cracked his head on the ground.'

'You mean Walter killed him?'

'It was an accident, but he couldn't say anything, could he? I mean, everyone knew there was bad blood between them, so who would have believed it was an accident? By then he was doing well in London and he couldn't afford to have the police involved so he put the body in the river and let everyone believe Wesley had fallen in when he was drunk.'

'He killed his own brother, and then dumped his body in the river! I've heard of getting away with murder, but blimey, can it get any worse?'

'It wasn't murder it was an accident.'

'You've only got Walter's word for that,' said Flutter.

'But why would he lie?' argued Doris. 'He didn't have to tell me any of it, did he? So why lie?'

'And he actually got away with it?' asked Katie.

'William suspected him, but couldn't prove anything. But it was the last straw for him and he told Walter he had to leave town, and never come back, or else he'd go straight to the police and tell them what he thought had happened. And Walter did leave town and he never came back until ten years ago.'

'And that's it?' asked Flutter.

'That's all I know about the family trouble.'

'Okay, so let's go back to my first question. Where did the money come from?'

'I told you, he had it when I met him.'

'Yeah, and technically that may be true,' said Flutter. 'But we both know that you know more than you're letting on, don't we? Let's start with when you met him. You told me it was a few years ago.'

'That's right.'

'How many years ago?'

'I don't know exactly. Time flies as you get older, and it's easy to forget these things.'

'That's very convenient for you, isn't it?'

'I don't know. I can't remember exactly.'

'And who was your boyfriend before my dad?'

'I can't remember.'

'Blimey, Doris, your memory! It's a wonder you can remember your name.'

'I told you. I'm getting old.'

'You told me the other day that sixty-two isn't old!'

'Did I? I don't think I remember that.'

'Okay, so why don't I see if I can help you remember a few things,' said Flutter. 'I'll tell you a name, and let's see if it helps you. How about a bloke called Jimmy Jewle? Does that ring a bell?'

The colour seemed to drain from her face as they watched and then she buried her head in her hands.

'Oh my God,' she said, looking up. 'How did you know?'

'I seem to have hit the jackpot with that one, don't I?' he said, turning to Katie who was looking totally bewildered.

'I'm sorry I didn't mention that before, Katie, but it will make sense in a minute.'

He winked at her before turning back to Doris.

'Actually, Doris, that was what you might call a lucky guess. The thing is I heard a rumour when I was inside that a gangster called Jimmy Jewle was looking for me in relation to some sort of debt he's owed. Now, of course, it could be a coincidence that he's looking for me at the same time I've just inherited a nice big house, but I don't think it is, do you?'

He waited for Doris to speak, but she seemed temporarily lost for words.

'It's amazing what you can learn in prison,' continued Flutter. 'Especially what you can learn about crimes. Some of them are legendary. For instance, did you know that about twelve years ago a jewellers was robbed, and a large amount of diamonds was stolen. Does this ring any bells for you, Doris?'

Doris sat stock still and said nothing, but once again she nervously licked her lips.

'A guy called Jimmy Jewle was believed to be responsible for the robbery,' continued Flutter, 'but although the police had been given a tip-off, no conclusive evidence was ever found to enable them to bring charges that would stick.

'This was very lucky for Jewle because he actually was responsible for the robbery and, had everything gone to plan, the loot would have been right where the police had been told to look.'

'So, what happened,' asked Katie, who was enthralled by the story. 'How come they didn't find any evidence? Did he know the police had been tipped off?'

'No, he didn't,' said Flutter. 'He just got lucky. According to the legend he had no idea the police were going to turn up. It came as a complete surprise, just as it was a complete surprise to discover his most trusted gang member had disappeared with all the diamonds.'

'And this was the guy who had tipped off the police?' asked Katie.

Flutter shrugged.

'No-one knows for sure, but it seems likely. I mean the guy ran off with the entire proceeds of the robbery, and get this,' he looked pointedly at Doris. 'He took Jewle's girlfriend as well.'

Katie had caught up with him now, and regarded Doris with renewed interest.

'And now, how's this for another coincidence?' added Flutter. 'It was about ten or eleven years ago that Walter David Gamble, or as he preferred to be know more recently, Walter David, moved into this very house.'

Then he turned back to Doris.

'So tell me, how am I doing so far, Doris?'

'I don't know what you're talking about,' she said, defiantly. 'You've got a vivid imagination, I'll give you that.'

'Now here's the thing you need to understand,' said Flutter. 'You think Jewle couldn't find you and Walter, but I think you're wrong. I think he knew where you were, but he's been biding his time.'

'Why would he do that?' asked Doris.

'The thing is he couldn't come looking too closely because he was being watched by the police. If he'd brought them down here it could have connected all of you to the robbery.'

'You're wrong,' said Doris. 'Walter laid a trail that led Jimmy to believe we'd gone abroad. If he knew where we were he'd have been here like a shot.'

'Trust me, Doris, if he got a message to me in prison, it means he knows who I am. And why would he waste his time with someone like me unless he's looking to reclaim the debt he's owed? And if I'm right about that it means he knows about the will and the house.'

'How could he possibly know about that?' demanded Doris.

'I have no idea, but by strange coincidence the old man's solicitor also died recently. Apparently he had a heart attack.'

'People die of heart attacks all the time,' said Doris.

'Or perhaps someone frightened him to death,' said Flutter.

'You've got no evidence to prove that.'

This was true enough, and Flutter wasn't going to waste his time arguing the point.

'Okay, so let's say you're right and he doesn't know about the will, or the house,' he conceded. 'But he definitely knows who I am, and he knew I was in the nick. What if he knew I was being released and he had me followed down here? He'll know all about the house now, won't he?'

'Why would he have you followed?'

'Because he thinks I'll lead him to Walter.'

'Well that'll be a waste of his time,' said Doris. 'Walter's dead.'

'Yeah, but what if Jewle doesn't care about that? What if he just wants what he thinks is rightfully his?'

Doris fidgeted in her seat and considered for a moment.

'D'you think he really will come here to claim the house?' she asked.

Flutter shrugged.

'I dunno. How does anyone know what a psychopath is going to do?'

'I hadn't thought of it like that,' said Doris. 'I thought once he knew Walter was dead he'd call off the search and that would be it.'

'So you finally admit the two of you were hiding from this Jimmy Jewle character,' said Katie.

'I didn't say that.'

'Actually, you did, near enough,' said Flutter. 'You also said earlier that the old man wanted to make sure I stayed on the straight and narrow, so that suggests he'd been keeping an eye on me, right? In which case he would have known I'd been setup and was going to prison. So, if he cared so much, why didn't he do something to stop it?'

'Oh, don't be so melodramatic,' said Doris. 'Anyway, you got this house, didn't you? I should think that's worth a few months of anyone's life!'

'Worth it?' asked Katie incredulously. 'Since when did you get to play God?'

Doris gave her a withering look.

'Listen here, girlie,' she said. 'D'you think it was any fun for Walter and me? Ten years we were in prison here.'

'Prison?' said Flutter. 'This isn't a prison!'

'It is when you daren't go anywhere, or do anything, in case you get recognised.'

'I'll swap you ten years here for a few months in a real prison any time,' said Flutter. 'Trust me, you'd soon notice the difference. Anyway, we can argue about this another time. Right now I need to know what I can expect Jimmy Jewle to do when he gets here.'

'How am I supposed to know?'

'Come on, Doris, don't play games. You used to be his girlfriend, so you must know something about him and what he's like.'

Doris sniffed huffily.

'I'll tell you this much. If I were you, I'd get as far out of town as you can. Jimmy bears a grudge, and he's been bearing this one for over ten years.'

'So, he wants me to hand over the proceeds of the robbery, right?' said Flutter. 'But I'm guessing this house is part of it and the rest has been turned into cash and tied up in a trust fund. How am I supposed to get my hands on that?'

'You're not listening,' said Doris. 'If he's still coming, even though Walter's dead, that means he wants everything. Not just the money and the house, but I reckon what he'll really want, most of all is your father's blood.'

'But the old man's dead!'

'Yes, but his son, isn't, is he?'

'But I had nothing to do with what happened back then.'

'D'you think he cares about that?'

'But I've just been inside. If he had wanted to get at me, he could have done it in there.'

'Even Jimmy Jewle doesn't have people everywhere.'

'Hang on a minute,' said Flutter. 'Are you telling me the old man knew all this was going to happen, but he did nothing to help me?'

'He was dying. He couldn't have done anything. That's why he left you the house. It was compensation.'

'I don't want compensation, and I don't want to to spend the rest of my life looking over my shoulder. All I ever wanted was the freedom to live my own life!'

'Listen to yourself,' said Doris, 'You do nothing but complain. You're free now, aren't you?'

'Hardly,' said Flutter. 'You seem to forget Attila the Hun is going to come riding over the brow of the hill at any minute, and he's looking to exact his revenge on me!'

'Well, it's your own fault you're still here. I've already told you to run,' said Doris. 'You should run while you can. I can deal with Jimmy Jewle.'

Flutter looked at her.

'Really? You think you can deal with him, but I can't? How are you going to do that?'

'Listen to me,' said Doris. 'You might think you're Jack the Lad, but you need to understand you're way out of your depth here. Jimmy isn't some petty thief you can smack around and send home. He's mean, and he's nasty. I don't want you to get hurt, and your father wouldn't want you to get hurt.'

'He didn't seem to give a damn about me going to prison, did he?'

'That was different. He couldn't do anything to help.'

'So what, are you saying we should just run away?'

'What I'm saying is this isn't your fight. There's no reason for you to get involved.'

'But I am involved aren't I? He knows who I am, and he knows where I am.'

'And if you get more involved now, what will happen? You could end up back in prison, or even die! How is that going to help anyone?'

'But what about you?'

'Look at me,' she said. 'I'm sixty-two years old, with nothing left to live for. What have I got to lose? You've still got your whole life ahead of you. Take Katie and get away while you still can.'

Flutter suddenly realised Katie was missing.

'Where is she?'

'I don't know,' said Doris. 'She must have slipped out while we were talking, but she can't have gone far.'

Just then, Katie appeared from the dining room.

'I thought you'd run off,' said Flutter. 'Mind you, I wouldn't blame you if you did.'

She had her mobile phone in her hand, and now she waved it at them.

'I was just calling the police.'

'The police!' said Flutter, 'Jeez, Katie, we're in enough trouble. We don't need dozens of coppers stomping around the place. The first thing they'll do is assume I'm involved with Jewle, and before you know it, I'll be banged up again.'

'It won't be like that. I've already explained what's going on.'

Doris tutted and shook her head.

'My Gawd, girl, you are so naïve. D'you really think they will believe that?'

'Yes, I do, actually,' said Katie, indignantly. 'I didn't call the local police station. I called my friend whose a detective in Birmingham. He knows the situation, and he's going to help.'

Flutter looked at Katie. She had meant well, but he felt the situation would only get worse if they involved the police.

'I really think you should get out of here,' he said.

'But what about you?'

'I can't leave Doris here on her own.'

'You don't owe me anything,' said Doris.

'Don't kid yourself,' said Flutter. 'It's not because I feel I owe you anything. I just can't leave a woman to face a gang of thugs on her own. It's not right.'

'Go on,' said Doris, 'Clear off, while you still can.'

The sound of the buzzer coming from the hall interrupted their discussion. Katie looked enquiringly at Flutter.

'There's someone at the gates,' he said, turning to Doris, 'Are you expecting anyone?'

She shook her head.

'Me neither,' he said.

'Then they must be here already,' she whispered, fearfully.

CHAPTER 12

FLUTTER CREPT out to the hall as if he expected to find someone waiting to jump on him. Katie followed and together they stared at the small CCTV screen that monitored the gate. A large black limousine was there waiting for the gates to open. The driver's door was open, and a man dressed in a smart black suit stood by the intercom.

'Is that them?' asked Katie.

'I don't think it's the man come to read the electric meter,' said Flutter, grimly. He pressed the button and spoke into the microphone.

'Hello?'

'Is that Mr Gamble?'

'Yes.'

'Can you open the gates, please?'

'Why would I do that? I have no idea who you are.'

He could see the beginnings of a smile on the driver's face, and he seemed to nod his head as if in approval of the question.

'I have Mr Jewle in the back of my car. I believe you know who he is. He would like to come in and speak to you.'

'Yes, I bet he would,' said Flutter, 'but you can tell him it's not going to happen.'

The driver turned back to the car, and the back window opened a couple of inches. The driver exchanged a few words with his passenger and then turned back to the microphone.

'Mr Jewle asks if you're sure you don't want to let him in? He says you should understand he will be very disappointed if you don't.'

A combination of adrenaline and impatient bravado fueled Flutter's reply.

'Why don't you tell Mr Jewle if he gets his arse out of the car he can speak to me now.'

A smirk flashed across the driver's face but vanished as he turned back to the car window to begin another muttered conversation.

After a further minute, to Flutter's surprise, the back door of the car opened, and another man emerged.

'Is that him?' asked Katie.

'I guess it must be. He looks full of his own self-importance,' said Flutter.

The man was wearing an expensive-looking, full-length, camel-hair coat with equally expensive, shiny shoes. An immaculate white collar and tie were all Flutter could make out beneath the coat, but he guessed the suit would be the very best from Saville Row.

As the man approached the CCTV camera, they could see his face. He looked grimly determined.

'He looks more like an undertaker than a gangster,' said Katie.

'They're both involved in death,' agreed Flutter. 'The difference is an undertaker prepares bodies for the afterlife, and this guy prepares them for the undertaker.'

On the screen, they watched as Jewle reached for the button.

'Mr Gamble? My name's Jimmy Jewle, but you already know that. I was rather hoping your father would be here, but I understand he's no longer with us.'

'Yeah, sorry about that. I'm afraid it looks like you've had a wasted journey,' said Flutter.

'Oh, I wouldn't say that. I'll admit I'm disappointed your father's not around because we had unfinished business, but that needn't be a major hindrance. Your name's Harvey, isn't it?'

'You know it is.'

'You sound angry, Harvey.'

'Too right I'm bloody angry. You're the arsehole who had me framed and sent to prison.'

'Actually, that was your father's doing, not mine.'

Flutter's heart sank. This wasn't what he wanted to hear.

'What d'you mean it was his doing?'

'He knew I was closing in, and that I'd figured out you were his boy. He thought if he put you inside you'd be safer than if you were on the outside.'

'Safer? In amongst all those thugs?'

'Oh, I understand how you feel,' said Jewle. 'He had some strange ideas, did Walter. Of course, that whole unhappy episode could have been avoided if your old man hadn't been such a coward.'

'That's rubbish. He was dying. He couldn't have done anything.'

'He could have done as I asked, and signed this house over to me, along with what's left of the money,' said Jewel. 'But he didn't, did he? He kept his head down, signed it all over to you, and left you to face the music. Those aren't exactly the actions of a superhero, are they? Anyway, it's all yours now, and we can avoid any further unpleasantness if you just sign everything over to me.'

'Even if I wanted to, I can't sign the money over. It's in a trust fund. Anyway, why should I give it to you?'

'Because it's rightfully mine.'

'Your argument is with my old man, not with me.'

'My argument is with whoever has my house and my money. As I already said, it's a pity your father isn't here in person, but there we are, it is what it is. As his heir, the debt passes down to you. It won't be quite as satisfying without seeing old Walter, but, to be honest, I can live without the gratuitous violence as long as I get what I want.'

A shiver ran up Flutter's back. He had come across one or two characters in prison who knew how to intimidate, but this guy was on another level altogether. He heard Katie gasp alongside him as she took an involuntary step back.

'My God,' she said. 'I've never seen anyone so sinister.'

'He's just trying to intimidate us,' said Flutter.

'Well, take it from me, he's succeeding,' she said.

'Remember, he can't hurt us from that side of the gate.'

'Yes, but how long can we keep him that side of the gate?'

Jewle had been studying the gates and the wall. As if he had heard the question, he spoke again.

'I'm not alone, you know.'

'I didn't for one minute think you were,' said Flutter. 'People like you always need plenty of back-up to do your dirty work for you.'

'There are two more cars, with my men inside, just down the road. If I wanted to escalate things I could easily send them over the wall.'

'Yeah, I'm sure you could,' said Flutter. 'But don't forget my old man made this place into a fortress. There are state of the art alarms everywhere and the system's linked to the local police station.'

'Is it?' asked Katie when he let the intercom button go.

'I've no idea,' said Flutter. 'I'd say probably not, but Jewle won't know that.'

'What if he figures it out?'

'Then we're ten miles up shit creek without a paddle, but I'm beginning to think we are anyway. If this works it might buy us a couple of hours so I can get you out of here.'

Jewle's voice filled the hallway again.

'You're bluffing.'

'You think? Go on then, try it. Send your guys over the wall and see how long it takes for the local plod to get here. I reckon we could easily hold out for the few minutes it would take.'

A scowl settled on Jewle's face, making him look even more sinister.

'I always thought vampires had to avoid sunlight,' muttered Flutter as he watched Jewel stalk up and down outside the gates.

Katie looked horrified as she turned to Flutter.

'How can you joke about this?'

'I can hide in the cupboard under the stairs if you prefer,' he said, 'but that sort of thing's never worked for me before.'

'So facing down gangsters is a regular occurrence for you, is it?'

'Don't be silly. That's not what I mean. It's just not in my nature to run away and hide. I'd rather face up to my problems and see if I can find a way out.'

'Well, this is definitely a problem,' said Katie, 'but if you ask me, he doesn't look the sort whose interested in negotiating.'

'Well, yeah, I'd sort of worked that one out for myself.'

'So what are we going to do?'

'I dunno yet. I'm still thinking. What the....'

Jewle had been pacing up and down outside the gate as Flutter watched on the screen. Now he stopped in his tracks and stared at something through the gates that Flutter couldn't see on the screen. Then, to his surprise, Jewle raised his hands and took two steps back.

'Bloody hell,' said Flutter moving to the window to get a better view. 'Take a look at this, Katie.'

He pointed down the drive towards the gates.

'This is a surprise,' he muttered. 'I bet when Jewle mentioned escalating he hadn't figured on it starting from our side of the gate.'

CHAPTER 13

Looking down the drive, they could see Doris marching away from the house towards the gate. There was something weird about the way she was walking, but Katie couldn't quite make out what it was.

'Why is Doris marching down the drive like that, and why has he got his hands up?'

'Didn't you see it on the screen?' asked Flutter.

'I wasn't looking.'

'He's got his hands up because Doris is pointing a shotgun at him.'

She raised her hands to her face.

'Oh my God. Tell me you're kidding.'

Flutter shook his head.

'No, I'm not, and look, Jewle doesn't seem to think it's a joke, does he? Let's just hope she doesn't pull the trigger. If she does, it'll start a bloodbath.'

He made towards the front door, but Katie grabbed his arm.

'Where are you going?'

'I'm going to try and stop Doris blowing his head off.'

'But you could get hurt.'

'It's better than being a party to murder, isn't it?'

He lifted her hand from his arm, opened the door, and ran down
the drive after Doris. He had no desire to startle her by his arrival, so
he called after her as he ran.

'Doris. Doris. Now don't do anything stupid, will you? Just hang
on a minute, until I get there.'

By the time he caught up, she was at the gate, still pointing the
shotgun at Jewle who was standing perfectly still, his hands still
raised.

Making sure Doris knew he was there, and keeping his distance,
Flutter carefully skirted around her until she could see him.

Jewle kept quiet as he waited for Flutter to settle. He seemed
remarkably relaxed considering his situation and appeared to be
thinking along similar lines to Flutter.

'Now look here, Doris,' he said, 'You really don't want to
shoot me.'

'Oh, but I do,' said Doris.

'But you've got no reason—'

'I've got plenty of reasons,' she said. 'Why d'you think I left you?'

'These things happen, don't they? But I don't hold it against you. I
expect it was Walter's fault. He could be very persuasive. He knew
how to charm the ladies.'

'You don't get it, do you?' said Doris. 'I didn't need Walter to
persuade me to leave you. I couldn't wait to get away.'

'But I don't have a grudge with you, Doris. It's Walter who
double-crossed me, and it's Walter who owes me. I just want what's
mine.'

'D'you really think I'm going to believe you, Jimmy Jewle? You built
your empire by telling people one thing and then doing the opposite. I
think it's better for all concerned if I just shoot you and have done with it.'

'If you shoot from this range you can't miss. You'll blow my head
off.'

'Which is precisely why I walked all the way down here to the
gate.'

'But that would be murder, Doris. They'd lock you up and throw away the key.'

Flutter was impressed by Jewle's ability to remain so calm and wondered how he would fare if their roles were reversed. He quickly realised he would almost certainly have needed a change of under-wear by now and had to admit to a certain grudging admiration for the older man's coolness.

'He's right, Doris,' said Flutter. 'It would be murder. You'd get life.'

'The thing is, I don't care,' said Doris. 'I mean, what have I got to live for now Walter's gone?'

'Sorry?'

'Walter was my life, but he's gone now, so what have I got to live for?'

Jewle took his eyes off the shotgun for a moment to glance at Flutter.

'No offence,' he said, 'but if her whole world revolved around Walter Gamble, she's not just a sandwich short of a picnic, she's missing the entire hamper.'

Flutter was desperately trying to think of an argument that might win Doris over, but so far he had come up with nothing. He could see she was getting close to the edge now, and Jewle taunting her wasn't helping. He wondered how much longer it would be before she snapped.

'Don't you bad mouth my Walter,' she snarled at Jewle. 'He was ten times the man you are.'

'That's your considered opinion, is it?' asked Jewle. 'I'll try not to lose too much sleep worrying about that.'

He glanced at Flutter again.

'You want to take the daft old bat back inside the house before she does something stupid,' he advised. 'It won't look good for you if you're an accomplice to murder, will it?'

It took a couple of seconds for Flutter to absorb Jewle's words.

Had he just been given an argument that might work? It was worth a try.

'Can I ask you a question, Doris?'

She looked at him uncertainly.

'What question?'

'Do you think Walter would want you to get me sent back to prison?'

'Of course not. You're all right, you are. Why would I want to do that to you?'

'The thing is, if you shoot him, that's what will happen to me.'

'But I'm the one pulling the trigger.'

'Yes, but I'm standing here next to you. I would be considered an accessory to the crime. In the eyes of the law, I might as well have pulled the trigger myself.'

'But that's silly.'

'You may well be right, Doris, but that's how it is,' said Flutter.

'He's right,' said Jewle. 'And he'd probably get twenty years minimum.'

'You don't want me to go back to prison, do you?' asked Flutter.

Doris looked at Flutter, then at Jewle, then at the gun. It was as if she hadn't seen the shotgun before. She was obviously confused, but after a few seconds, she seemed to make sense of everything.

'No. I don't want you to go to prison,' she said.

Jewle was watching the exchange, and as he saw the confusion clear from Doris's face, he breathed a silent sigh of relief. As he watched her hand the shotgun over to Flutter a momentary, ghostly smile appeared on his face. The object of his revenge had just saved his life, and he thought it was almost a pity to have to hurt Flutter after that.

Then again, he had never been one to allow sentiment to get in the way of business for long. And, right now, business dictated that, if he had to hurt someone to reclaim his property, then Flutter should be the victim. But these were exceptional circumstances so perhaps, just this once, as a gesture of goodwill, he could allow the victim the opportunity of safe passage.

Katie had come down to the gate and was now escorting Doris back up to the house. Flutter had broken the shotgun to make it safe and now watched as Jewle came right up to the gate.

'Thank you. You saved my life,' he said.

'Don't kid yourself,' said Flutter. 'I couldn't give a damn about your life. I would have been happy to see her blow your head off, but I don't want to end up in prison again.'

Jewle sniggered.

'You talk like a proper hard nut, don't you?' he said. 'But, the thing is, we both know it's all show. It takes a particular sort of person to take a life in cold blood, or even stand by and watch someone else do it, and we both know you're not like that.'

'I think Doris might have done it,' said Flutter. 'Does that mean she's special?'

'Doris isn't special, she's just crazy, and always has been,' said Jewle. 'Walter did me a favour when he persuaded her to leave me. Anyway, I don't want to talk about Doris. I still want my house, and my money, but as you just did me a favour, I'm willing to do you one in return.'

'Oh, yeah? I can't wait to hear it.'

'I still intend to take what's mine, but now I'm prepared to make it easy for you. I came here intending to hurt anyone who got in my way, but I quite like you, so I'm going to make you an offer you can't refuse.'

'I'm sure I will refuse it, but go on, let's hear it.'

'I promised my wife I'd be home in time to take her out to dinner but, because this has taken a little longer to resolve than I intended, I'm in danger of being late. So, as a gesture of goodwill, I'm going to back off, go home, and give you time to consider what to do.'

'How much time?' asked Flutter.

'I'll give you 24 hours, and then I'll be back.'

'I should warn you, my friend called the police earlier.'

Jewle feigned surprise.

'Oh, really? Well, all I can say is they don't seem to be in a hurry to get here, do they? Is this the same police that will be here within minutes if we breach your security?'

Flutter had forgotten about that little lie.

'The thing is, you can't afford to have the police involved, can you?' said Jewle. 'Apart from anything else they'll ask is if that shotgun's licensed.'

Flutter looked down at the shotgun in alarm.

'My guess is it's probably not,' said Jewle, 'but that would be enough for starters. And, of course, once they get a little suspicious who knows where it will all end.'

Dismayed, Flutter looked up at Jewle who offered a sinister smile as he spoke again.

'You see, you thought Walter had done you a big favour, didn't you? But the reality is he's lumbered you with a ticking timebomb. I mean, just suppose someone was to suggest the police should look into where the money came from to buy this place?'

'You wouldn't,' said Flutter.

Jewle's smile widened.

'Of course, I wouldn't, but someone else might.'

'You mean you'd tell someone else to do it, right?' asked Flutter.

Jewle winked at Flutter.

'The thing is, can you afford to take the risk?' he asked. 'Whichever way you look at it, you could end up back behind bars, and you don't want that, do you?'

Flutter knew Jewle was right. Getting the police involved would almost certainly be a disaster.

'Oh, one other thing,' said Jewle, opening the door to his car. 'If you don't open the gates when we come back tomorrow, I might feel the need to send my guys over the wall, and if that happens, you need to understand they won't be taking prisoners. Know what I mean?'

'I already told you what will happen if you do that,' said Flutter.

Jewle smiled another mirthless smile.

'You mean about the security system being linked to the local police?'

Flutter hadn't really expected him to be fooled by his claim, but even so...

'Don't look so surprised,' said Jewle. 'I mean, you could have been telling the truth, but I thought it was highly unlikely. So, while we were here at the gate, having our little chat, one of my guys went around to the other side of the house and climbed over the wall. He even walked across the garden and went into the house to see if he could trigger an alarm.'

'I don't believe you,' said Flutter.

'Why would I lie?' asked Jewle, strolling to his car. 'Anyway, now I've had time to get to know you a little, I find you're nothing like Walter, who would almost certainly have encouraged Doris to pull the trigger. The truth is I quite like you so I want to give you a chance to walk out of here without getting hurt.'

He climbed into the car and closed the door. He appeared to exchange a few words with the driver, then the window slid silently down, and he spoke again.

'I can see you're still doubtful, so consider this: even that weird, smelly, guard dog in your kitchen doesn't work. My guy says he snored his way through the whole episode. Now, ask yourself, how could I possibly know that?'

Flutter was suddenly so worried he had no response.

'You've got 24 hours,' called Jewle.

The window slid silently closed, then the driver started the car, reversed off the drive and headed towards town.

CHAPTER 14

As FLUTTER WATCHED the car drive away and then turned to walk back to the house, he realised it was getting dark. He was still carrying the shotgun which he placed down inside the front door, making a mental note to get rid of it as soon as he could. He hadn't bothered turning on the security lights before, but after what had just happened, he thought tonight would be an excellent time to start using them.

'Where's Doris?' he asked Katie. 'She hasn't gone back to her flat, has she?'

'No. She's upstairs.'

'Good, because we need to have a little chat and she needs to clarify a few things.'

'What about Jewle? Has he gone?'

'For now. As a reward for persuading Doris to put the gun down and not to blow his head off, Mr Jewle has very generously decided to give me 24 hours to get out, or else.'

'Or else, what?'

'Or else he's sending his troops over the wall to take the house by force.'

'He can't do that!'

'Guys like Jewle can do whatever they want.'

'I'll speak to my friend. He'll stop him.'

'I admire your faith, Katie, but coppers don't usually rush to help people who've just come out of the nick. I mean, he didn't exactly rush to the rescue this afternoon, did he?'

'He's not going to get here in five minutes from Birmingham, is he? Let me call him and find out where he is.'

'Yeah, right, you do that,' said Flutter.

As Katie headed for the dining room, Flutter made his way to the kitchen and walked over to Winston, who was still snoring peacefully. He prodded the dog to wake him.

'Come on, wake up, Winston. It's dinnertime.'

As the dog slowly came to full consciousness, Flutter poured him a bowl of food. The dog wagged his tail as he made his way over, then sat in anticipation of the meal he could see in Flutter's hands.

'I really ought to dock you a day's dinner for dereliction of duty,' said Flutter. 'Apparently, we had an intruder in the kitchen, and you slept through it.'

Winston aimed his big sad eyes at Flutter and scored another direct hit on his heart.

'I'm wondering which of us is the master, here,' said Flutter, 'and the more I think about it, the more I realise it's not me.'

He patted the old dog's head, placed the bowl of food in front of him, and watched as he proceeded to devour it.

'You really don't care who was in the kitchen, do you, Winston? Just so long as the food keeps coming, right?'

Winston was far too busy to look up, but he wagged his tail, which Flutter took as a sign of agreement.

Katie was back in the kitchen.

'He says he couldn't get away, but he called the local police and they sent a patrol car over. The officer called back to say it was all quiet and there was nothing to report.'

'What did I tell you?' said Flutter, 'they don't give a damn about people like me.'

'If he says he asked them to send someone, then he asked them to send someone!' snapped Katie. 'You might think he doesn't give a damn about you, but he certainly cares about me!'

'All right, Katie, I'm sorry. I'm not having a go at you. It's just that, right now, I feel as if I'm on my own, against the world.'

'I'm here!'

'I know, and I appreciate it, honestly. I guess I'm just a bit stressed.'

'I think you have every right to feel stressed,' she said. 'And I have to admit, I'm a bit confused by what Robbie has just told me. If someone from the police came out here, they couldn't possibly have missed Jewle's car at the gate.'

Flutter was thinking the same thing, but he had taken it a step further.

'Did he say who they sent?' he asked.

'No, why?'

'The local guy who patrols this area is PC Blackwell.'

'Of course, my older brother.'

'Are you thinking what I'm thinking? About your own brother?'

'My brother's always walked a fine line. I wouldn't put anything past him.'

'It's too much of a coincidence to mean anything else, isn't it?' said Flutter. 'And, if Blackwell is in Jewle's pocket, he would say it was all quiet over here!'

'I need to call Robbie back and tell him what we think has happened.'

At that moment Doris came into the kitchen.

'Oh,' she said as she saw Winston, 'I was just going to feed him. Well, if you don't need me anymore I suppose I'd better get off home.'

'Not so fast,' said Flutter, drawing a chair out at the table. 'Before you go anywhere I think you should come and sit down. You've got some explaining to do.'

'I told you what was going to happen, and why.'

'Yeah, you did, sort of, but you were a bit sketchy on the details, and you forgot to mention the fact you had murder on your mind. And as Katie's been dragged into this situation as well, I think you owe us both a proper explanation, don't you?'

He nodded pointedly at the chair. Doris looked from Flutter to Katie, but it was obvious whose ally she was. Doris sighed, walked over to the chair and sat down.

'All right. What do you want to know?'

'How about I tell you what I've worked out, and then you can tell me where I'm wrong and fill in the blanks.' said Flutter.

'Go on, then.'

'Jimmy Jewle's gang raided a jewellers and nicked a load of diamonds, and my old man was one of gang, right?'

Doris nodded.

'You were Jewle's girlfriend at the time, but you were also having a fling with my old man.'

'I wasn't having a fling with anyone,' said Doris. 'I made a mistake getting involved with Jewle. He was a nasty piece of work, and he used to knock me about. Walter was the only one who showed me any respect. He treated me like a lady. He told me that one day he'd take me away from there.'

'So, Walter's plan was to run off with the diamonds after the job, and take you with him, right? And then what, vanish into thin air?'

'I didn't know what his plan was, he didn't tell me. I didn't even know they were doing a job that weekend. I just got a phone call from him telling me where to meet him if I wanted to escape and start a new life. I was that miserable I jumped at the chance.'

'But how did you manage to disappear in England? Surely a bloke like Jewle would have been able to hunt you down?'

'Walter was clever. He bought flight tickets and arranged for people to travel as us. He laid a trail that showed we'd flown off to South America.'

'And Jewle fell for it?'

'We were really careful. Like I said before we were like prisoners here. You say he knew we were here, but I think you're wrong.

Walter's plan must have worked because this is the first contact we've had in all that time.'

'But Jewle knew I was Walter's son. How did he know that?'

'I don't know. Why do you ask?'

'Well, for a start, I got a warning in prison that he was looking for me,' explained Flutter. 'And then the minute I come out of prison and find out where the house is, Jimmy Jewle pops up. You have to admit it's a bit of a coincidence.'

'I don't understand what you're getting at,' said Doris.

'Well, it's obvious,' said Flutter. 'Someone must have told Jewle who I was, and then, when I was released, he had someone follow me down here.'

'I don't know anything about that,' said Doris.

'Going back to the diamonds,' said Flutter. 'How did Walter manage to get his hands on them?'

'Jimmy trusted Walter, so when they all split up after the job they all went off in different directions. Walter was entrusted with the diamonds, but instead of making his way to the hideout, he met up with me and we ran off together.'

'Wait a minute,' said Flutter, thoughtfully. 'So, you're saying Walter had all the diamonds?'

'That's right.'

There was silence for a moment then he spoke again.

'Now something else is bothering me,' he said.

'What is it?' asked Katie.

'Well, the thing is someone framed me with a tiny diamond from that robbery. If Walter had all the diamonds...'

'Oh Gawd,' said Doris. 'Moan, moan, moan, is that all you're going to do?'

'Answer this one question, and I'll stop,' said Flutter.

'What question?'

'Was it Walter who set me up?'

Doris looked horrified.

'Wherever did you get that idea from?'

'I got sent down because there was a minute diamond from that robbery in my rucksack. And the legend says Walter got away with the entire proceeds of the robbery. That means every single diamond, even the tiny ones.'

'You don't seriously think everything you hear in prison is true, do you?'

'But you just said it as well. You said Jimmy had entrusted Walter with the diamonds.'

'Your father loved you, he wouldn't have done anything like that.'

'Dream on, Doris. He didn't love me.'

'So, why did he leave you this house, and all that money?'

'Guilt,' said Flutter.

'How can you say that? You never even met him!'

'As I've said before, that was his choice, not mine,' said Flutter.

'If Walter had all the diamonds he must have been the one who planted one in your rucksack,' said Katie.

'Or he got someone to plant it for him,' said Flutter, glaring at Doris.

'He was dying and he had heard that Jewle was closing in on you,' she said, hastily. 'He was in no fit state to protect you. He thought you would be safe in prison.'

'Safe?' exploded Flutter. 'Safe? In prison? Do you have any idea what sort of people end up in prison?'

'He knew he was going to die before you came out and he thought Jimmy would stop looking once he knew he was dead.'

'So he made sure Jewle knew he was dead?'

'Oh, yes. He got his solicitor to notify Jimmy after the event.'

'Oh, great,' said Flutter. 'And this was an official communication was it?'

'How d'you mean, official?' asked Doris.

'The same solicitor wrote to me about this house. He sent the letter in a nice envelope with his address on the back. I'm guessing the letter to Jewle was sent in a similar envelope, and now, quite by coincidence, the solicitor's dead.'

'You think Jewle murdered him?' asked Katie.

'I don't suppose he got his own hands dirty, but it explains all these coincidences, doesn't it?'

'I don't understand where the solicitor comes into it,' said Doris.

'If he was Walter's solicitor he would have information Jewle wanted to know,' said Katie.

'Yes, but why murder him?'

'Maybe it was an accident,' said Flutter. 'Perhaps they were in his offices and he surprised them, or they threatened him and his heart couldn't take the stress.'

In silence they each considered the implications.

'He did it with the best intentions, you know,' said Doris.

'Who did?'

'Your father. He was just trying to look out for you.'

'His best intentions have lumbered me with a criminal record,' cried Flutter. 'His best intentions didn't keep me safe, they just made it easier for Jewle to find me, and then follow me to this house.'

'You just said he threatened the solicitor,' said Doris.

'I said it was possible he could have, and that the solicitor might have told him before he died.'

'Well, he wouldn't have needed to follow you here then, would he?' said Doris, triumphantly. 'So that means it's not Walter's fault, doesn't it?'

'Oh, come on, Doris, stop defending him and open your eyes. If Walter had left things as they were, and quietly popped his clogs, Jewle might have been none the wiser. But the way he went about things he might just as well have sent Jewle a map and told him to come and help himself!'

There was a tense silence, until finally, Doris sniffed loudly and got to her feet.

'I can't believe you're so ungrateful,' she said, huffily. 'Walter was only trying to do his best to make amends. He wanted to leave you something to remember him by.'

'Well, he's certainly done that,' said Flutter. 'I'm not likely to forget spending time in prison, having a gangster threaten me, nor having to stop you from blowing his brains out. I never asked for him to leave me a big house or anything else. I'd much rather he'd been a real father when I was a boy. That would have been worth so much more.'

'Now, if it's alright with you, I'd like to go back to my flat,' said Doris.

'I think that's probably a good idea,' said Flutter.

CHAPTER 15

Unsurprisingly Flutter spent a troubled night tossing and turning, but barely sleeping, finally giving it up as a lost cause and heading downstairs at 6 am. He might not have slept very well, but at least he'd decided what he was going to do.

It was too early for Doris to be around, but this was probably for the best after yesterday. He made his way into the kitchen, knelt down beside Winston and poked him in the ribs several times. For a dreadful moment he thought the dog had passed away in the night, but then those big doleful eyes opened and the tail slapped against the side of the bed a couple of times.

Flutter breathed sigh of relief.

'Jeez, Winston, I wish you didn't sleep so deeply, mate,' he said, stroking the dog's huge ears. 'Come on, you can have your breakfast now and then we'd better decide what we're going to do with you.'

The dog gave him a reproachful look.

'Well, I can't leave you here, now can I?' said Flutter. 'Somehow I can't see a bloke like Jewle wanting to take on an old codger like you, so we're going to have to think of something else.'

Now the eyes seemed to sag more than ever.

'Don't look so sad. I promise I'm not going to abandon you. I just want to make sure you're going to be okay.'

He filled a bowl with food and set it in front of the dog who started eating before the bowl had even reached the floor. Flutter smiled indulgently.

'Ah, I see. It's the food thing, right?' he said as he stood up. 'As long as it keeps coming, you're happy enough. I understand where you're coming from.'

He left Winston to his breakfast, put the kettle on, and whistled quietly to himself as he found a mug to make tea. Now that he'd made up his mind what to do when Jewle arrived he felt relieved. What did he want with a huge house like this anyway? He was lost with all this space to himself. Jewle could have it. He could even have the money for all Flutter cared. He'd been broke, or very close to it, for most of his life, so it wasn't something he couldn't cope with.

The morning passed by quite uneventfully. The only event of note was a phone call from Katie to see if he wanted her to come over and offer more moral support.

'I think I'd prefer it if you stayed away, Katie. I'd never forgive myself if you got hurt.'

'You're not going to fight him are you?'

'No, I'm not. What would be the point of trying to fight a guy like Jewle? Besides, I'm trying to start over, and now I know for sure where the money for the house came from I really don't want it.'

'How is Doris this morning?'

'I haven't seen her. I assume she's still mad at me and keeping away.'

'Are you going to tell her what you're going to do?'

'Oh, yeah, I'll go across and talk to her in a while.'

'But where will you all live?'

'Well, it just so happens I have a plan for that, but you'll have to wait and see what it is. Let me deal with the gangster, and then when I'm sure I've got rid of him I'll reveal what happens after that.'

A buzzer sounded from the hallway.

'There's someone at the gate.'

'He's not here already is he?' asked Katie.

Flutter carried the phone out to the hall. On the monitor he could see a man standing by the buzzer, and a car behind him. The man was Jimmy Jewle.

'Oh, crap!' muttered Flutter. 'What's he doing here this early?'

'Is it him?' Katie demanded in alarm.

'Yeah, it's him all right.'

'What are you going to do?'

'I don't think ignoring him is going to work so I guess I'm going to have to speak to him. I'll call you back later.'

'You can't deal with him on your own, I'm on my way right now,' said Katie in alarm.

But Flutter had already taken the phone from his ear and missed Katie's words.

He watched on the monitor as Jewle leaned forward and pressed the button and the buzzer sounded again.

'Hallo,' said Flutter.

'Jimmy Jewle here—'

'Yes, I can see who you are,' said Flutter. 'But why are you here so early? You said I had 24 hours.'

'Yes, sorry about that,' said Jewle. 'There's been a slight change of plan, but it's to your advantage.'

'Somehow, I doubt that,' said Flutter. 'So, what is this change of plan?'

'Why don't you let me in, and I'll explain.'

'How do I know you won't just come in and kick me out?'

Even on the small screen he could easily see Jewle's face crease into a smile as he replied.

'You don't, do you? You'll just have to trust me. Or, of course, I could send my boys over the wall. You choose.'

'It's not much of a choice, is it?'

'What I'm suggesting is that I come in alone, on foot, and my boys will wait outside.'

Flutter wondered how likely it was that a man like Jewle would be prepared to expose himself to risk like that.

'How do you know I won't blow your head off with the shotgun?' he asked.

Jewle laughed.

'You won't do that.'

'How can you be sure?'

'Because that might be the sort of thing Walter would do, but I'm a good judge of character and I reckon you're a much better man than he was.'

'And you'll come in alone?'

'I give you my word,' said Jewle.

Flutter considered for a minute. How much could this man's word be relied upon? But, there again, what choice did he have? Reluctantly he pressed the button and watched on the monitor as the gates began to open. Jewle turned to his driver and exchanged a few words, then strode through the gates and up the drive. To Flutter's surprise the car stayed where it was.

Once Jewle was through the gates Flutter stabbed his finger on the "close gates" button. The gates stopped opening and slowly began to close but Jewle didn't turn around or break his stride. Flutter let out the breath he had been holding and felt himself relax. A tad.

He opened the front door and stepped outside as Jewle reached it.

'Good morning,' said Jewle. He looked past Flutter at the house, then turned and looked back down the drive.

'He actually seems to have made a nice job of it,' he said. 'Is it as nice inside?'

'You'll see for yourself later,' said Flutter. 'I'm not going to fight you. You can have the damned house.'

'Don't you like it?'

'Not especially,' said Flutter. 'It's too big for me.'

'That's a pity,' said Jewle, 'because I'm going to offer you a chance to keep it.'

Flutter couldn't hide his surprise.

'Oh, yeah, and why would you do that?'

'I never thought it would be possible to warm to the offspring of a snake like Walter Gamble, but there's something about you I actually like. And what's even better for you is my wife has taken a shine to you as well.'

'But I've never met your wife.'

'This is true, but I told her about how you stopped that daft old bat Doris from shooting me yesterday. My wife was so pleased she made me promise I wouldn't hurt you, or kick you out on your arse, and insisted I should give you a fair chance to keep the house.'

'And you'd do that just because your wife says so?'

'Believe me, son, my wife is the last person I would want to cross. She alone has the power to make my life a misery so I never argue with her, and if she says "jump" I always ask "how high, luv." It makes for a much easier life.'

'All right,' said Flutter. 'So, what's the catch?'

'I want you to find something out for me.'

'Like what?'

'My wife has a sister called Julia. When she was younger she had a little boy, Stephen. He was my only nephew, and he was the light of her life. Then, one Spring morning, when he was just ten years old, he went off to school as usual, and that afternoon he didn't come home. He was never seen again. She was heart-broken, still is really. I want to know what happened to him.'

'Isn't that a job for the police?'

Jewle scowled.

'The thing is I'm not happy with the way they carry out their investigations. I'm willing to give you a month to prove they could have done much better.'

'You think I can do better than them in a month? With all their resources?'

'I like to do my homework on people before I negotiate with

them, and I've done mine on you. I've heard it on good authority that you've always fancied yourself as something of a detective.'

'I think what I actually said was I wouldn't mind being one of those detectives on TV. It was just talk. I wouldn't know where to start for real.'

'Well, now's your chance to learn,' said Jewle. 'And I've also done my homework on your friend Katie Donald. She's a journalist, so that means she knows how to find things out!'

'This is a joke, right?' asked Flutter. 'You just want to send me on a wild goose chase for a month before you kick me out of the house. Well, don't bother. I'll move out today and save us both a whole load of time.'

Jewle smiled at Flutter and spread his arms appealingly.

'Look, I'm not joking. If you get to keep the house you don't have to live here. If you really don't like it you can sell it and buy somewhere smaller. This house must be worth well over a million. You could buy something decent for half that. Think of all the cash you'd have in the bank.'

Flutter studied Jewle's face looking for the tiniest sign that would give him away, but there was none.

'You're serious aren't you?'

'Of course I'm serious. I saw the two of you together yesterday - you make a great team.'

'When did this little boy disappear?'

'1985.'

'Sorry? Did you say 1985? That's thirty-five years ago!'

'So you're good at maths, too,' said Jewle. 'That might come in handy.'

'How do you expect me to find out what happened in a month, if the police haven't succeeded in over thirty years?'

'Because you're going to come at the problem from a different direction.'

'What?'

'It's my belief the police never found out what happened because the senior detective in charge of the investigation steered them away from the truth.'

'And why would he do that?'

'That's exactly the question you need to start with because I reckon, if you find out why, you'll probably be able to find out what happened to Stephen and then I can give some peace to my sister-in-law. And my wife will award generous helpings of brownie points to both of us.'

'Do I have a choice?'

Jewle pulled a face and thought for a few seconds.

'You see the problem is I told my wife you could do this, and you really don't want to fall out with her, because if you do, you'll fall out with me, and that really wouldn't be a good idea.'

'So, I don't have a choice.'

Jewle patted Flutter's shoulder.

'Good boy,' he said, 'I knew you'd see it my way. People usually do.'

'Yeah, I can understand that,' said Flutter. 'It must be that winning charm of yours.'

'Oh, you've got a sense of humour, too,' said Jewle. 'That is good.'

'You're just setting me up to fail here, aren't you?'

'On the contrary, I'm going to give you a head start by naming the detective you need to focus on. His name is Hammer. Detective Chief Inspector Raymond James Hammer as he was back then. He's retired now, of course, but he still lives not far from here.'

'Here? He lives near near here?'

'Oh, didn't I say? We all used to live down here back then. That's how me and Walter came to be in business together. We started here before we opened our London branch.'

'So this little boy disappeared in Waterbury?'

'My, you catch on fast. See, I said you could do this.'

'Yeah, very funny,' said Flutter. 'What if Katie won't help me?'

'Of course she'll help you. As I said, I've done my homework, and I know for a fact her local newspaper is a money drain, and it's only a matter of months before it disappears down the plughole and takes her with it. So, tell her there's a reward and I reckon she'll bite your hand off.'

He raised his wrist and glanced at his watch.

'Wow! Look at that,' he said. 'Isn't it amazing how the time flies when you're enjoying yourself? It's a good job we've sorted out our business because I have to be somewhere else now. It's been lovely, but I really have to go.'

'Hang on a minute,' said Flutter. 'I told you I've never done anything like this before. I need a bit more information than one name.'

'Then talk to Katie. She has the local news archive, and it was the biggest local news story in years. Don't forget you've got four weeks.'

With that he set off back down the drive. Flutter watched as he stopped to press the button to open the gate, walked through the gates, turned to wave to Flutter and then climbed into his car. Then, as the gates began to close, the car slowly backed away from the gates on to the road and disappeared from view.

As Flutter stared down the drive another, familiar, car suddenly appeared beyond the gates. It was Katie. He hurried inside to open the gates for her then came back out as she pulled up and jumped from her car.

'Are you okay?' she asked.

'Yeah, I think so, physically anyway.'

'I was expecting to find you out on the street. What happened? I thought you were going to give him the house.'

'I was, but then the weirdest thing happened,' said Flutter. 'He's given me a chance to keep it.'

'Is that likely? There must be a catch.'

'Oh, there's a catch all right. We've got to solve a 35 year old mystery, that's the catch.'

'What? Did you say "we"? Where do I come in to it?'

'His nephew disappeared 35 years ago, and he wants us to find out what happened to him.'

'That's nothing to do with me, or you. It's a matter for the police to investigate.'

'Oh they did, but Jewle thinks the guy in charge of the investigation covered up what really happened.'

'Why would he do that?'

'I dunno. That's what we have to find out.'

'Why did he ask you to do that? Wouldn't he be better employing a private detective?'

'The thing is I once said I fancied being a detective.'

Katie rolled her eyes.

'Right. I see. And what makes you think we can prove Jewle's theory is right?'

'I have no idea, but he says that's where you come into it.'

'Me? How can I help? I wasn't even a twinkle in my dad's eye 35 years ago.'

'Nor was I, but Jewle tells me it was the biggest thing that ever happened in Waterbury and you must have everything about it in your archive.'

'It happened here, in Waterbury?'

'Yeah, I was surprised, too, but as you said we weren't born then, were we? He says he's prepared to offer you a reward if you'll help.'

'I don't need his dirty money,' snapped Katie.

There was a broody silence which Flutter felt he had to break.

'You're right, it's a crazy idea,' said Flutter. 'I shouldn't have even asked you. I can walk away and give him the house - it's what I was going to do anyway.'

'Did he actually give you the option of walking away?'

'Er, no, not exactly.'

'What do you mean, not exactly?'

'He says I'll be doing it for his wife, and if I fail her I'll upset her, and if I upset her I'll upset him, and, well, you get the picture, right?'

'D'you think he can be trusted to let you keep the house?'

'Gawd, I don't know, Katie. How could anyone know for sure

with a guy like him? The only thing I can say is he sounded genuine enough.'

'So, you've got to do it, whether I help or not?' she asked.

'It looks that way,' said Flutter. 'I feel I shouldn't be asking as we've only just met and you hardly know me but, will you help me?'

Katie thought for a few moments, then smiled.

'I've always fancied doing some sort of investigative work, and as your friend Jewle pointed out I do have the archive. I can't make any promises about finding the answer though. How long do we have?'

'A month.'

'A month? He's got to be joking!'

'I'm afraid not,' said Flutter.

'Did he give you any information to get started?'

'He gave me the name of the detective. DCI Hammer.'

'Hammer? He's a Detective Inspector at the local nick. He's another one with an attitude like my brother. But he'd be too young, he must be mid-forties... Oh, hang on, now I remember. His father was also a detective, here at Waterbury. He would have been the one leading that investigation.'

'He must be in his seventies or eighties by now,' said Flutter. 'If he's still around.'

'I can soon check that out.'

'Even if he's still around, we can hardly ask him if it's true he suppressed information, can we?' asked Flutter. 'And why would he speak to someone like me, anyway?'

'Good point,' said Katie. 'But he might be prepared to speak to a journalist whose willing to massage his ego.'

'Even so, I still don't see why he'd tell you about the case.'

'What if I'm doing a piece about missing children who were never found?'

'Are you?'

'No, I'm not, but he doesn't know that.'

'D'you think it would work?'

'We won't know that until I ask him,' said Katie.

· · ·

Katie and Flutter spent that afternoon searching through the archive for stories about the missing boy. Jewle had been correct, it was massive story that occupied page after page for several weeks. Just before 5pm Katie called a halt.

'It's a long time since I've done research like this,' she said. 'I'd forgotten how tiring it can be. I think we should call it a day now.'

'You're right about it being tiring,' said Flutter. 'I'm exhausted. But still, we've come up with quite a lot haven't we?'

'To be honest I think we've barely uncovered the tip of the iceberg. Of course, in an ideal world access to the police files would tell us a lot more.'

'Yeah, well, dream on, Katie,' said Flutter. 'Somehow I don't see them offering to hand over those files any time soon. Anyway, it's not all bad news. We've got the gist of the story, haven't we?'

Katie had been compiling notes on a pad as they had been searching. Now she flipped back to the beginning.

'Let me see,' she said, reading from the notes. 'According to the stories in the newspaper it was a perfectly normal school day. As usual, school finished at three-thirty. All the kids headed homewards, or for the bus stop outside the school to catch the school bus home. That's all the kids except for Stephen and the other members of the choir, who stayed behind for choir practice.

'Choir practice ended at 4.30. Stephen was expecting his mother to be waiting outside, but she had been delayed in heavy traffic several miles away. If parents didn't show up, or were delayed, the kids were supposed to go back into school and ask a teacher for help, but for some reason Stephen didn't do that. One of the other boys in the choir said he saw Stephen walking away from the school on his own.

'It's believed he decided to head into town to catch the later, regular bus home. It was a journey he had made before, so he knew exactly where he was going, and how to reach his destination, and which bus to catch. It should have taken him no more than twenty minutes to walk to the station which would have given him plenty of time to catch the 5pm bus. But he didn't get on that bus, and he didn't even make it to the bus station and despite extensive appeals no-one ever came forward to say they had seen him after he left school.'

'So somewhere between the school and the bus station he just vanished,' said Flutter. 'Jeez, I bet his poor mum has never forgiven herself for being late. Even if we could tell her exactly what happened I'm not sure it would take that away from her.'

'We're a long way from doing that,' said Katie. 'As I said, we've barely scratched the surface.'

'Don't forget you're planning to see DCI Hammer tomorrow,' said Flutter, optimistically. 'You never know, he might be willing to help.'

'Hmm, I'll reserve judgement on that until after I've spoken to him.'

CHAPTER 16

THE RETIRED DCI Hammer owned a small bungalow in a village about ten miles from Waterbury. He sounded surprised when Katie asked if she could come and speak to him about the disappearance of Stephen Bowles, and was rather reticent at first, but when she explained she was writing a series about missing children who had never been found he seemed to relax a bit.

'I suppose it'll be okay then,' he decided. 'You can come over this afternoon, if you like. I shan't be going anywhere, and there's not much you can do in the garden this time of year. About two-thirty suit you?'

Katie agreed. Two-thirty would be perfect.

Later that morning she gave Flutter her spare laptop and gave him a quick lesson in how to locate people and settled him with a list of teachers who were working at the school at the time of Stephen's disappearance.

Number Twenty-two Ridgeway Gardens was a neat corner plot at the end of a cul-de-sac. Even now, in November, it was obvious the owner was a keen gardener with the greenest of fingers. As Katie parked the car and walked up the path to the front door she couldn't help but admire the neat and tidy garden. Hammer must have been watching through the front window because the door opened just as she got to it.

'Mr Hammer? I'm Katie Donald. Thank you so much for agreeing to speak to me.'

As they shook hands, Katie thought it would do no harm to start with a little flattery.

'You have a lovely garden,' she said. 'It's very neat and tidy.'

Hammer beamed a smile.

'Not much else to do at my age. It keeps me active and reasonably fit.'

He spoke with a slight northern accent which was still there even though he had lived in Waterbury for forty years. It was faint enough that Katie hadn't noticed it over the phone, but it was discernible now she was speaking to him in the flesh.

He ushered her inside and it became clear she had started him on his favourite subject, as he pointed through the window at the back garden which was filled with fruit bushes of varying types and small fruit trees.

'Wow!' she said. 'This lot must really keep you busy.'

'Oh yes,' he said proudly. 'I used to have an allotment down in Waterbury as well. But I'm too old to look after both now. I used to grow all my vegetables down there, and the fruit up here.'

He pointed Katie to an armchair and sat down opposite.

'But you didn't come out here to ask me about my fruit and vegetables, did you?'

It was almost as if a physical barrier had suddenly been placed between them, and to emphasise the point he crossed his arms and his chin jutted defiantly. But Katie had faced reluctant interviewees before and his attitude didn't faze her.

'I don't want to upset you, Mr. Hammer,' she began. 'As I said on the phone I'm writing a series about unsolved missing children cases, but I'm not looking to point the finger at anyone. I'm just trying to get a feel for what happened, and what you feel stopped you from solving the case.'

He looked thoughtful for a few moments.

'It was the worst case of my whole career,' he said and, as he said it, he seemed to sag in his chair.

'I knew the boy must have been taken, and murdered, and I was one hundred per cent sure who'd done it, but we just couldn't find the evidence to prove it.'

'So you actually knew who had taken the boy?'

'It was the school teacher, Rooke. There was no doubt in my mind at all. He didn't even have an alibi, just said he was at home on his own. I knew he was lying, I just couldn't prove it.'

'Didn't he take his own life?'

'That's right. Two years later. I reckon he couldn't live with the guilt. If that doesn't prove I was right, I don't know what does.'

'Didn't anyone else come under suspicion?'

'No-one else even came close. I had a nose for these things and I'd been doing the job long enough to know I could trust my instincts.'

His tone, and manner, made it clear there was no room for discussion on this. Katie thought it was a bit odd that no one else had even been considered worthy of suspicion, but she felt sure this wasn't the time to argue with him. Carefully, she tiptoed around the subject for a few more minutes trying to prise a little more from him, but his answers became increasingly evasive and the longer it went on, the more hostile he became.

But Katie felt this was a clear indication that there had really been nothing to suggest the teacher Mr Rooke was guilty apart from former DCI's "nose for these things". She thought it was no wonder the case had never progressed far, if the lead officer had such a blinkered view.

Once Hammer had begun to turn hostile, Katie knew it wouldn't be long before his patience was exhausted so it was no surprise when he finally snapped at her.

'I don't know why you're poking your nose in now, anyway,' he said. 'It was over thirty years ago. What makes you think you can do any better than I could with the whole damned police force behind me?'

'I'm not suggesting I can do any better, Mr Hammer. It's just that I met Mrs Bowles a few weeks ago, I heard her story, and I saw the pain she still endures. Stephen was just ten years old when he disappeared, and here we are thirty years on, and she still doesn't know what happened to him.'

'Do you think I don't know all that? You're way out of order coming here asking me about this. My own son was ten at the time so I could easily understand what she was going through. I tried my hardest to prove that man was guilty, but I just couldn't.'

Hammer was visibly upset now, and Katie began to feel uncomfortable. Maybe he was right and she was out of order. He certainly seemed genuine enough.

'Look, Mr Hammer, I'm sorry. I didn't mean to upset you. Maybe I'd better go.'

'Yes, I think you should go. You can see yourself out.'

Dismissed in such a fashion, Katie crept guiltily out of the room to the front door.

'Goodbye,' she called out, as she opened the door, 'and I'm sorry for upsetting you.'

'Just bugger off,' he called, bitterly, 'and don't come back.'

As Katie drove back to Waterbury she felt she should probably be feeling guilty about upsetting the old man, but any guilt she felt was being suppressed by her excitement. She had the distinct feeling there just had to be more to this than first meets the eye. It seemed Jewle might be onto something when he suggested the case had been steered in a particular direction. It was hard to believe there wouldn't have been any other suspects, yet Raymond Hammer was adamant there were none.

. . .

'I've been following up on the teachers who were at the school at the time,' Flutter announced when Katie got back to the office. 'It was only a small school, with not many staff. Two of them have passed away and, of course, Mr Rooke took his own life two years after the boy went missing. But I have managed to track down a lady teacher, Miss Goodie. She was quite new to the school at the time and was actually off sick on the day in question.'

'Well done,' said Katie. 'That's great work. Do you have an address for her?'

'I have,' said Flutter, proudly, 'and a telephone number. I even called her and she said she would be happy to talk to us tomorrow morning. I said we'd be there at about 11.'

CHAPTER 17

Miss Goodie was tiny, and at first glance Flutter thought she appeared fragile-looking, but the spark in her eyes suggested he should not be fooled by that. She still had a sharp mind and could be feisty enough if the need arose.

In her seventies now, she was on her own and wanted to be useful so she had chosen to live in the retirement home where she saw herself as one of the staff and made a point of looking out for many of the less able-bodied residents.

At first she was suspicious of her visitors but, once Katie had convinced her they weren't intending to pin responsibility for the disappearance of Stephen Bowles on David Rooke, she began to relax and warm to them.

'It was all very unpleasant,' she said. 'That policeman wouldn't believe David even though there was no evidence against him. I knew David Rooke very well. There was no way in the world he could be guilty of such a crime. He was such a kind, sweet man.'

She had become more animated as she spoke, her hands making small fluttering movements rather like a pair of butterflies dancing in the air.

'The policeman you're referring to,' Flutter asked, just to make sure. 'That was DCI Hammer?'

'Oh, yes, that's him.' She pulled a face. 'Ghastly man. And those terrible accusations; David wasn't guilty, you know, but when you get labelled with suspicions like that...'

She paused as if lost for the right words.

'It ruined his career, and he lived for teaching...'

The butterfly hands settled in her lap, and she became lost in her thoughts for a moment.

'That's what drove him to commit suicide, you know.' Her voice wobbled as she said it. 'And it could have been avoided so easily if it hadn't been for his wife.'

This was something new.

'I'm sorry,' said Katie. 'His wife? How do you mean?'

'It was all a misunderstanding, you see. David and I were just good friends, but his wife thought it was something more. I could have told everyone where he was that afternoon, but he wouldn't hear of it. He didn't want his wife to know, and he didn't want to get me involved in a scandal. He made me promise, you see, promise not to tell anyone.'

She was off on another silent reverie, but deep inside Katie, something was beginning to tingle. She glanced at Flutter. He seemed to be equally aware that this could be important. She tried to be patient and wait for Miss Goodie to continue, but she seemed to be lost in her thoughts.

'He made you promise not to tell what, Miss Goodie?'

She looked up at Flutter, then turned her gaze on Katie. Finally she made a decision.

'Well, I suppose it can't hurt now, can it? They've both passed away now and David's reputation was ruined years ago, and there really was nothing wrong.'

The butterflies fluttered from her lap to her face, as she dabbed at her eyes with a tissue.

'You see David was with me when Stephen went missing.'

Katie and Flutter exchanged a glance.

'How do you mean he was with you?' asked Katie.

'He was with me, at my house. I had been off sick that day and he came to my house after school to see if I needed anything. He was very kind, and thoughtful, you see, a real gentleman.'

'And the police were never told this? He had an alibi and you didn't tell them?'

'He wouldn't let me. I wanted to, but he wouldn't let me. He said it wasn't necessary because he was innocent, and everyone would realise this when they caught the...'

Her voice trailed off to a silent sob, and the butterfly hands settled to cover her face, as the enormity of it all hit her. A minute or two later, she continued, almost in a whisper.

'But, of course, they didn't catch anyone else, and the suspicion stuck to him. Although he was released, and never charged with anything, the damage had been done, and by then it was too late, and it couldn't be undone.'

It took some time for Miss Goodie to regain her composure, but eventually she managed to pull herself together, apologising profusely for being upset. Before they left she made Katie and Flutter promise they would do their utmost to make the world understand David Rooke had been an innocent man, on a mission of mercy that day, and not the bad man DCI Hammer had made him out to be.

'What did you make of that?' asked Flutter, as Katie drove them away.

'You mean about the alibi? I believe he was there, but I think she's being naive if she thinks anyone would believe the reason for him being at her house was as innocent as she claims.'

'Yeah,' agreed Flutter. 'It's more likely people would point out the man's wife had been suspicious and there's no smoke without fire. And anyway, if it was all so innocent, why didn't she come forward and say so at the time?'

'Maybe she was in love with him,' said Katie.

'But she says it was all innocent.'

'You don't have to have an affair to fall in love with someone, you know.'

'I dunno,' said Flutter. 'Maybe being inside has made me cynical, but I don't buy it.'

'You'd be surprised,' said Katie. 'A naive young woman in love with an older man can easily be persuaded to do as he says. It happens all the time.'

Flutter looked across at her but she kept her eyes focused on the road ahead. He wondered if she was speaking from experience, but something told him this wasn't the time to pry into her past.

'Okay,' he said, 'does that mean we're going to take Miss Goodie at her word?'

'She convinced me,' said Katie. 'I can't see how she could possibly gain anything by lying after all this time.'

'Okay. So, she said David Rooke was with her from around 4pm until 5.30 that afternoon. And her house was on the other side of town from the school and nowhere near the route to the bus station. That rules him out as a suspect for me. What d'you think?'

'Oh, I agree. He can't have been in two places at once.'

'Okay, so we've very quickly eliminated the one and only suspect the police had, so what do we do now?'

'We have the names of all the teachers who worked at the school back then,' said Katie. 'The first thing we need to do when we get back to the office is see if we can find a suspect among them.'

'And if we can't?'

'Then we work out who else might have been working at, or near, the school who could have been in a position to abduct the boy.'

'What if it was nothing to do with the school? What if it was a random stranger?'

'Then we've got no chance in a million years of finding out who it was,' said Katie.

. . .

It was several hours later when Katie sat back at her desk, stretched and yawned.

'God, look at the time,' she said. 'It's gone 7pm.'

She pushed her chair back, stood up and walked across to a second desk. Where Flutter was bent over her spare laptop.

'I'm sorry I had to do all that catching up,' she said.

'Don't apologise, Katie. It should be me apologising to you for taking you away from your job.'

'Are you kidding?' she said. 'Do you really think I'd rather be creating classified ads when I can be doing proper investigative work? Anyway, how are you getting on?'

'I've done everything just as you showed me. The good news is, it was only a small school and several of the teachers were accounted for in the newspaper stories so there weren't too many names left to go through. The bad news is I haven't found anyone I could point a finger at.'

'I said it was a long shot, didn't I? But well done for getting through them all.'

'So what should I do now?'

'Honestly? I think you should probably go home and get some rest, then come back in the morning at 9am and we can start afresh.'

CHAPTER 18

Next morning Flutter was waiting outside Katie's office when she arrived, a sad looking Winston peering up at her from behind his legs.

'Are you hoping he can sniff out the bad guy?' she asked, pointing at the dog.

'Er, yeah, I'm sorry about him. I hope you don't mind, but I can't leave him at home on his own all day. A couple of hours is okay, but not all day.'

'I thought Doris looked after him while you aren't there.'

'Yeah, so did I, but it seems she's packed her bags and left me and Deputy Dawg here to our own devices.'

'She didn't tell you she was going?'

'Not a word, but then I haven't set eyes on her since the night of the shotgun incident.'

'That's not very good. She's supposed to be your housekeeper, isn't she?'

'I don't care about her leaving me,' he nodded down at Winston, 'but this poor old thing was on his own all day and starving by the time I got home last night, and I'm not happy about that. It's not right.'

Katie studied Flutter's face. He seemed genuinely upset on Winston's behalf.

'You really mean that don't you?' she said.

'Yeah, well, I can't stand people who do things like that to animals. He trusted her and she walked out on him. If she had told me she was leaving him I would have gone home much earlier.'

Katie unlocked the door.

'So, is it all right to bring him in?' asked Flutter, uncertainly.

'Does he still smell as bad as he did the other day?'

'No, I put him in the shower and shampooed him.'

'And he is house trained?'

'He's got a bladder like a football. He can last all day. And he'll probably sleep all day anyway.'

'In that case,' she said, 'you'd both better come on up.'

They followed Katie up the stairs to her office. Flutter slipped Winston's lead off and left him to find somewhere suitable to sleep, then slipped into the tiny kitchen to make Katie a drink.

'I couldn't stop thinking about this case last night,' he said, carrying two mugs of coffee into the office. 'I'm not sure if my instincts count for anything, or even if following them is the right thing to do, but my feeling is that rather than waste time looking all over we should focus on people connected to the school.'

'Don't forget all the teachers have been accounted for,' said Katie, accepting her coffee. 'Even David Rooke is ruled out now.'

'Yeah, but a school doesn't just have teachers, does it?'

Katie nodded thoughtfully.

'That's true enough,' she agreed. 'And I believe you should never discount your gut feelings, so what are your instincts telling you?'

'I was thinking about when I was at school as a ten-year-old,' said Flutter. 'I was trying to remember the people at the school who weren't teachers, like the caretaker, the dinner ladies, and that sort of thing. And I got to thinking, if my mum usually met me after school and then one day she wasn't there to meet me, and I didn't know why, how would I feel? I'd probably be a bit upset, and even though I knew my way to the bus station I might even be a bit scared, right?'

'Yes, that wouldn't surprise me.'

'And then I got to thinking if I was scared, would I look it? And, if I did look scared, would someone offer to help?'

Katie wasn't sure where he was going with this, but she could see how excited he was.

'Yes, go on,' she urged.

'Now, if a stranger approached me, I would probably refuse their help, I might even run away. But what if someone I knew, and trusted, offered to help me?'

Now Katie began to understand.

'Just imagine it,' continued Flutter. 'There I am, a bit lost, and scared, and then someone I know and trust, offers to accompany me to the bus station. How do I feel about that?'

'You feel relieved,' said Katie.

'Of course I do.'

'They can see you're scared so they reassure you and take your hand--'

'Then they tell me they know a short cut to the station, and next thing you know--'

'You've been whisked off never to be seen again,' finished Katie.

'It makes sense, doesn't it?' asked Flutter.

'Absolutely,' said Katie. 'But would a dinner lady still be in the vicinity at the end of school?'

'Maybe not, but there's nothing to stop her coming back, is there? Anyway, I wasn't thinking of a dinner lady. I may be going out on a limb here, but I think we're more likely to be looking for a man.'

'I don't know the exact figures,' said Katie, 'but I think you're probably right. There again, the only man who worked at the school and wasn't a teacher is the caretaker and he was in school when Stephen went missing. He was polishing the floor in the main hall when Stephen's mother arrived looking for him. So, unless I'm missing something, that's all the men accounted for.'

'But that's just it, Katie. You are missing something. Stephen's mum used to collect him from school because she finished work early enough to do that but, because she had to get to work in the mornings, she didn't have time to take him to school.'

'Of course. She used to put him on the school bus every morning.'

'Exactly! And school buses usually have the same driver every day, and back then I'll bet there weren't many women drivers. It was only a small school so there were probably only a handful of kids who made that journey every day, which means the driver would have known them all fairly well, possibly even by name.'

'You're right,' said Katie, 'and if he was the first person those kids saw every morning after they left home they'd certainly recognise him if they met him on the street.'

'And you'd trust him, wouldn't you?' added Flutter. 'I mean, if your mum is happy to put you on his bus every morning, he must be someone you can trust, right?'

He looked at Katie for her approval but he couldn't read her face.

'Well, what do you think?' he asked. 'We've got nothing else have we?'

'I think you could be on to something,' said Katie. 'There's just one problem, wouldn't the bus driver have been driving the bus taking the other kids home when Stephen disappeared?'

'Crap!' said Flutter. 'I hadn't thought of that.'

'Don't be too disappointed,' said Katie. 'When I worked as an investigative journalist I used to have moments like that several times a week.'

'I was so sure I was onto something.'

'There again,' said Katie, 'having eliminated the inquiry's one and only suspect we've got to start somewhere, and that somewhere might as well be with the bus driver.'

'Really? But how could he be in two places at once?'

'I'm not saying he's guilty but it's somewhere to start. If you check the route the bus followed it might suggest he had time to get back before Stephen went missing.'

Flutter smiled.

'That's quite a smile,' said Katie. 'But I wonder if it will last.'

'Sorry?'

'Well, it's a great theory, but the problem with theories is they have to be proven. And, now I think about it, I don't seem to recall seeing anything about the bus driver in the archive. That suggests we either missed him, or he's not mentioned.'

'Either way we'll have to go through all the stories again to see what they can tell us about him. Right now we don't even have a name. The only thing is you're going to have to start on your own because I have my own work to do today.'

'Ah, right. I see what you mean,' said Flutter.

'You'll be fine. Just remember what I showed you yesterday and don't expect too much. There's a limit to what you can find in public records.'

'I suppose practice makes perfect,' said Flutter, heading for the spare desk and laptop.

Katie pulled a chair across to her desk ready to sit down but Winston had decided to make himself comfortable under her desk, and now he gave her the full sad eyes treatment.

'Oh,' she said, 'someone seems to have beaten me to it.'

'Oh, sorry,' said Flutter getting to his feet. 'Let me get him out of there.'

'Oh, look at his face,' said Katie. 'He looks so sad.'

'Don't be fooled by that,' said Flutter. 'He's not sad, he's manipulating you.'

'You can't move him.'

'Of course I can, he won't mind.'

'No, honestly, leave him. He's not doing any harm, and it doesn't seem fair to move him now he's settled. And anyway, he doesn't take up too much room.'

'There, you see,' said Flutter settling back into his chair. 'I told you. He's a devious old devil. He's got you wrapped around his little finger already. You're going to regret it.'

Katie bent down and stroked Winston's head.

'He's just a cute old dog.'

'Yeah, well, if you say so, but don't say I didn't warn you,' said Flutter, going back to his laptop.

'Oh, nonsense,' said Katie, carefully placing her feet either side of the old dog and shuffling her chair up to her desk. 'He'll be fine.'

Two minutes later they were both busy with their work.

It was half an hour later when Katie let out a cry.

'Oh, my God,' she said, hastily pushing her chair back and jumping to her feet. 'What is that smell?'

Flutter looked up innocently.

'Ah, yeah, sorry about that. It's probably Winston,' he said. 'He gets a bit windy sometimes.'

'What d'you mean he gets a bit windy?'

'I mean he farts. And they're usually silent ones, so you don't know until it's too late.'

Katie looked down at Winston who continued snoring loudly.

'In his sleep?'

'It seems to be worse when he's asleep.'

Now she turned to Flutter, hands on hips.

'I suppose you think it's funny.'

'Not if I'm within range when he does it,' said Flutter, trying hard not to grin.

'Ha, ha, very funny. What have you been feeding him?'

'It's normal dried dog food, expensive stuff, supposedly the best, according to Doris. But the problem isn't the food, it's the dog. He's a thief, you see. He might look slow, but he's like greased lightening when there's food lying around, and he'll steal anything that's left where he can reach it.'

'What on earth could he have stolen that makes him smell that bad?'

'Because Doris had gone and it was getting late I ordered a Chinese takeaway last night, and I ate it in front of the TV.'

'And you gave some to Winston? Isn't that cruelty to animals?'

'I didn't give it to him. I put the dishes on the coffee table, and he helped himself when I went to the kitchen to get a drink.'

'What exactly did he steal?'

'A portion of duck in black bean sauce. Enough for two.'

'Enough for two?'

'Turns out I wasn't as hungry as I thought I was.'

'Is he going to keep on doing it?'

Flutter shrugged.

'I dunno,' he said. 'I've only known him for a few days, so your guess is as good as mine.'

'He's not sleeping under my desk if he's going to keep doing that.'

'Well, don't blame me,' said Flutter. 'I did try to warn you not to leave him there, but did you listen? No you didn't because you were so busy allowing him to hypnotise you with those big sad eyes and saying how cute he was, you chose to ignore my advice.'

Katie couldn't argue with those facts.

'Does he have any other bad habits I should know about?'

'Apart from snoring, stealing, farting, and being manipulative? No, he's more or less perfect, apart from those.'

'You think this is funny, don't you?'

Flutter did his best to look innocent.

'The smell usually disperses quite quickly so you should be safe to sit down again now,' he said.

Katie looked uncertainly at her desk and the snoring dog.

'If he does it again...'

'If he does it again, I'll make him move, I promise,' said Flutter.

'You'd better,' grumbled Katie, as she returned to her seat, gingerly placing her feet either side of Winston as if he were an unexploded bomb.

. . .

The rest of the morning passed without further incident from under Katie's desk. It took Flutter most of the morning, but by lunchtime he had finally found something he felt was worth sharing.

'This is interesting, Katie,' he said, finally. 'It says here that the guy who drove the school bus that day was a relief driver. The regular driver had called in sick. That's the sort of thing the police would have checked out wouldn't they?'

'It's certainly something they should have checked out,' she agreed.

Flutter sighed.

'But, of course, without the files we'll never know if they did,' he said. 'This is frustrating. We can't check anything. It's like trying to tie your shoelaces with one hand tied behind your back.'

'Is there a name for the relief driver?' asked Katie.

'Steve Grant.'

'See if you can find an address or a phone number for him. Maybe he's still in the area and willing to help us.'

It took Flutter half an hour, but he was lucky; Steve Grant still lived in Waterbury. He was 70 now, but he could still recall what happened that day.

'I was supposed to be off for the whole week, but they were short staffed so when he called in sick they called me and asked me to work. I didn't really mind because I thought it was only going to be for one day, and I needed the money.'

'It sounds like there's a "but" after that sentence,' encouraged Flutter.

Steve Grant chuckled.

'The "but" is that the guy never came back so I had to work the rest of my week off.'

'What happened to the other driver?'

'I've no idea, mate. We never saw him again.'

'Did the police know he'd gone off sick that day?'

'You mean did they think he was a suspect? It was a long time ago now, and my memory's not what it was, but as I recall the detective in charge checked him out. I think they found he had an alibi so he couldn't have had anything to do with it.'

'Do you remember the driver's name?' asked Flutter.

'Terry Harrison.'

'You remembered that okay,' said Flutter.

'I never forgot his name because of what happened that day.'

'Is there anything else you can tell me about him, like how old he was, or where he lived?'

'He didn't work for us for long so I never really got to know him. I've no idea where he lived, but I'm guessing it was in town some-where because I'm pretty sure he didn't have a car. As for how old he was...' There was a pause while he tried to recall. 'I'd say he was prob-ably around my age, so that would make him about seventy now, but again I can't be sure.'

'You say he didn't work there for long. Can you remember how long?'

'If I had to make a guess, I'd say two or three months. I'm not much help with the details, am I?'

'I disagree,' said Flutter. 'As you say, it was a long, long, time ago and, thanks to you, I definitely know more than I did five minutes ago.'

'I do remember one or two of the other drivers thought he was a bit strange.'

'Strange in what way?'

'He was a bit of a loner. Kept himself to himself, you know? Although whether that makes him strange is a matter of opinion I suppose. Maybe he just liked his privacy. I don't think any of us really knew him well enough to judge, d'you know what I mean?'

'Yes, I know exactly what you mean,' said Flutter. 'Some people find it all too easy to judge without knowing all the facts.'

'I try to keep an open mind about people.'

'Well, that's good to hear,' said Flutter. 'I think the world would be a better place if we were all like you. Anyway, thank you for speaking with me, Mr Grant, you've been very helpful.'

He hung up the phone and turned to Katie.

'I've got a name for the driver who went sick that day.'

'Oh, well done,' she said.

'His name is Terry Harrison, and not only did he go sick that day, but he never returned to work again.'

'What? Never?'

'Steve Grant says no-one at the bus depot ever saw him again. He hadn't been there long either. I don't know what you think, but this Harrison bloke sounds a bit iffy to me.'

Katie grinned.

'Iffy? Is that a technical term?' she asked, tongue in cheek.

Flutter chose to ignore her teasing.

'Don't tell me you're not curious about him.'

'Didn't the police check him out?'

'If Steve Grant's memory can be relied on he seems to think the detective in charge of the case checked him out. That would be Hammer, wouldn't it? Is checking out an alibi a job for the boss? I would have thought that's the sort of job you delegate to someone a bit lower in the pecking order, wouldn't you?'

'Perhaps Steve Grant got it wrong,' suggested Katie. 'Or, perhaps Hammer was already in the locality. If he was already there it would be a waste of time to send someone else.'

'Yeah, maybe,' said Flutter, thoughtfully. 'But if he was so convinced David Rooke was his main suspect, how thorough would he have been checking out a bus driver who was off sick that day?'

'You think the senior investigating officer would have cut corners? Are you sure you're not just following an anti-police agenda because of what happened to you?'

'No, it's not that at all. Don't forget you're the one who interviewed him, and you came back and told me he was obsessed with David Rooke. All I'm saying is if that's the case, then isn't it possible he could have ruled out other possible suspects just because they didn't fit his scenario?'

Katie regarded Flutter with a faint smile of approval.

'D'you know,' she said. 'I think you've got a feel for this.'

'Maybe I'm just suspicious of everyone.'

'And you seem to be enjoying it.'

'Enjoying it? I don't know about that. Don't forget I'm doing this because I have to, not because I want to.'

'But even so, you are enjoying it, aren't you?'

'It's different from what I used to do, that's for sure.'

'I reckon we could make a pretty good investigator out of you.'

'It's good of you to say so, but I think it's probably a bit soon to start talking like that,' said Flutter. 'Let's see if I can dig up anything interesting about Terry Harrison before we start celebrating.'

'I think we should have a bite to eat before you start that,' said Katie.

'Now that sounds like plan,' said Flutter.

'We must have the wrong name for this bus driver,' said Flutter, later that afternoon. 'I've spent two hours searching, and you won't believe how many Terry Harrison's there are! I thought I'd narrowed it down to three Terry Harrisons who might be possibles, but now I've found two of them were overseas in the forces when Stephen disappeared, and the third one was doing time for armed robbery.'

'Have you tried widening the search age-wise? Steve Grant said he was guessing they were about the same age.'

'Yeah, I thought of that. I had to try ten years either way to find those three. There is one other guy who might have fit the bill, but it can't be him because he died when he was twenty. So, unless we're saying a ghost abducted Stephen, I don't know what else to suggest.'

'We could try the bus company.'

'Are they still going?'

'They have new owners, but they are still operating. They advertise with us.'

'If they have new owners, they won't remember, will they?'

'Rule one for investigators is that you have to be optimistic. If you're always going to expect to get nowhere, you probably will.'

'Yeah, but if the people are different...'

'They might still have old records.'

'After all this time?'

'I know it's a long shot, but it's worth a try. Let me give them a call.'

'Okay,' said Flutter. 'While you're doing that I'll take Winston round the block. I could do with stretching my legs for five minutes.'

It was twenty minutes before Flutter returned.

'I was beginning to think you'd got lost,' said Katie.

'Winston hasn't walked around here before so he had to stop and sniff everything we passed. We might have been gone twenty minutes, but we've barely walked a hundred yards in that time!'

'Anyway, we're in luck,' she continued. 'I spoke to Evelyn whose co-owner of the bus company. Of course she doesn't know anything about what happened back then, but she says when they took over the business they inherited a whole room full of box files which they've never opened. She has no idea what we might find in there but we're welcome to take look and see if there's anything relevant to our investigation.'

'Oh, cool,' said Flutter. 'When do we start?'

'I said you'd be there first thing tomorrow morning.'

'Just me?'

'Sorry, I've got work to do here.'

'How long will it take?'

'I've got no idea. Does it matter?'

'Not to me,' said Flutter, looking down at Winston, and then back up at her. 'But I have to think of the old boy here. It doesn't seem right leaving him on his own all day.'

As if on cue, Winston gave Katie the full beam of his big, sad eyes, and thumped his tail on the floor a few times.

Katie sighed.

'All right,' she said. 'I suppose you can leave him here.'

Flutter bent down and patted the old dog's head.

'There you go, mate,' he said. 'I told you she wouldn't be able to resist the eyes.'

'Not so fast,' said Katie. 'There is a condition. He can only stay here with me if you promise not to feed him anything untoward.'

'Untoward?' echoed Flutter. 'What does that mean?'

'It means if he's going to keep farting all the time, then tomorrow will be the first, and last, time I dog-sit for you.'

'But he only did it once and then he was okay. I think you must have scared him.'

'Scared him? Don't talk rubbish, Harvey Gamble. He's not scared of me. It's the rubbish you fed him—'

'I didn't feed it to him, he stole it!'

'Whatever, you just make sure he doesn't come laden with gas in the morning, or there will be trouble. Okay?'

'All right, keep your hair on,' said Flutter. 'Trust me, he'll be on his best behaviour.'

'You make sure he is.'

CHAPTER 19

As USUAL, Flutter was waiting outside her office when Katie arrived next morning.

'Remember what I said,' she warned him.

'I've brought a blanket for him,' he said, 'and a water bowl just in case he gets thirsty.'

Winston immediately chose to re-install himself under Katie's desk, totally ignoring the blanket Flutter had so carefully arranged for him under the spare desk. And despite several minutes of cajoling from his owner, he resolutely stayed where he was.

'I don't mind, as long as he's not going to start making smells again,' Katie told Flutter. 'You haven't given him anything that will set him off, have you?'

'Scout's honour, I've only given him dog food,' said Flutter, making a little salute.

'Right. Well, you'd better get going,' said Katie.

'Off into the unknown,' said Flutter.

'Yes, something like that,' agreed Katie. 'Evelyn runs the office there. Be nice to her and I'm sure she'll keep you supplied with tea.'

'Okay, let's do this,' said Flutter. 'I'll see you later.'

'Good luck,' said Katie.

. . .

Evelyn hadn't been exaggerating when she had told Katie there was a whole room full of paperwork that had never been touched.

'Blimey,' said Flutter, when she had opened the door to the room. 'Is it in any particular order?'

'I did have a quick look when we first took over in case there was anything we needed, but that was nearly ten years ago now. I did think I might try to put it all onto the computer, but then my husband pointed out that even the taxman only expects you to keep stuff for seven years, so why bother?'

'So you've never actually gone through any of it?' asked Flutter.

'Like I say, I only had a quick look at a couple of boxes. Can I ask what you're looking for?'

'Employment records for 1985 would be good. Do you think there's a chance?'

'I seem to recall it was all old stuff that preceded computers, and one of the boxes I opened even dated back to the 70s. One thing I can tell you - whoever kept these records did at least label them by year, so if it's in here you should be able to find it.'

Flutter looked at the shelves piled with box files.

'Oh well,' he said. 'I'd best get started or I won't find anything.'

'Call me if you need anything,' said Evelyn. 'I'll be in the main office.'

Evelyn had been correct when she said someone had labelled each of the boxes by date, but unfortunately that was about as far as things went in terms of organising. Flutter soon discovered that whoever had stored them in this room either hadn't realised (or perhaps hadn't cared) that it would be easier to find things if all the labels were visible.

It would have been equally helpful if all the boxes that related to one year had been stored together, but instead of discouraging him, this further hindrance to his progress just served to spur Flutter on. There appeared to be five boxes to each year, and after a quick count

Flutter estimated there must be somewhere in the region of a hundred and fifty boxes.

'Jeez, there must be thirty years of records here,' he muttered. 'There again, I only have to find the five relating to 1985. How hard can that be?'

As it happens it wasn't so much hard for Flutter, as time-consuming. He quickly found three boxes dated 1985, but of course none of those had the employment records. Sod's law then dictated that the remaining two boxes would be the last two on the shelf.

Hardly daring to breath he opened the first of the two boxes, removed the contents and thumbed through them.

'Gotcha, you little beauty,' he said, triumphantly.

'I've just brought you a cup of tea,' said Evelyn from the doorway.

'A cup of tea for me? Evelyn, you're an angel,' said Flutter, clutching the box as it were gold.

'I thought it might be thirsty work, what with all that dust. Have you found what you were looking for?'

'I think so,' said Flutter. 'Is it okay if I sit here and read through it. I need to make a few notes.'

'You don't need to do that. You can take the box with you.'

'Are you sure,' asked Flutter. 'Aren't there rules about privacy and what have you?'

'I don't think it applies to stuff as old as this,' she said. 'You just check through it while you drink your tea, and if it's what you want, you can take it with you.'

'I'll do that, Evelyn. Thank you.'

It was 1.30 when Flutter rejoined Katie in her office, triumphantly waving the box file, but one look at her face told him she wasn't quite as pleased as he had hoped.

'Everything all right?' he asked.

Katie pointed beneath her desk at the slumbering dog.

'What have you been feeding this dog?'

'I told you he's only had dog food.'

'Well, perhaps you need to change to another brand.'

'Oh, did he, er...'

'Yes, he did.'

'Was it bad?'

'I'll say it was bad. I had to evacuate the room.'

'Ah. That'll be the liver, then.'

'Liver? Are you serious? That's not dog food. Who feeds their dog liver?'

'I didn't feed it to him. Doris left it in the fridge. I can't stand the stuff so it put it by the bin ready to throw it out. I was sure he was asleep, but the minute I turned my back he was there like a shot. He ate the paper it was wrapped in as well. I was hoping it would pass through without mishap.'

'Pass through without mishap? Well, that's a good one,' said Katie. 'I suppose I should think myself lucky it didn't come out gift wrapped.'

'Look, I'm sorry, but I didn't do it on purpose. I haven't had a dog before, and I'm still getting used to his thieving ways.'

Katie had an appropriate retort about thieves on the tip of her tongue, but chose to keep it to herself.

'Well, I hope you're going to keep better control of him in future,' she said.

'How am I supposed to do that? Fit him with a stopper?'

If Flutter was hoping to lighten the mood, he'd missed the mark by some way.

'Instead of trying to be clever, how about you just make sure he doesn't eat the wrong stuff?'

'Right, yes, I'm sorry. I'll try to do better.'

Unimpressed, Katie returned to her work leaving Flutter in no doubt about how she felt. Feeling somewhat deflated, and let down by the comatose Winston, Flutter made his way to the spare desk and settled down with his box file. He thought about trying to improve the atmosphere but when he looked across at Katie she appeared to be engrossed in her work so he decided it would probably be best to leave her to it.

'This is interesting,' said Flutter, a couple of hours later.

'Mmm, what's that?' asked Katie.

'According to the guy's employment record, he was renting a flat here in Waterbury when he worked for the bus company.'

'Did he leave a forwarding address?'

'There's no record of it. And he was owed half a week's wages.'

'Sounds like he left in a hurry,' said Katie.

'Yeah. Suspicious, right? But it gets even better. When I tried searching his previous address near Manchester, no-one by the name of Harrison is ever recorded as living in that house.'

'It's possible he was an unregistered lodger,' said Katie. 'You know the sort of thing; you pay the owner cash in hand and no-one needs to know anything about you. It wasn't so easy to cross-check these things back then.'

'That just makes him even more suspicious as far as I'm concerned, but how am I supposed to find out about his past if he was living off the radar?'

'He can't have always been off the radar, can he?'

'Are you sure about that? I mean, I didn't find his birth certificate, did I?'

Katie pursed her lips.

'I wonder,' she said, thoughtfully.

'You wonder what?' asked Flutter.

'Didn't you say you found a Terry Harrison who was born around the right time but had died a young man?'

'Yeah,' said Flutter. 'He died aged twenty. But I don't see how that helps.'

'What if the man we know as Terry Harrison is actually someone else using the deceased Terry Harrison's identity?'

'Why would he do that?'

'I don't know,' said Katie. 'Maybe he was in hiding for some reason.'

'You mean like if he was on the run?'

'Exactly. Perhaps he was wanted by the police somewhere else and he changed his identity and then moved down to Waterbury to hide.'

'Yeah, I suppose that might work as long as the local police don't check him out,' said Flutter. 'Because if I could find a death certificate in his name, they sure would.'

'Only if they had reason to look,' said Katie. 'If he kept out of trouble they wouldn't have reason to check.'

'Don't you think a kid going missing would be a good reason to check out the boy's regular bus driver?'

'Of course, and if he was on a wanted list he probably disappeared when Stephen went missing because he was frightened the publicity around the case might reveal his whereabouts.'

'Going missing should have given them a perfectly good reason to be checking him out, but you're missing my point,' said Flutter. 'Steve Grant says the police **did** check up on Harrison. Now if they did, wouldn't they have found there was a death certificate in his name? That would make this guy pretty suspicious in my eyes.'

'Yes, but if he had a cast iron alibi maybe they didn't feel the need to check him out.'

'I don't buy that,' said Flutter. 'I mean, I'm no police detective, but surely they would have checked everyone out before it even came to alibis. It would be the first thing they'd do, wouldn't it?'

'You can't just assume he's guilty because he disappeared. You need a bit more evidence than that?'

'Why? Hammer seems to have assumed David Rooke was guilty, and from what I can make out he had no evidence whatsoever.'

'I think he ran because he was frightened of being arrested for whatever he did before he came to Waterbury.'

'That doesn't mean he didn't disappear because he took the boy,' said Flutter.

'I'm not saying he's not involved,' said Katie. 'I'm just pointing out there could be another reason he ran away.'

Flutter thought for a minute.

'Of course, there's always the possibility we're both right,' said Flutter.

'What d'you mean?'

'Suppose he changed his ID and went into hiding because he was a kiddie fiddler?'

Katie frowned.

'I hate that expression' she said. 'It almost makes what they do sound like harmless fun.'

'I appreciate it might sound a bit flippant,' said Flutter, 'but where I come from it's just the word for what they do, it's not a sign of approval, nor is it trying to trivialise it. I definitely don't see it as fun, and I don't know anyone who would.'

'Well, I don't like it.'

'Okay. I'm sorry. I didn't mean to upset you, but you have to admit it's a possibility.'

'Would a bus company really employ someone like that to drive kids around? I don't think so,' said Katie, dismissively.

There was an uncomfortable silence as she turned back to her work.

'Maybe they didn't know,' said Flutter.

He would have preferred to keep the discussion going, but something about her posture told him that might not be a good idea right now. Mindful of her suggestion an investigator should always be optimistic, he returned his attention to the box file. The list of employees names and addresses had been close to the top and he was hopeful if he delved a bit deeper he might find evidence in support of his theory, however unlikely Katie might think it was.

He lifted the remaining papers onto the desk and began to sort through them. As it was the employment records box file, he wasn't surprised to find a number of application forms. He quickly sifted through them until he found Terry Harrison's and read through it.

It soon became apparent Harrison had entered the bare minimum in answer to every question. Flutter immediately thought this was suspicious but there again, he wondered, was he was now guilty of doing exactly what Hammer had done with David Rooke?

A letter of reference was stapled to the application form. Flutter read through what appeared to be an unlikely character reference for Terry Harrison. He did a double take when he got the signature at the end of the letter, and then let out a low whistle.

'How much credence would you place on a character reference if someone was applying for a job, Katie?' he asked.

'That would depend on what it said, and who wrote it.'

'Well, according to this character reference with Terry Harrison's application form, the guy was a saint,' he said.

'Well, there you are then,' said Katie. 'Perhaps he wasn't what you said he was.'

'You don't think it's unlikely he's such a good bloke, given we think he may have been on the run?'

'It was just a guess he's on the run,' she said.

'Yeah, but even so, the guy's applying to be a bus driver, not an angel. It just seems a bit too good to be true if you ask me.'

'Can I see it?'

She reached a hand out, but Flutter didn't pass it across to her.

'If it was written by someone with a bit of authority, you'd tend to take it more seriously, right?'

'Yes, I suppose so.'

'Katie, I think I might know why Terry Harrison was never a suspect.'

'Why? Who wrote it?'

'See for yourself,' he said, reaching across to pass her the letter.

She took the letter and quickly read through it until she reached the signature and then she looked up at him, open-mouthed.

'I don't know about you,' he said, 'but I'm asking myself how a guy like Hammer would know a bloke a good ten years younger who

had just arrived in town. And how does he know him so well that he
can give him such a glowing reference?'

'Maybe they knew each other before Hammer came to Waterbury. Hammer does have a slight trace of a Northern accent. Perhaps
they were once neighbours, or Hammer knew his parents.'

'Yeah, maybe,' said Flutter, doubtfully, 'but to my mind there's
only one answer; Harrison had something on Hammer.'

'You don't know that,' said Katie.

'No, I don't know that,' agreed Flutter. 'And I understand you
think I'm anti-everything-police, but you've read the letter. He's a
Detective Chief Inspector. People look up to a bloke in his position,
and yet he's almost pleading with them to employ this new guy in
town. Why would he do that?'

'I don't know,' said Katie.'But I can hardly go and ask him, can I?
Excuse me Mr Hammer, but was Terry Harrison blackmailing you?
He didn't exactly welcome me with open arms last time, so you can
imagine what his response would be.'

'Well, if it's innocent enough, he should be willing to talk,' said
Flutter. 'I mean, it hardly matters after all this time, does it?'

'But what about the theory you're developing? If you're right, and
Harrison took Stephen, and then Hammer covered it up for some
reason, then of course it matters. It matters a lot.'

'If you're frightened of him, I'll go and ask him,' said Flutter.

'I'm not frightened of him,' said Katie, indignantly, 'but, if we're
going to confront him, we need to have some sort of proof or he'll
know we're guessing and, if knows that, we're sunk before we start.'

'But how can we prove any of this without asking him? asked
Flutter.

'We'll just have to dig into Hammer's past. Maybe we'll get lucky
and learn where their paths cross.'

'Can I take this laptop home?'

'I don't think that's a good idea,' said Katie.

'Why not? I can make a start on it tonight and save us some time.'

'It sounds fine in theory,' said Katie. 'I even used to think like that myself but, trust me, you'll find it doesn't work that way. Yes, you'll probably save a few hours now, but if you keep on doing nothing but work you'll end up so tired you become less and less efficient. In the end things will take longer to do, and you may end up missing little details that you would have spotted if you were more alert.'

'Blimey, that sounds like a lecture.'

'It's a lesson I learned the hard way, and I'm passing it on to save you from yourself. I see it as part of my job to pass on my knowledge to help you learn.'

'So, what am I going to do tonight?'

'Do what I do. Relax, chill out, have a glass of wine, watch some TV, watch a film, read a book.'

Flutter grinned.

'It must take you all night to do all that,' he said, flippantly.

She smiled, secure in the knowledge she was going to have the last word.

'Of course not. As a multi-tasking woman I can do them all at the same time.'

She licked the end of a finger and used it to mark her score in the air.

'Ha! Right. Point taken,' laughed Flutter. 'I know better than to argue when I can't possibly win.'

'Clever boy,' said Katie. 'There's hope for you yet. Now get off home, and take your smelly friend with you.'

Beneath her desk Winston was slowly emerging from his slumber. He yawned expansively, stretched, and reluctantly emerged.

'Same time tomorrow?' asked Flutter.

'I'll be here first thing,' said Katie.

'And so will we,' said Flutter. 'Come on Winston, get your arse into gear. We're going home which means it's walkie time.'

CHAPTER 20

IT WAS MID-AFTERNOON. Katie had been out most of the day, leaving Flutter and Winston to their own devices, but now they could hear her heels clattering up the stairs.

'I know it's a bit late but I've bought us lunch,' she said producing sandwiches and coffees from the shop downstairs.

'Katie, that's magic,' said Flutter, getting to his feet to help her. 'What have we got?'

'Because it's so late there wasn't much left so I got BLT, because everyone likes BLT, and I know you don't really like my instant coffee so I thought I'd treat us to cappuccinos.'

'You're spoiling me.'

'Don't kid yourself,' she said. 'It's just lunch. I guessed you wouldn't bother to eat if you were alone, but you can't work on an empty stomach.'

They took a fifteen minute break to enjoy their sandwiches.

'So how have you got on?' asked Katie. 'I would imagine it's pretty slow going.'

'Actually, the first bit wasn't too bad. There aren't many Raymond James Hammer's to sort through, and we know his age so finding his birth certificate was quite easy, and I've also managed to track the major events in his life from the time he was born.'

'Where was he born?'

'Stockport, which is—'

'—not far from Manchester,' finished Katie. 'I said he had a bit of an accent.'

'He did his National Service in the military police, then went on to join Greater Manchester police where he worked his way up to detective inspector. He transferred to Waterbury in April 1982, rising to DCI a year later.'

'Do we know why he transferred down here?'

'Your guess is as good as mine,' said Flutter. 'It could be any one of a hundred reasons.'

'I'm guessing it was a career move, as he became DCI within a year,' said Katie.

'Yeah, maybe,' said Flutter.

'And we think Harrison could have been from the Manchester area, so there's every possibility their paths could have crossed long before Hammer moved down here,' said Katie.

'Yes, it's possible you were right and they knew each other before Harrison came here, but I still think that reference is too good to be true.'

'You've done well to get that far already. I said you could do it.'

'Er, actually, I've done a bit more than that.'

'You mean there's more about Hammer?'

'When I found his birth certificate, I got a bit nosey and dug a little deeper into his family. I found he had a couple of brothers. Now, one of them, Harold, is two years older. He was also in the military police and became a police officer, too, but he emigrated to Australia in 1982. He's now long retired and living near Perth.'

'He's no use to us then,' said Katie.

'No, he's not. The interesting one is the younger brother. His name was Barry, and he was born when Hammer was twenty.'

'He was a late addition to the family.'

'His mother was forty-five when he was born.' said Flutter. 'My guess is he could well have been a mistake.'

'You can't be sure of that,' said Katie.

'I said it was a guess,' said Flutter. 'Anyway, that's not important. The interesting thing about Barry is that he's no longer around.'

'You mean he's dead?'

Flutter shrugged.

'I mean he's no longer around. If he is dead, I haven't found a death certificate to prove it. He just seems to have vanished from all records some time in the early 8os.'

'People don't just disappear.'

'Barry did.'

'Are you sure?'

'The last record I can find is from January 1982 when a police warrant was issued for his arrest.'

'Do we know why the police wanted him?'

'No idea,' said Flutter. 'Maybe was waiting to go to court and he skipped bail.'

'What do you think happened to him?' asked Katie.

'Well, I'm no Sherlock Holmes, and I'm probably jumping to conclusions, but I couldn't find any trace of the supposedly deceased Terry Harrison until he applied to become a bus driver in Waterbury in December 1984.'

'You're not serious...'

'You were the one who suggested he might have changed his ID,' said Flutter.

'Well, yes I did, but I didn't know he might be Hammer's younger brother when I said that.'

'Are you saying his big brother being a policeman meant he couldn't possibly do anything so devious?'

'Well, no, but... maybe Hammer didn't know anything about it,' suggested Katie.

'Oh, come on, Katie. Of course he knew; he would have recognised his own brother, whatever he was calling himself. And he wrote the guy a glowing reference to get him a job.'

'Yes, bu—'

'Maybe it was Hammer's idea to use a dead man's ID.'

'Now you're going too far. He was a senior detective; he wouldn't do a thing like that.'

'Why do you keep defending him?' asked Flutter.

'He has a son who works for Waterbury police, and he's not someone we want to be antagonising even if we're absolutely certain of our facts. And, in case you've forgotten, right now this is all speculation. Anyway, why are you so keen to prove he was up to no good?'

'The only thing I'm keen to do is find out what happened to an innocent little boy, or had you forgotten that's what we're trying to do?'

'Of course I haven't forgotten what we're trying to do, but I like to think the police can be trusted.'

'Most of 'em can be,' said Flutter. 'But at the end of the day they're human beings just like everyone else, and we know not all humans are good people. Maybe Hammer was just trying to protect his brother. I mean, would you give up your little brother if you could offer him an escape route?'

'That would depend on what he'd done.'

'Would it? Don't forget blood's thicker than water. And what if the repercussions might tarnish your reputation and ruin your career?'

'Now you sound like you're willing to turn a blind eye and forgive him,' said Katie.

'I'm not forgiving him for anything,' said Flutter. 'I'm just saying he might have given credence to a false alibi to protect his little brother and, at the same time, save his own reputation. If it was about evading an arrest warrant for petty theft or something equally trivial, then I don't really care, but if he knew his brother had something to do with Stephen disappearing, we're getting into a totally different ball game, and I won't turn a blind eye to that!'

'Did Hammer know about the arrest warrant?' asked Katie.

'He was a police officer working in Greater Manchester when it was issued, so I find it hard to believe he didn't know. Anyway, if my brother suddenly turned up with a new name I'd want to know why, wouldn't you?'

'Harrison could have lied about what had happened.'

'That only works if Hammer didn't know what his brother had done, but he was a DCI. He would have been able to check it out quickly enough and, unless Harrison was a fool, he'd have known his brother would suss out his lies. But I don't think it would have come to that. I reckon he did something big, and the whole family knew what it was.'

'Why do you say that?' asked Katie.

'Look at the dates, Katie. In January 1982, an arrest warrant is issued for Barry Hammer; within weeks big brother Harold heads off to Australia, and our man Raymond transfers south. In the meantime, Barry goes off the radar. I don't think that's a coincidence.'

'You can't just emigrate to Australia on a whim. These things take time to set up.'

'whose to say he didn't apply a year before? Perhaps they all knew what Barry was up to and that it was only a matter of time before he got caught. Maybe Harold was hoping to get as far away as he could before the shit hit the fan and they all got splashed.'

'What d'you think he did?'

'I dunno, but it looks as if it was serious enough for the other two to want to escape the fallout. And one of the things that might trigger a reaction like that brings us right back to little boys and girls.'

'But they would have stopped him, wouldn't they?'

'Maybe they tried but couldn't.'

'Okay, so let's assume you're on the right track, and that the older brothers washed their hands of Barry, who then went into hiding and changed his identity. So, why did he then come down here to Water-bury?' asked Katie.

'I can think of a couple of reasons,' said Flutter. 'Maybe they'd kept in touch and put together some sort of deal to get him down here where big brother Raymond could keep an eye on him and keep him out of further trouble.

'Or, as I suggested before, maybe little brother knew something about big brother that would have destroyed his career. Hammer wasn't married, was he? So, maybe his career was his life and he'd do anything to protect it.'

'I'm not sure I can live with this idea that Harrison took Stephen, and then Hammer covered it up,' said Katie. 'That makes him an accessory to the crime, doesn't it?'

'Hammer would certainly be guilty of perverting the course of justice, at the very least. I'm just surprised you find it so hard to believe. I'm not being funny but, for someone who used to be an investigative journalist, you seem pretty unaware of a lot of things that go on in the real world.'

Katie sighed.

'It's not that I don't believe it, it's more that I don't want to believe it. Perhaps you're right and I've been down here in my little Waterbury bubble, cocooned from the real world, for too long. But what about his alibi? What if it was genuine?'

'I'm starting to think there was no alibi. All we know is that he was supposedly off sick that day, and Hammer personally ruled him out of the enquiry.'

'Yes, but you said he did that because the arrest warrant was for skipping bail.'

'My first thought was that it could be something like that, but what if it was for something worse?'

'Like what?'

'Like I suggested before, something to do with kids.'

'You mean he'd done it before?'

'Maybe, or perhaps he was a suspect in a similar case. Once you get tarnished with that brush it's probably a good idea to change your name and move away. It would certainly explain why his brothers didn't want to be caught in the crossfire.'

'But then Hammer got him a job driving a bus full of children,' said Katie, appalled. 'That would be like starting the clock on a time bomb.'

'Well, like I said, perhaps Harrison had something on him.'

'Terry Harrison should have been an automatic suspect in any investigation involving a small boy.'

'Yep,' said Flutter. 'You'd think he would have been at the top of the list, but it seems Hammer deliberately steered the enquiry away from him.'

'And straight towards David Rooke,' said Katie, 'who was innocent but couldn't escape the accusations, and eventually killed himself.'

'And then, within days of Stephen disappearing, Terry Harrison vanished into thin air and, because Hammer had cleared him, no-one in the police team seemed to find that even remotely suspicious.'

'It's hard to believe, isn't it?' asked Katie.

'But it's all very convenient, if you're Harrison or Hammer,' said Flutter.

There was an uncomfortable silence as they absorbed the enormity of what Flutter seemed to have uncovered.

'Harrison did vanish, too,' said Flutter. 'Into thin air. I can find no trace of him anywhere after that.'

'He could have changed his name again,' said Katie.

'If he did I've got no chance of finding him.'

'So he could have literally got away with murder,' said Katie, 'aided and abetted by his older brother.'

Flutter felt as though the sky had suddenly darkened.

'I suppose in my head I knew Stephen had probably been murdered,' he said, gloomily.

'I'm sorry. After what you just said I thought I should try be more realistic,' said Katie.

'Oh, I know you're right, it's just that none of us had actually said as much before. Even Jewle avoided that word, but now you've said it everything has suddenly changed. Before this case was just something to do, a bit of a diversion almost, but now it's like, well, I'm not sure I have the right words to describe it. I'll tell you one thing though, I'm going to find out what happened and if old Hammer is involved I'm going to make sure he gets what's coming.'

'Now let's not get carried away,' said Katie. 'I understand where you're coming from but it's no good rushing in. We're going to have to tread very carefully. At the moment, we have our suspicions, but without proof we've got nothing. And once Hammer knows we've found out this much, who knows what will happen. I'm sure his son will be on the warpath.'

'Yeah, you're right. We need a plan,' said Flutter.

Katie looked at the clock. It was just gone 4.30.

'You seem to have covered an enormous amount of ground in just a few hours,' she said. 'I'm very impressed.'

'I've been lucky I guess,' said Flutter.

'Well, as a reward I think you should stop now, go home, and put your feet up.'

'Really? It's a bit early.'

'Nonsense. Get away while you can. If you want something to do, you can think about what we're going to do next. I'll do the same tonight and then, in the morning we'll put our heads together and see what we can come up with.'

CHAPTER 21

NEXT MORNING the sky was filled with foreboding and by 11 am it was covered by a thick blanket of oppressive, dark grey clouds which appeared set to spend the rest of the day sharing their contents with the residents of Waterbury. As Katie started the car and pulled away she looked out at the weather and muttered a gentle curse. Flutter smiled in agreement with her sentiment, but neither of them could have any way of knowing the weather was simply providing an appropriate backdrop to what was going to prove to be a disturbing day.

'Are you sure this woman's going to speak to us?' asked Flutter.

'We won't know that until we get there. I couldn't phone her and ask as I couldn't find a number for her.'

'I don't know how I missed her. I was sure I'd already found all the witnesses,' said Flutter.

'Don't worry about it. Anyone could have missed her name. She wasn't in any of the main stories, she was almost an afterthought. It was pure luck that I noticed her. Anyway, she might have nothing to tell us, but she was the same age as Stephen and in the same class, so I'm hoping she can give us something.'

The Woodlands estate was just a twinkle in an architects eye when Flutter had left town fifteen years ago. A collection of just 50 houses built around a central, circular green on the outskirts of Waterbury sounded idyllic but, sadly, the reality was rather different and as a result it had earned the local nickname of "The Dump". It was the sort of small estate that would love to look clean and tidy but, as the locals name for it suggested, it had failed. Or, to be more accurate, the people who lived there had failed it.

As Katie turned onto the estate the first thing they saw was a collection of dead cars, broken bicycles, and a rusting fridge and matching washing machine, which littered the roadside and spilled onto the green.

'Blimey,' said Flutter, as he took in the scene. 'It looks like the inner city. You don't expect to see this sort of thing out in the sticks.'

'Welcome to the hidden side of rural living,' said Katie. 'People have this absurd idea it must be wonderful living out in the country, and that everywhere is clean and fresh, but there's just as much deprivation and squalor out here. It's just easier to hide it away.'

There seemed to be shopping trolleys everywhere, gathered in small groups, almost as if they had stopped for a chat. As Flutter took in the scene he wondered how on earth they had got there. It had to be at least two miles to the nearest supermarket. It all seemed depressingly appropriate for such a damp, grey, morning.

They were looking for number eighteen and as Katie pulled up outside they could see it was the stand-out house in the street. Not because its occupiers had made the effort to make a showpiece of their small front garden, but because it was the only house with its own mountain of rubbish. A huge pile overflowed from the wheelie bin at the side of the house. It was already blocking access to the side door and was slowly spreading along the path towards the street.

As they climbed from the car and contemplated this amazing sight, a woman emerged from the front door carrying a bin bag full of rubbish. Flutter couldn't decide which was more attractive; the cigarette dangling from her lips, the shapeless tracksuit bottoms that seemed to be in danger of bursting at the widest part of her backside, or the grubby vest she wore.

Totally unaware of her visitors she walked halfway to the river of rubbish and heaved the latest bag roughly in the right direction, watching with disinterest as the sack curved upwards in a gentle arc, missing the pile and landing instead on the concrete path where it burst and spread its contents in all directions.

'Sod it. Missed,' she muttered.

She scratched disinterestedly at an armpit then tugged at the backside of her trousers, which appeared to be in danger of being swallowed up and lost forever. As she turned back to the house, she finally noticed the visitors watching her from the roadside, and her eyes narrowed as she focused on Flutter. She snatched the cigarette from her mouth and tossed it aside.

'Wotchoo starin' at?' she snapped.

'Helen Dawson?' asked Katie

'No,' she snapped.

'If there's an award for the world's most unconvincing liar, she's got it in the bag,' whispered Flutter to Katie.

'You were formerly Helen Linden, isn't that right?' asked Katie.

'If it's about money, the pair of you can piss off,' she yelled. 'I don't owe you nuffink, an' I ain't got none anyway.'

Flutter stepped towards the rickety garden gate.

'It's not about money, Helen.'

'Well, piss off anyway!'

She looked warily towards the front door, apparently calculating whether she could get there before him.

'Go on. Sod off, oo'ever you are,' she shouted. 'Whatever it is, I never done it! I wasn't even there.'

'Flutter, step back and let me try,' warned Katie, quietly. 'If she bolts indoors we'll never get to speak to her.'

Reluctantly Flutter stepped back towards the car.

'Helen, listen,' pleaded Katie. 'We're not here to ask you for money, and we're not here to accuse you of anything. We want to talk to you about something that happened thirty-five years ago.'

Helen's eyes narrowed even further and she pointed at Flutter.

'He's one of them dirty pervert people, isn't he?' she asked Katie.

'What me?' asked an incredulous Flutter. 'Where d'you get that idea from?'

'I know your sort and, for your information, I don't do that sort of fing no more, and I never wanted to back then. So, like I already said, you ca-'

Katie thought she now understood what Helen's problem was.

'Helen, he's not going to do you any harm, I promise,' she said. 'We want to ask you about Stephen Bowles. You remember? He's the little boy who disappeared when you were at school.'

This seemed to stop Helen in her tracks, and she stared at Katie as her words sank in.

'I didn't have nuffink to do with that, neither.'

Unlike Katie, Flutter hadn't worked out Helen's problem and he was beginning to wonder how much of a persecution complex one woman could have.

'Helen, listen,' insisted Katie. 'I promise we're not here to accuse you of anything. We just want to ask you what you remember about the day Stephen disappeared.'

'I told the coppers back then. They already know what I saw.'

'We're not with the police, so we don't know what you told them. We're trying to find out what happened because we think there's something fishy about the whole thing.'

Helen eyed them suspiciously as she considered this new information.

'What? Bent coppers, you mean?'

'That's what we're trying to find out.'

That was Katie's breakthrough moment. As soon as Helen re-alised Katie wasn't with the police, but might actually be working against them, she was no longer the enemy but had just become a potential ally. Unfortunately, this wasn't to be the case for Flutter.

'Okay. Whatcha wanna know?'

'Just tell me what you remember from that day.'

Helen cast a wary eye over the neighbouring houses.

'Lots of ears out 'ere,' she warned. 'You better come inside.'

Katie eased the gate open and started up the path to the front door. Flutter began to follow.

'Where d'you think you're going?' asked Helen.

He stopped dead in his tracks.

'I'm just comi—'

'Oh no, you're not,' said Helen. She pointed at Katie. 'She can come in, but you can wait outside. This is a no man zone. I don't let men inside my house.'

'Yeah, bu—'

Katie turned to Flutter, and offered him the car keys.

'Do as she asks, please.'

'But I—'

'Wait in the car. I'll explain afterwards,' said Katie.

Helen offered Flutter a self-satisfied smirk as he reluctantly took the keys and made his way sulkily back to the car. He slammed the door closed and watched as Katie followed Helen into the house. He consoled himself with the thought that if the house was as bad on the inside as it was on the outside, he'd probably got the better deal.

As Katie approached the front door she was having a similar thought, but she had that tingling feeling that told her Helen was going to be a crucial witness and, if they were going to hear what she had to say, there was no other choice but to go inside.

As she entered the house she took a quick look around. To her surprise, and relief, the inside of the house was nothing like the disaster area outside. Helen certainly wasn't ultra house-proud, but the house was untidy, not dirty, and it was surprisingly cosy. It was almost as if she occupied two different worlds.

Helen was watching her, and as Katie caught her gaze, she realised her face was obviously far too easy to read. Helen laughed quietly.

'That surprised yer, dinnit?' she said. 'You thought you were coming into a pigsty, didn't yer?'

Katie really didn't know what to say, and wondered if she was going to be on the receiving end of another outburst but, instead, Helen offered a warm smile.

'Me house is like me life,' she explained. 'I'm like two different people. Inside my home, in my own little world, I can just about keep fings under control, but out in the open I turn into a complete mess. They messed me up when I was a kid, see, an' I ain't never been right since.'

She seemed to withdraw into herself for a few moments leaving Katie to struggle for something meaningful to say. She had guessed Helen was a victim, but just saying "sorry" seemed totally inadequate. Then a little smile flitted briefly across Helen's face and she was back.

'Is that why you don't allow men into your house?' asked Katie.

'Only my husband, Billy,' she said. 'He's definitely not the sharpest knife in the box, but he's the only man I can trust. He's got a heart of gold, he loves me, he keeps me safe, and asks for nothing in return. You can't ask for more than that, can you?'

There was another brief pause as Helen became lost in her thoughts again, and then, just as suddenly, she was back again.

'But you didn't come 'ere to listen to me praising Billy, did you? Come in and siddown.'

She led the way through to a surprisingly clean and tidy living room and pointed to an armchair. Katie sat down and Helen slipped into a similar seat opposite her.

'Right,' she said, giving Katie her full attention. 'I'm all yours.'

'In the newspaper story at the time it says you told the police you think you might have seen Stephen in town the day he disappeared.'

'Oh, there was no "might" about it. I definitely saw him,' she said. 'I told that detective I saw Stephen that afternoon, and he was with uncle Terry.'

Katie felt she would burst, but she had to keep clam.

'Did Stephen often spend time with Uncle Terry? Or was it just on the one occasion?'

'It weren't just that day,' said Helen. 'It weren't that simple.'

And then she told Katie her story...

An hour later Flutter watched Katie pull the front door closed behind her and, head bowed, walk slowly down the path. He thought she was avoiding his gaze and guessed this probably meant he was in trouble. As she opened the car door and climbed in he studied her face. Her eyes were distinctly red and a bit puffy.

'Are you okay?' he asked. 'Did she give you a load of verbal? Is that what's upset you?'

She reached for a tissue and wiped her eyes.

'No, she didn't give me any verbal. She's actually a very nice lady, but she's been messed up by her past. That's what's upset me.'

'She didn't come across like a lady when she was snarling at me.'

'Yes, well, she's a classic example of why you shouldn't judge a book by its cover.'

'Eh?'

'She was abused as a child. Why d'you think she's so anti-men? All that aggression is her defence system.'

'Oh, shit,' said Flutter, suddenly feeling about an inch tall. 'I had no idea.'

'It's not your fault.'

'No, but that doesn't make it any better does it? I was happy to think she was just some rough old bird who didn't give a damn. Now I feel terrible.'

'Come on,' said Katie. 'Let's get out of here.'

'I'm almost frightened to ask now, but what did she have to say?' asked Flutter, as Katie started the car.

'Oh, she had quite a story to tell, and I will share it with you but, first, I think I need a stiff drink.'

CHAPTER 22

TRUE TO HER WORD, Katie stopped at the first pub they came too.

'Will you drive us back?' she asked as they stood at the bar waiting to be served.

'You're not going to get hammered, are you?' asked Flutter.

'No, I'm not, but I meant it when I said I needed a stiff drink.'

'Okay, I can do that,' said Flutter. 'Now, what do you want to drink?'

'I'll have a large gin and tonic please,' she said to the waiting barman.

'I suppose I'd better have an orange juice,' said Flutter, unenthusiastically.

Katie smiled sympathetically, and winked at him.

'Never mind,' she said. 'You know it makes sense. I'll drive next time.'

'Yeah, right,' he said.

When they were settled at a table, Katie took a large slug of her drink and then began to speak.

'You were right about Harrison.'

'Right about what?'

'He had a liking for little boys, and little girls.'

'Oh, no. Really? This is what Helen told you?'

Katie nodded.

'So, being handed the keys to the school bus must have seemed like the perfect job to him,' finished Flutter.

'He told the kids they should call him "Uncle Terry". Helen Linden was just ten years old when he arrived. Things weren't good at home for Helen and, being the predatory manipulator that he was, Harrison soon identified her as his first victim. It wasn't long before he began abusing her.'

'Why didn't she tell anyone?' asked Flutter.

'Why do you think? Her parents were always arguing, she felt neglected, and was unhappy. Then this man came along, paid attention to her and made her feel as if she mattered. He ensured her silence by telling her that what they were doing was their special secret and that something terrible would happen if she ever told anyone.'

'What about Stephen?'

'According to Helen, Stephen was a beautiful child, with an angelic face, blue eyes, and blond hair. It was in his nature to trust everyone and by the time he went missing he had become one of Uncle Terry's "favourites" although Helen didn't think he had actually abused Stephen at that time.'

'Did Hammer know all this?' asked Flutter. 'Because, if he did...'

'According to Helen, the day Stephen disappeared, she saw him walking along with Harrison when he was supposed to have been on his way to the bus station. Harrison was holding the boy's hand and they were walking down a quiet alleyway away from the safety of the town and the bus station. She told this to DCI Hammer, but he had told her it was important she didn't tell anyone else unless he said it was okay.'

'So he frightened her into suppressing the evidence?'

Katie nodded.

'It gets even worse,' she said. 'Next day, "Uncle Terry" came to her and told her she had been a bad girl for speaking to Inspector Hammer and that they were both angry with her. He told her that, if she ever mentioned the story again, he would tell Inspector Hammer she had been a bad girl again, and then she'd be in real trouble and they would lock her up and throw away the key.'

'How long will I get if I murder someone?' asked Flutter.

'That's not going to help Stephen is it?' said Katie.

'No, of course not, but I just feel so bloody angry...'

'Getting angry won't do anyone any good, either. Angry usually means acting hastily, and we need to stay cool or this will all have been for nothing.'

'It explains a lot about Helen Linden and why she hates men so much.'

'It's nothing personal against you,' said Katie. 'She was a bright, intelligent kid who was left terrified and confused. She became regarded as a hopeless case by those trying, and failing, to educate her. And she was so traumatised she kept her terrible secret to herself, knowing she would surely be locked away if she so much as mentioned it to anyone, ever.

'Even when she grew up she never told anyone because she didn't think anyone would take the word of a failure like her against that of a man like Detective Chief Inspector Raymond Hammer.'

'Oh, I totally understand where she's coming from,' said Flutter. 'Why should she trust any man she doesn't know after she's been through something like that? And she's never going to get any justice now, is she?'

'Not against Harrison,' said Katie, 'but I think we should make sure her story comes out. Maybe then she'll get some help. It's bit late now, but her life was completely messed up and I think it's the least we can do.'

'So, what are we going to do?' asked Flutter. 'Confront Hammer and tell him we know what he's done?'

'It's tempting,' said Katie, 'but not just yet. I was wondering what might happen if we were to speak to the brother in Australia.'

'D'you really think he'll co-operate?'

'Willingly? Who knows? But it's worth a try. Maybe we can learn something about what was going on before he emigrated.'

'Okay, let's do it,' said Flutter.

'Not so fast,' said Katie. 'There's something like a nine or ten hour time difference, and the guy's in his eighties. If we call him now it'll be after midnight, and he doesn't know us from Adam. D'you think he'll be more, or less, willing to co-operate in those circumstances?'

'Good point,' said Flutter. 'Perhaps we'd better wait until the morning.'

'I'm thinking between nine and ten,' said Katie. 'It'll be early evening over there, which is a much more sociable time to call.'

'So what do we do now?' asked Flutter.

Katie looked at her wristwatch.

'How about we take the rest of the day off?' suggested Katie. 'I don't know about you, but I have stuff that needs to be done during business hours.'

'I've some shopping I need to do,' said Flutter.

'There you go then, that settles it,' said Katie.

CHAPTER 23

'HALLO? Is that Mr Harold Hammer? My name is Katie Donald. I'm a journalist, calling from England.'

'A Journalist? From England, you say? Well, Katie Donald, what can I do for you?'

'I'm doing a story about a case your brother Raymond worked on. He's reluctant to talk about himself so I was hoping you might be able to give me some information about him.'

'What information? Are you trying to blame him for something?'

'Good heavens, no. We're doing a story about unsolved missing children investigations. We're not trying to blame anyone for anything, we're talking about how detectives trying to solve the cases are affected by them. I'm just looking for a bit of background about his younger days. School days, family stuff, that sort of thing.'

'I'd love to help you, but I don't think my brother would be very happy if I spoke to you without asking him first.'

'I'm not asking you to tell me anything embarrassing.'

'It's not that. I haven't spoken to Raymond since I came to Australia, and I don't feel inclined to start now.'

'Oh, that's a shame,' said Katie. 'What caused that? Was he upset you were leaving?'

'We'd already fallen out before that. Family business.'

'Can I ask what that was about?'

'Yes, you can ask, but you can also mind your own business.'

'Oh, right. I'm sorry, I didn't mean to pry.'

'Of course you did,' snapped Harold. 'You're a journalist. It's what you people do, isn't it?'

Katie felt Harold was about to hang up the phone. She was sure if he did, they'd never get another chance, so she took a risk and changed the subject.

'Can I ask you about your younger brother, Barry?'

'Barry? What's he got to do with anything?'

'He was a lot younger than you, wasn't he?'

'Over twenty years. Twenty-two in fact.'

'He spent time in Waterbury with Raymond, didn't he?'

'Isn't that the town Raymond transferred to?'

'Yes, that's right. Did Barry stay there with him?'

'I wouldn't know about that. As I said, I haven't spoken to Raymond in years, and I never had much to do with Barry. I'd already left home when he was born.'

'Did you know he'd changed his name to Terry Harrison?'

'What? When did he do that?'

'Early in the eighties.'

'But, why?'

'I was hoping you could tell me that.'

'No, you must have got that wrong. He called me once, right out of the blue. Must have been 1985. He said he was coming to Australia and asked if he could stay with me. I didn't want him here, but what could I say? I'm sure he didn't say anything about changing his name.'

'And did he come to visit?'

'No. I even went to meet the flight he said he was arriving on, but he wasn't on it. When I checked later I found he'd never even booked a ticket. He always was a waste of space that boy.'

'Did a man called Terry Harrison book a ticket?'

'I don't know. I was looking for a ticket in the name of Barry Hammer. Anyway, what's this got to do with your story?'

'The thing is, we think your brother Barry, or Terry Harrison, as he was calling himself then, may have abducted a little boy in Waterbury in 1985.'

'Holy God, I hope you're kidding.'

'I'm afraid not, Mr Hammer. And it gets worse. Raymond was leading the investigation and we think he may have known Barry was responsible and let him get away with it.'

'Oh, christ, not again.'

It was almost a whisper, and at first Katie wasn't sure what she'd heard.

'I beg your pardon, Mr Hammer, what was that?'

There was the faintest of clicks, the line went dead, and then a few seconds later Katie could hear the dial tone.

'Damn it. He's hung up,' she said. 'Did you hear it all?'

'Yeah,' said Flutter. 'He distinctly said "oh, christ, not again" before he hung up. It's all recorded.'

'We're not supposed to record conversations without telling the person we're talking to,' said Katie. 'It's against the law.'

'Yeah, and so is grabbing little boys on their way home,' said Flutter. 'Anyway, it's not as if we're going to be using it as evidence in court, is it?'

'I suppose not,' she said.

'You should be happy,' said Flutter. 'Now we know Barry had done it before, there's a good chance he took Stephen. And didn't I tell you the family knew what he'd been doing?'

'We still don't have any concrete proof,' said Katie.

'And after 35 years I'll be very surprised if we find any,' said Flutter.

'Do you think Harold knew about Barry? Because if Harold knew, and stood back and did nothing, he's just as bad as Raymond.'

'Thirty-odd years is a long time for two brothers not to speak,' said

Flutter. 'I would imagine it would take something pretty big to cause that sort of rift and Barry could well have been that reason. Perhaps Harold wanted to hand him over to the police, but Raymond didn't.'

'So why didn't Harold speak up anyway?'

'I dunno, Katie. I don't have brothers so I'm only guessing, but maybe it's that brotherly love thing. Maybe giving up a brother you hardly know is easy, but giving up one you grew up with is something else. Perhaps Harold went to Australia so he wouldn't have to give up Raymond as well.'

An hour later Flutter suggested it was his turn to go out and buy lunch.

'Did you get your shopping done yesterday?' asked Katie.

'Yes, I did, thanks.'

'Buy anything exciting?'

'Actually, I bought a laptop.'

'Really? You do know I have a spare one here?'

'Yeah,' said Flutter, 'but I wanted one of my own that I can keep at home so I can do personal stuff.'

'Is it secret personal stuff, or something I can help you with?'

'I think it's high time I found out exactly what happened when I was a kid, so I thought I'd start by doing my family tree.'

'Oh, right. That's very brave. You might find things you'd rather not know about.'

'Maybe I already have,' said Flutter. 'I always thought there were three brothers, Walter, William and Wesley, but it turns out there was also a half-brother called Andrew, born some fifteen years after the others.'

'Half-brother?'

'Different mother. I suspect grandad was a bit of a frisky old devil and had an eye for an attractive younger woman.'

'Where's he now?'

'Who, Grandad? I've no idea. I never met him, and no-one ever spoke about him. I assume he's dead but I don't know for sure.'

'No, silly. I mean Andrew, the half-brother.'

'I didn't get that far. I know his mother was called Isabella Agostini, and she was only twenty when he was born, and grandad was in his fifties.'

'That would have been awkward if your grandmother was still around.'

'Yeah. I don't suppose she nominated him for husband of the year. Maybe that's why he's dead.'

'You don't seriously think—'

'Actually, Katie, I was joking. But the fact is I don't know anything about either of my grandparents, and what I thought I knew about my parents has turned out to be a load of lies. That's why I want to learn about them now.'

Katie nodded her understanding, but said nothing.

'Anyway,' said Flutter, 'I'm just going to nip down the road and get us something to eat. Is there anything you really don't like?'

'Not really, but you don't need to go to any trouble. Just a sandwich will do.'

'I thought we could have something a little better than a sandwich today.'

'Like what?'

Flutter smiled and winked.

'It's a secret. You'll just have to wait and see. I won't be long.'

Flutter smiled to himself as he made his way downstairs. He didn't for one minute think he was any sort of detective, but he had to admit he was beginning to like this investigative work. And he was enjoying Katie's company even though she could be a bit prickly at times.

As he pushed the door open and turned left onto the street he began to whistle quietly to himself.

CHAPTER 24

ACROSS THE STREET, two men were sitting in the back of a parked car, with a third in the driving seat.

'That's him,' said one man in the back of the car as Flutter appeared.

'Thank gawd for that,' said the driver, Denny, as he started the car. 'I thought we were going to be sitting here forever.'

'Wait a minute,' said the man in the back, whose name was Tommy. 'Let's see where he's going first. We don't really want to create a scene in public.'

'D'you think he'll put up a fight?'

'I dunno, Denny, but ask yourself, would you choose to get in a car with three strangers?'

'But what if he stays on the High Street?'

'Then we'll have to ask him politely to get in the car but, if he says no and we have to grab him, it's going to cause a scene. It would be much better if we could be a bit discreet about it.'

'We're in luck,' said the second man in the back. 'Look, he's going round the corner. It'll be much quieter down there.'

They watched as Flutter turned left off the High Street and disappeared from view.

'Where's he going?' asked the driver.

'I don't know, and it doesn't matter, Denny,' said Tommy. 'You just follow him.'

The driver drove the car carefully across the street and turned left. Flutter was strolling along, lost in his thoughts, about thirty yards ahead.

'Perfect,' said Tommy. 'Not another soul in sight. Right, Denny, you know what to do.'

'No problem,' said Denny, slowing the car and pulling in to the kerb.

'Okay, Bob, you ready?'

'Don't worry, Tommy. I've got him,' said the third man.

As the car stopped, he slipped from the back seat and began purposefully walking after Flutter, quickly gaining ground on him. In the car the two remaining men watched as Bob gradually caught up with Flutter until finally Tommy tapped Denny on the shoulder.

'Right, Denny, let's go,' he said.

In one smooth, well-oiled manoeuvre, the car moved alongside their victim. Startled from his daydream, Flutter stopped and his mouth dropped open as the car appeared from nowhere. The door swung open in front of him and a rough-looking man leaned out.

'Want a lift?'

'What, me? A lift from you? You must be joking,' said Flutter.

'Oh, that's a pity. I was hoping we could do this without a lot of fuss.'

Flutter tried to back away, but before he knew what was happening, he was grabbed from behind, lifted from his feet and bundled into the back of the car. The man who had pushed him inside jumped in next to him and slammed the door, squashing Flutter between himself and Tommy.

As the car accelerated away, Flutter could barely breathe for the two huge guys either side of him. Involuntarily, he braced himself for a beating.

'There's no need for that,' said Tommy, as Flutter flinched. 'We're not here to beat you up.'

Flutter looked at the two guys on either side of him.

'How do I know you won't beat me up?'

'You don't,' said Tommy. 'But it would make a terrible mess in the car, and then we'd have to clean it. Trust me, we've got better things to do.'

'Of course, if you want a fight, that's a different matter,' said Bob.

Flutter turned to look at Bob. He was at least a foot taller than Flutter, and his fists seemed enormous. Flutter had no intention of getting into a fight with people like these guys, but he wasn't going quietly.

'What is this?' he asked. 'I thought we had a deal. I was told I had a month.'

'I don't know what you're talking about,' said Tommy. 'All I know is my boss would like a word with you.'

'Then that just proves Jimmy Jewle is a lying shit,' said Flutter. 'I knew I shouldn't have trusted him.'

'Jimmy Jewle? We don't work for Jimmy Jewle.'

'You don't? Then who the hell do you work for?'

'Why don't you stop complaining and chill out. You'll find out who soon enough.'

Flutter felt he had plenty more to complain about, but he knew he'd be wasting his breath so he kept quiet, folded his arms petulantly, slumped back in his seat and focused on the road ahead. He had no idea where they were going but he thought, if he could spot a few landmarks, it might help if he had a chance to escape.

The car was heading out of town, so he prepared himself for a long, silent journey, possibly even as far as London. Then the car slowed and turned off the main road onto a mixed estate of industrial and business premises on the outskirts of town. Flutter suddenly sat bolt upright.

'Where are we going now? This isn't London.'

Denny, the driver, looked at Flutter in his driving mirror.

'London? Why would we be going to London? Who said anything about London?'

'I dunno,' said Flutter. 'I assumed if Jimmy wanted to see me...'

'Will you stop blathering on about Jimmy Jewle,' said Tommy. 'For the last time, this is nothing to do with him.'

'So who—'

'Just wait a couple of minutes and you'll find out.'

A short distance onto the estate, the car turned right through a set of gates. Ahead of them stood a rather tatty looking building. Above the main door a sign read "Bennet's Snooker Hall".

'whose Bennet?' asked Flutter.

The car pulled up outside the main door and they dragged Flutter from the back of the car and led him into the reception area of the building.

'Right,' said Tommy, pointing to a flight of stairs. 'Walk up those stairs, and at the top you'll find a corridor. Doors to the left and right are toilets and kitchen, the one straight ahead is the office. The boss is expecting you.'

Flutter stared at him.

'You're joking, right?'

'I think you'll find I'm not known for my sense of humour.'

'He's right,' said Bob. 'Wouldn't know a joke if it slapped him.'

Tommy glared at Bob.

'You seriously think I'm going to walk up there like some sort of sacrificial lamb?' asked Flutter.

'Yes, I do,' said Tommy. 'Unless you'd like me to ask Bob, here, to escort you.'

'I can carry you if you're tired,' suggested Bob.

Flutter looked at Bob, and then at the stairs. Reluctantly, he headed for the stairs.

'And don't even think about trying to escape,' added Tommy. 'The only way out is back down this way and we'll be waiting here.'

Flutter made his way up the stairs. The doors to left and right were just as Tommy had said. There were windows in both rooms, but there were also bars across them, so there was no escape there. The door ahead at the end of the corridor was marked "office".

Flutter considered his options and quickly realised there were none. If he didn't enter the room of his own volition, it was obvious Bob would be more than happy to assist him. So, one way or the other, he was going to have to face whatever awaited him beyond that door.

He swallowed hard, marched up to the door, and knocked.

'Come,' boomed a voice from inside.

Flutter turned the handle, took a deep breath, swung the door open, and marched inside.

CHAPTER 25

THE OWNER of the voice was sitting back in a luxurious leather chair behind a large mahogany desk. He was a swarthy looking man with jet black hair, and he peered intently at Flutter over his steepled fingers as if waiting for an explanation.

'What is this?' demanded Flutter. 'And who are you?'

The man raised a single eyebrow to acknowledge his irritation at Flutter's impertinence.

'My name's Bennet,' he said. 'That's all you need to know right now, and you should understand I'm not the one whose here to answer questions. It doesn't work like that. You're the idiot whose causing me grief so that entitles me to ask the questions, and you to provide the answers.'

'Causing you grief?' asked Flutter. 'What, me? I don't know what you mean.'

'Really? Then let me explain,' said Bennet. 'Forty years ago this area was awash with police trying to keep control of a couple of tearaways called Jimmy Jewle and Walter Gamble.'

Flutter's ears pricked up at the mention of the two names.

'Ah!' said Bennet. 'So you admit you know the people I'm talking about.'

'I admit I know their names,' said Flutter cautiously.

Bennet scowled. He knew Flutter was being economical with the truth, but he decided they could come back to that. For now, he continued speaking.

'Anyway, those two young men were so mean everyone around here hated and feared them but then they took off to London to make their fortunes and things slowly got back to normal. The police presence became smaller, and smaller, until, about thirty years ago, Waterbury and the surrounding area became the perfect spot for me to go about my business with no interference from anyone. And it's been like that ever since.'

He smiled sweetly at Flutter, then suddenly jumped to his feet, slammed his fist down on the desk, and shouted.

'But now, suddenly, someone's arrived in town and started rocking the boat. That someone is you, and I want to know why you're making waves!'

Despite Bennet's anger, Flutter couldn't help but notice the man's suit.

'Cor. Nice threads,' he said. 'Italian isn't it?'

Bennet's vanity took momentary control, and without thinking he looked down at his suit and brushed an imaginary speck of dust from his jacket.

'Yes, it is Italian,' he said warmly. 'If you can afford the best you shou — Hang on a minute! Never mind about my suit. I want answers, not flattery. For a start, why is Jewle in town? Did you invite him?'

'Look, it's not my fault,' said Flutter. 'And I certainly didn't invite him. I'd never even met the man until he turned up at my house.'

'Why would he come all the way down here to see you?'

'Because I've just inherited a house which he claims should be his by rights because the owner bought it with the proceeds of a robbery which was stolen from under his nose.'

'And you say you've inherited this house?'

'That's right, yeah.'

'From Wally Gamble?'

'That's right.'

'So, you really are Wally's boy? I figured you must be.'

'If you know all this, why did you kidnap me and bring me here?'

'Because this is my turf, where we do things my way. And I wanted to make sure I'd got it right.'

'What's it got to do with you, anyway?'

'As I said, this is my turf and I don't need someone stirring things up and attracting attention from the boys in blue.'

'Yeah, well, I don't want any trouble either,' said Flutter. 'I just seem to attract it at the moment.'

'What about this girl you're working with, the journalist?'

'How do you know about that?'

'I make it my business to know what's going on locally. And once you know whose arm can be twisted it's relatively easy to find out things out,' said Bennet. 'What with that and the internet you can learn just about anything about anyone. Anyway, why has she been out to see old man Hammer?'

'What difference does it make to you?'

'It could make a lot of difference to me. The thing is, he's got a son with the local plod, goes by the nickname of Sledge.'

'Sledge?'

'Yes, Sledge, as in, Sledge Hammer. Now it doesn't take a genius to figure out why he's got a nickname like that, and you can take it from me that annoying him is rather like sticking your finger in a hornet's nest.'

'But it's our fingers that will get stung, not yours,' said Flutter.

'Not if he finds out we're family,' said Bennet. 'Once he knows we're connected, that will be just the excuse he needs to come swarming all over me and my business.'

Flutter's mouth dropped open and he was momentarily lost for words, but only momentarily.

'I think I must have heard that wrong,' he said. 'I could have sworn you said we were family.'

'That's right. We are family.'

'How does that work, then?'

'I'm Andrew,' said Bennet. 'I was your father's brother, or at least his half-brother. I guess that makes me your uncle, or should that be half-uncle?'

'This is a joke, right? I mean, you can't be serious.'

'Why is it so hard to believe?'

'Because for the ten years since my aunt and uncle died I've believed I had no family left, and now they seem to be popping up all over the place. How do I know you're not making this up?'

'Why would I make it up? Do you think I'm proud to admit I'm a Gamble?'

'But your name's Bennet.'

'Oh, well spotted. You should be a detective.'

'It's funny you should say that, because Jimmy Jewle has turned me into one.'

'How's he done that?'

'It's a long story. Basically, he wants my house, and he came down here to throw me out, but then I stopped someone blowing his head off, and now, because I saved his life, his wife insisted he had to give me a chance to keep the house. So he's come up with this crazy task, and if I can solve it, I can keep the house.'

'That sounds very generous of him to offer you a deal. Normally he'd just send his heavies in and throw you out on your arse. He must have mellowed in his old age. So, you solve the case and you get to keep the house, is that it? What's it worth?'

'It's worth over a million, but the thing is, I don't want the damned house. Walter paid for it with dirty money and I don't want it.'

Bennet looked at Flutter in amazement.

'Are you sure you're Wally's boy? He never would have encouraged an attitude like that.'

'Yeah, well, he never got to encourage me to do anything. I didn't even know he was my dad until he was dead.'

'Now that sounds more typical of the Walter I knew and hated. He never accepted responsibility for anything. Just like his father, really.'

'At least your father took you in and raised you,' said Flutter.

'That's not quite how it was,' said Bennet. 'My mother was twenty when the old man seduced her. She was beautiful, way too good for him, but he knew how to charm the ladies, and she was a bit naive. In the end she fell for his patter and he got what he wanted. She actually thought he was going to leave his wife and set up home with her. It was all great until she told him she was up the duff.'

'What happened then?'

'He told her to clear off. He said he'd deny ever knowing her if she tried to cause trouble.'

'So how come you became a Gamble?'

'Because your grandfather wasn't as clever as he thought he was. Her name was Isabella Agostini. The clue was there in her name. It should have been easy enough to work out for anyone with half a brain, but thinking with his brain wasn't his forte, and he missed it.'

'Right,' said Flutter, realising he didn't get the clue any more than his grandfather had. 'And what does that mean, exactly?'

'Isabella was from an Italian family. An Italian family with connections in Sicily. What do you think it means?'

'Oh, right,' said Flutter as the penny finally dropped. 'I see what you mean. And he didn't even think it was a possibility?'

'Not until her father arrived on his doorstep with Isabella holding a newly born baby. Daddy made it clear what the consequences would be if the child's father didn't face up to his responsibilities. Apparently the old man thought he was bluffing, but then the rest of the Agostini family emerged from their cars, armed to the teeth with shooters, and he realised they didn't intend to leave until he did the right thing.'

'And what was that?'

'You can work it out, can't you? I mean my surname's Gamble. Or, at least, it was until I changed it.'

'You mean they left you here?'

'They had high hopes for Isabella marrying someone who could improve the family connections back home, but arriving back in Sicily with a little bastard in tow wasn't part of the plan. And let's be honest, it wouldn't have looked good, would it?'

'So, they abandoned you?'

'It's not as bad as it sounds. They made sure I never went without, and kept in touch now and then. I've even had financial help here and there since I went into business. And Sheila was a good mum to me, even though I was her husband's bastard son.'

'What happened to the old man? He was my grandfather, yet I don't recall ever hearing him mentioned.'

'Yeah, it's funny that. He disappeared not long after I arrived on the scene, and no-one ever heard from him again.'

'Did he run away?'

'If he did, he took nothing with him. My guess is it's more likely he's dead.'

'D'you think that was down to Isabella's family?'

'If I was a betting man, my money would be on Sheila.'

'Wow! Do you really think she could have done something like that?'

'Oh, yes. That woman had a fearsome reputation and, don't forget, he had seriously humiliated her. I mean everyone knew I wasn't her son, and she had to face everyone knowing they knew. It can't have been easy for a proud woman like her.'

'Hell hath no fury, like a woman scorned. Isn't that what they say?' said Flutter.

'Exactly,' agreed Bennet. 'Anyway, I didn't bring you here to talk about me. What about this task Jewle has set you?'

'He's got this mad idea that I can find out what happened to his nephew, who disappeared over thirty years ago. An entire police force couldn't solve it, but he thinks I can, with Katie's help.'

'Katie?'

'The journalist, Katie Donald.'

'I think I remember that case,' said Bennet. 'The police never found the boy, did they?'

'Never even got close according to Jewle.'

'And they arrested no one?'

'Hammer fixed on one teacher, and wouldn't consider anyone else. Jewle reckons Hammer deliberately focused on the teacher to steer the inquiry away from the truth.'

'So that's why this journalist friend of yours went to see him?'

'Yeah, and she's convinced he's hiding something.'

'What about the teacher?'

'As far as we can tell there was never any evidence against him, and we now know he had an alibi so he couldn't have done it.'

'I was too young to be in the know back then,' said Bennet. 'But I heard later that there had been rumours about Hammer.'

'What sort of rumours?'

Bennet settled back in his chair.

'There were a couple. Word had come down from Manchester that Hammer had a problem family member. A brother, I think it was. This was of interest because it was suggested this information could be used to blackmail Hammer. Of course that meant someone had to find the guy and prove he existed, and then find out why he was an embarrassment, but as far as I know no-one ever found him. Of course in those days we couldn't jump on a computer and find things out like you can now.'

'Well, I can tell you Hammer has two brothers. The older one is a retired detective in Australia, but the younger one is the one you heard about. It turns out there was warrant for his arrest.'

'What was the warrant for?'

'Dunno,' said Flutter, 'but it fits with your story, doesn't it? What was the other rumour?'

'It concerned Hammer's mental health. Apparently he had taken to digging at night instead of sleeping.'

'Digging? You mean like in his garden?'

'I don't know. Nowadays I make it my business to find out as much as I can about local police officers, but back then I was just a kid and I had no business to protect. And, of course, old Hammer had retired by the time I needed to know. But you can't deny it sounds bizarre behaviour for a guy working such a big case, and if it's true it would make you question his sanity, wouldn't it?'

'Katie said he's a keen gardener.'

'He'd have to be if he was digging all night. There again, if that's true then maybe the whole story is a load of cobblers started by someone who took the facts and twisted them to create a rumour.'

'It would be nice if we could find something to use as leverage,' said Flutter. 'We want to speak to him again, but with nothing new to put to him, he'll probably just show us the door.'

'You want to be careful,' said Bennet. 'His son, who happens to be the local Detective Inspector, will go bananas when he finds out you've been trying to ruin his dad's reputation.'

'He must know by now,' said Flutter.

'Yeah, he probably does,' said Bennet, 'but you're in luck. He's on a month's vacation in Portugal right now, so there's nothing he can do. But he won't be there forever, and when he comes back, he's going to go berserk.'

'How d'you know he's in Portugal?'

Bennet tapped the side of his nose.

'It pays to know these things,' he said. 'Keep your friends close, and your enemies even closer, that's my philosophy.'

There was a brief silence as Flutter tried to take in all this new information.

'D'you know you're the only family I've got,' said Bennet. 'We should celebrate. Why don't we go down to the bar so I can buy you a beer?'

'I really should get back,' said Flutter. 'I told Katie I was only going to be a few minutes.'

'But we've got so much to talk about,' said Bennet. 'Just have one, and then I'll get one of the guys to drive you back.'

'I suppose one won't hurt, as long as it's a quick one.'

CHAPTER 26

When Flutter finally got back to the office and pushed open the door, the expression on Katie's face was somewhere between fury and despair. Combined with the angry pout and the folded arms, it told Flutter he wasn't exactly going to be welcomed like a returning hero.

'Has Winston been farting again?' he asked.

'No, Winston hasn't been farting. Winston has behaved impeccably all day,' said Katie through gritted teeth.

'Oh, so what's wrong?'

'What's wrong?' fumed Katie. 'Where the hell have you been? When you left you said you'd be a few minutes, not three and a half hours! If you have places to be, all you have to do is say, and you can go, but just wandering off without a word is so, well...' she paused for breath, and Flutter could see she was so angry there were now tears in her eyes. 'Well,' she continued, 'apart from anything, it's just plain bad manners. I mean, where were you? I was worried. I didn't know what to think.'

Flutter raised his hands in surrender as he waited for her to finish letting off steam.

'Katie, I'm sorry, really I am, but I can explain.'

'Oh, please do. I can't wait to hear it.'

'I got kidnapped.'

Katie rolled her eyes so expansively that, for a split second, Flutter could only see the whites of her eyes.

'Kidnapped?' she repeated. 'I suppose next you'll be telling me there's a pirate ship moored down by the river.'

'No, there aren't any pirates, but there were three guys in a car. They followed me round the corner and dragged me into the car.'

'And why would they do that?'

'Because there's a guy running things around here, and he's upset we've been making waves in his patch.'

'A guy running things? You mean like a gangster?'

'Not the sort of gangster you're thinking of. He's more a sort of "gangster light", if you see what I mean.'

'No, I don't see what you mean. This is ridiculous. Next you'll be telling me this man has mafia connections.'

'Well, it's funny you should say that...'

'Don't you dare try to make fun of me, Harvey Gamble.'

'On my life, I am not making fun of anyone. D'you think I enjoyed being dragged into the back of a car?'

'You can't seriously expect me to believe gangsters with mafia connections kidnapped you. For goodness' sake, there are no gangsters here. This is Waterbury, not Sicily.'

'You're right, this isn't Sicily,' said Flutter. 'But what about Jimmy Jewle? He was genuine enough, wasn't he?'

'Well, yes, but he was from London.'

'Yeah, but he was here, so why can't there be someone like him in this area?'

'I'm sorry, but I find it hard to believe there's a gangster in every town.'

'Walter Gamble lived here.'

'Yes, but he wasn't running the town, he was running away.'

'That's correct, he was running away, but why did he come back here?'

'I don't know.'

'Because, once upon a time, this town, and the surrounding area, was run by two young guys called Jimmy Jewle and Walter Gamble. Thanks to those two, and especially to Walter, the Gamble name was feared by many people around here.'

'I didn't know that.'

'Of course you didn't. This was before you were born,' said Flutter. 'Even I didn't know about it until today. Apparently, old Wally and Jimmy were the local gangsters back then, but their behaviour attracted a lot of attention from the boys in blue. Finally, when things got too hot for them, they moved on to bigger things in London.'

'How do you know all this?'

'Remember the half-brother called Andrew? Well, he's still here in Waterbury, but he was so ashamed of the Gamble name he changed his name by deed poll. He now goes by the name of Bennet, and he runs things around here. He wanted to know why we were causing the sort of trouble that might become a problem for him.'

'What trouble?'

For the next half hour Flutter explained the family history he had just heard about to Katie, including how Walter had mercilessly bullied the much younger Andrew, and how Walter dumping Wesley's body in the river had convinced Andrew he never wanted to be associated with the Gamble family name.

'So you're telling me that your uncle Andrew—'

'Step-uncle, and he prefers to be called Bennet,' corrected Flutter.

'Okay, your step-uncle, whose called Bennet, runs the local area,' said Katie with a heavy dose of scepticism.

'That's right. Once the police had faded into the background, his family connections enabled him to go into business.'

'And he says there was a rumour Hammer had an errant brother, but no-one ever found him.'

'You have to admit it sort of confirms what I suggested.'

'And he also claims Hammer senior is off his head because he liked gardening.'

'The rumour was he spent his nights digging, instead of sleeping. It wouldn't help him do his job, would it?'

'Maybe, but it doesn't prove he misled the inquiry, does it?'

'You don't believe any of this, do you?' asked Flutter.

'Can you blame me?' asked Katie.

'I swear it's all true. How can I prove it to you?'

'Right now, I don't know,' said Katie.

'I think you need some time to yourself, so you can cool down,' said Flutter. 'I'm gasping for a drink so I'm going to the coffee shop for a while, and then when I come back I'll collect Winston and go home.'

CHAPTER 27

BROODING on what he perceived to be the injustice of Katie's mood, Flutter pushed his way through the door into the coffee shop. He had been hoping for a bit of peace and was disappointed to find it was heaving with noisy customers.

Disconsolately, he carried his coffee to the only empty table in the room, sat down and stared out of the window. Someone had left a newspaper on the table and, after a minute or two, he opened it and read absently just for something to do. He'd been minding his own business in this way for a few minutes when he became aware someone was standing by the empty chair next to him. He looked up and a little old man met his gaze and nodded a greeting.

'Mind if I sit here?'

Flutter looked at the old man and saw an opportunity to divert his attention away from Katie and her foul mood and perhaps lift his spirits.

'No, of course not,' he said, moving his cup and newspaper aside to make room. 'Sit yourself down.'

The old man sank down into his seat with an enormous sigh. He had what appeared to be a bag full of vegetables, which he tucked under his seat.

'My name's George Wilkins,' said the old man, offering his hand. Flutter shook the hand.

'People call me Flutter,' he said. He pointed to the bag. 'Been shopping, George?'

The old man looked down at the bag. 'Oh, no, I'm waiting for the lady who runs the shop. I'm hoping she's going to buy from me.'

'You're selling then?'

'I'm from the local allotment association,' he explained. 'If we can flog some of our stuff to local shops and restaurants, we can make a few quid. It makes the pension go a bit further.'

'Now, that's a good idea,' said Flutter. 'Have you had the allotment long?'

George smiled fondly.

'Longer than I can remember. I used to manage the place, but I'm too old for that now. Still grow some good stuff, though. Keeps me fit, you know? I'm eighty-two. You wouldn't believe it, would you?'

'You do look pretty fit,' agreed Flutter. 'I bet I won't look that good when I'm your age.'

The old man accepted the compliment with a nod of his head.

'You can't beat an allotment to keep you fit,' he said.

Flutter had a hunch.

'I was speaking to someone just the other day,' he said. 'He's about the same age as you. He had an allotment around here a few years ago. If you used to manage the place, maybe you remember him?'

'Oh yes? What's his name?'

'Raymond Hammer, he used to be a detective inspector with the police.'

George creased his brow and thought for a few moments.

'Oh, yes, I remember him,' he said. 'That must have been thirty-odd years ago. He was a bit of a loner, nearly always kept himself to himself.'

'That sounds about right,' said Flutter. 'Your memory's pretty good.'

George pulled a face as he searched for more memories.

'I seem to remember he waited months for his allotment, and then, when he finally got it, there was some big case on and he didn't have any spare time.'

'There was a young boy went missing,' prompted Flutter.

'That's right. I remember now. He couldn't sleep at night thinking about that boy so he asked me if he could start coming down at night.'

Flutter thought this was sounding interesting.

'He used to work on the allotment at night?'

'That's right. He reckoned working on the allotment helped him to cope. We all thought it was weird, but there must be a lot of stress trying to solve a case like that. I suppose it would be enough to keep anyone awake at night.'

'Yes, you're probably right,' said Flutter. 'I think I'd probably have nightmares.'

'Worked like a Trojan, too,' continued the old man. 'He double-dug the whole blooming plot. He used to turn up late evening just when everyone else was going home, and he'd dig well into the night. By morning, he'd be gone, but you could see how much he'd done. I thought he was mad. I told him he didn't need to dig so deep but he said he was going really deep because he wanted to improve the drainage.'

Flutter didn't have a clue what his new friend was talking about, but he felt it was important to keep him talking.

'Is it common up there, bad drainage?'

'In all the years I've had my allotment, I've heard no one else complain about it. The soil is mostly sandy, so it drains and dries out quickly, but it was his plot, so he could dig as deep as he wanted as far as I was concerned.'

'It takes all sorts, I guess,' said Flutter.

The old man looked off into the distance to draw on his memory.

'He must have had a good supply of manure, too, although he wouldn't tell anyone where he got it from. I tell you what, though,' he finished, turning to Flutter and giving an approving look. 'It all paid off. He grew some cracking vegetables.'

Flutter's scalp was tingling.

'I've only just moved here and I haven't got my bearings yet,' said Flutter. 'Where are these allotments?'

'Take the north road out of town, and after about a mile you'll see a recreation ground with a kids' play area and a couple of football pitches. The allotments are just after. You can't miss them.'

'If I went up there, would I be able to find his old plot?'

'Oh yes. My grandson's got it now. He's nearly always there. Just ask for Geoff Wilkins. He's still growing great vegetables.'

Flutter was nearly bursting. He gazed up at the clock on the wall.

'Wow, look at the time. I'm afraid I've got to go now, George. It's been really nice talking to you. I'll definitely pop up and see Geoff. Will he be there in the morning?'

'He's bound to be. He's always up there.'

'Right. Maybe I'll see you up there, too,' said Flutter.

'It's nice to sit with someone who wants to talk these days,' said the old man, smiling. 'Thank you for taking the time to listen.'

'My pleasure,' said Flutter, shaking his hand.

Then he jumped up and almost ran from the shop.

CHAPTER 28

FLUTTER STUMBLED BREATHLESSLY into Katie's office.

'Katie, listen to this,' he said, then stopped speaking as he realised a tall man in a cheap-looking suit was leaning against the wall next to Katie's desk. For a minute he feared it was trouble.

'Flutter, this is Robbie,' said Katie. 'Robbie, this is Flutter.'

The man stepped forward and offered Flutter a hand.

'Robbie Bright,' he said, then deliberately added. 'That's detective sergeant Robbie Bright.'

Flutter knew a threat when he heard one, but he resisted the urge to take a step back and shook the man's hand. Warily, he looked from Katie to Bright and suddenly made the connection.

'Ah, I get it. You're Katie's detective friend,' he said.

Bright looked at Katie.

'I like to think we're a little more than friends,' he said. Then, turning back to Flutter, 'So, you must be the ex-con whose got Katie involved with a London gangster.'

'Robbie!' snapped Katie. 'It's not like that. You make it sound like I've become a gangster's moll. We're just looking into an old unsolved case, that's all.'

Flutter had thought he had detected an atmosphere as soon as he walked into the office. Now he understood why.

'Just down for the day, are you?' he asked, hoping to change the subject.

'Didn't Katie tell you? We wanted to be closer to each other, so I applied for a transfer to Waterbury. This is my first day.'

Flutter felt his heart sink.

'Oh, right,' he said. 'That's nice for you.'

'You had something to tell Katie when you came in,' said Bright.

'Eh? Oh, no, it's not important,' said Flutter.

'But you sounded excited,' insisted Bright.

Flutter didn't know Bright from Adam, and after the start they'd just made, he wasn't sure the guy could be trusted. He decided he was going to busk it.

'I was just going to say I've found out where I can get an allotment.'

'Keen gardener, are you?' asked Bright.

'I'd like to grow my own, help save the planet, you know the sort of thing.'

'But I thought you had this enormous house with a vast garden,' said Bright.

'That's just temporary,' said Flutter. 'The place I'm moving to has only got a small garden.'

'But why would you want to move?' insisted Bright.

Flutter bristled.

'What is this, twenty questions?' he asked. 'It's my life, I thought I could do whatever I wanted.'

Bright smiled as he studied Flutter's face.

'And so you can,' he said. 'Just as long as it's legal.'

Flutter looked at Katie, who looked distinctly embarrassed, and mouthed "sorry" to him.

'Has Winston been okay?' he asked.

'Winston has been an angel,' she said.

'Can you wake him up for me, then?'

As Katie prodded the old dog to life, Flutter glared at Bright.

'If it's not against the law, I'm going to walk home with my dog.'

'As long as he's on a lead and doesn't poo on the pavement,' said Bright. 'I believe there are bylaws against that sort of thing.'

Flutter fished a handful of small plastic bags from his pocket and held them up so Bright could see.

'Poo bags, mate,' he said. 'I pick up after my dog because I'm a responsible owner.'

'Good. I'm pleased to hear it,' said Bright.

'Will you two stop it,' said Katie, handing Winston's lead to Flutter. 'You're behaving like two little boys.'

'C'mon Winston, let's get out of here,' said Flutter. 'The atmosphere's not so good today and, for once, it's not your fault.'

Bright thought about a response, but a fierce glare from Katie made him reconsider.

'Goodbye,' she called to Flutter. 'See you in the morning?'

'I dunno,' said Flutter. 'There's somewhere I have to be.'

'Later, then,' said Katie.

'Yeah, I expect so.'

She watched as Flutter and Winston left and made their way out of the office. As soon as the door closed, she rounded on Bright.

'What was that all about?'

Bright tried to look innocent.

'What was what all about?'

'I don't know what you were trying to prove, but if you think that sort of behaviour is going to impress me I'm afraid you're way off the mark.'

'I was just letting the guy know I'm on his case and I've got my eye on him.'

'Why can't you just give him a chance?'

'Katie, these people never change. He's only been out of prison five minutes and already he's got you eating out of his hand.'

'Rubbish!'

'You're working for a gangster, for goodness' sake.'

'Flutter is not a gangster.'

'No, but Jimmy Jewle is, and your man Flutter seems to be well in with him.'

'Flutter didn't choose for this to happen. He'd never even met Jewle until he turned up on his doorstep.'

'That's what he says. Anyway, you're still working for the man, whether or not your friend knew him.'

'I'm not working for anyone. I'm helping to investigate an old missing person case. A case which, I might add, the police made a complete mess of.'

'You can't know that,' argued Bright.

'Actually we do,' said Katie. 'We know for a fact that the one and only suspect had an alibi and was nowhere near the scene of the crime.'

'How do you know?'

'Because we took the trouble to check out everyone who might have been connected and interviewed them. Obviously your lot either didn't think to do that, or chose not to do it. We also know there was something funny about the school bus driver but, again, your lot don't seem to have bothered to check him out.'

Something had been bothering Bright, and now he knew what it was.

'What were you doing at his house that day?' he asked.

'What day?'

'The day you called me about Jewle. You were at Flutter's house. Why were you there?'

'If you must know, I was there to help him question his housekeeper.'

'Oh, yeah, right,' said Bright. 'That was his excuse for getting you to his house, was it? Is there something going on that I should know about?'

Katie bristled with indignation.

'No, there is not something going on, and how dare you suggest it.'

'You seem to know a lot about him, and you're very close.'

'I like him, okay? He's a nice man. He just needs someone to give him a chance and he'll surprise you all, but you're so quick to write him off. Are you like this with everyone who makes a mistake?'

'You need to understand these people never change, Katie.'

'Are you perfect?' she demanded.

'What? No, of course not.'

'So, you've made mistakes in the past.'

'Yes, of course.'

'And were you given a chance to redeem yourself?'

'Well, yeah, but I didn't go to prison for my mistake.'

'So it's simply a matter of degree. Is that what you're saying?'

'This is crazy—'

'I think you should leave,' said Katie. 'And don't think you can come creeping round my house tonight because you won't be welcome. You need to understand that I choose who my friends are, and I will not be told otherwise by you or anyone else. And to suggest I can't be trusted? Well, you'd better make your mind up what you really want from this relationship.'

'But, Katie—'

'Don't even think about trying that "but Katie" business.'

'But I've just moved all the way down here to be with you!'

'Yes, but if you think this is just about what you want, perhaps you should have stayed where you were.'

'This is because of him, isn't it?' asked Bright.

'As I just said, I think you should leave,' insisted Katie. 'And I don't want to see you again until you've had time to think. I suggest that will take at least 48 hours. Now please go.'

She turned back to her work and ignored all his further attempts to engage with her until he finally left.

· · ·

Meanwhile, Flutter was making his way home with Winston. It annoyed him he'd let Bright get under his skin, and he wondered why Katie was involved with such an idiot.

He was also disappointed with himself for thinking he ever had a chance with Katie. I mean, who was he kidding? She had a lot going for her. She was bright, clever, and attractive. What could an ex-con with no prospects offer someone like her?

'To be honest, mate, I suppose I was being optimistic,' he said to Winston as they walked along. 'But I'm sure she was giving off the right signals. I mean, those tears when I got back this afternoon; were they angry tears, or were they relieved tears? I could have sworn it was relief, so that means she cares about me, doesn't it?'

The dog looked up and wagged his tail.

'What's that you say?' asked Flutter. 'You don't know because you were asleep? You're not much help, are you?'

Winston wagged again, and this time Flutter stopped and bent to stroke the enormous ears.

'But I like you, even though you're no help,' said Flutter. 'And do you know why? Because you accept me as I am, and don't judge me on my past, that's why.'

CHAPTER 29

FORTUNATELY IT WAS a pleasant morning because even though it was barely 2 miles from Flutter's house to the allotments, at Winston's pace, with his need for many stops to sniff various items, and then urinate on them, it took over an hour to get there.

Flutter was sure a snail had overtaken them at one point but, when he pointed this out to Winston, the old dog responded with a single wag of his tail but made no attempt to go any faster.

The allotment site comprised thirty good-sized plots. Flutter asked the first person he saw if he knew where Geoff Wilkins was and they directed him towards the far end of the site where a big, round man with huge hands was standing by a shed pouring himself a drink from a thermos flask.

Flutter made his way to the shed, introduced himself and then explained how, even though he was a complete novice, he was thinking about applying for a plot, and how Geoff's father had suggested he come and speak to him. Geoff was happy to welcome Flutter and show him proudly around his plot. As he pointed out various vegetables growing in neat rows, he gave Flutter a commentary on how each was growing and how this year's weather was affecting them.

Now he was here, Flutter's resolve weakened as he realised he had no idea what he was hoping to learn. He wondered if perhaps he should have sought Katie's advice before coming, or perhaps brought her with him. Then, as he thought about Katie, he recalled what she had said about trusting your hunches and being optimistic, and suddenly he understood this was a situation where his past could help him.

He'd made a living winging his way through life, and now he had the opportunity to use that skill for the good. He was sure if he did his best to nod and smile in all the right places, it would encourage Geoff to keep talking, and sure enough it seems to work. They were back by the shed now, and he noticed Geoff seemed particularly proud of his sweetcorn patch.

'Grows like mad just there,' he said, pointing out the area in question. 'I tried celery and marrows in that spot, but they were terrible. I don't know why, but it suits the sweetcorn just right.'

Flutter didn't need to be an expert on sweetcorn to see how well it was growing. He compared the nearby plots. Two or three others were growing similar crops, but none came close to the success Geoff was having.

'I see what you mean,' said Flutter. 'When it comes to sweetcorn, you seem to have the magic touch.'

'The others think I cheat somehow, but I don't have to. I just stick it in the ground and away it goes. It's weird because sweetcorn grows best on chalk, but there's no chalk here. It's amazing. I've never been able to grow it like this before.'

It would be fair to say Flutter hadn't been an exceptional student at school, but an odd collection of random facts had stuck in his mind for whatever reason, and now he recalled one of them.

'You say it grows best on chalk. That's calcium carbonate, isn't it?'

'That's right, but as I say, there's no chalk here, it's more sand than anything. Anyway, what d'you think? Are you after a plot up here?'

'Er, well, after speaking with your grandfather, and now I've had a chat with you, I'm certainly considering it.'

'In that case...'

Geoff reached into his shed and unhooked a clipboard with a pencil attached by a piece of garden twine.

'... we need to get your name on this list, pronto.'

He offered the board to Flutter.

'Well, I'm not sure—'

'Don't worry, it's not legally binding or anything. If you decide you don't want to join us, just let me know and I'll cross your name off. There are lots of names on the list already so you'll have plenty of time to reconsider.'

'I'm pushed for time right now,' said Flutter, looking at his watch.

'Just write your name and number. It'll only take a minute.'

Flutter hadn't intended to take things this far, but Geoff had willingly given up his time, so now he felt obliged to play along. He took the board and jotted down his details.

'Is it okay if I bring my partner along so she can have a look around?' he asked as he handed the board back.

'For sure. Bring her along and let her have a chat with some of the other guys. They're a friendly bunch and they like to help newcomers get the best out of their plot. She'll love it.'

'I'll do that,' said Flutter. 'Well, thanks for your time, Geoff. I'll see you again. C'mon Winston, we're late.'

Winston's urge to leave a urine trail diminished on the way back into town but, as they had further to walk, it still took over an hour to get to Katie's office. By then, Flutter's imagination was running wild, and he eagerly explained where he'd been and what he thought he'd discovered.

'So, what do you think?' he asked when he'd finished.

'You mean, do I think there's a body buried there? Or, do I think your man cheats at growing his sweetcorn?'

'Oh, come on, Katie, don't joke. I'm serious. He said sweetcorn grows best on chalk. Chalk is calcium carbonate, and human bones are made of calcium.'

'Yes, I get that, but we're talking about a body being buried over thirty years ago. There wouldn't be anything left by now, would there?'

Flutter's shoulders slumped.

'D'you know, I hadn't thought of that.'

'Wait a minute,' said Katie. 'We can check. Now, let's see...'

She tapped away at her keyboard for a moment.

'Right, here we are,' she said reading from her laptop, 'it says here a body buried underground decomposes naturally to a skeleton in anything from a few months to a few years, depending on the conditions, and then the acids in the soil can take as much as another twenty years to destroy the skeleton.'

Flutter sighed.

'So you're right,' he said. 'There's probably nothing left.'

'Hang on, there's more,' added Katie, still reading. 'If the soil is neutral-PH or sand, it can take hundreds of years. And in really dry, or salty, soil the body may simply become mummified and not decompose at all.'

She looked up at Flutter.

'I'm guessing the soil's not dry, or salty, or they wouldn't be able to grow anything there.'

'No, it's not salty,' said Flutter, 'but old George said it was quite sandy. What if it's sandy enough to slow the process down?'

'I think you might be clutching at straws there,' suggested Katie.

He sighed again.

'I really thought I was onto something,' he said. 'Why else would anyone be digging that deep, and in the middle of the night?'

'I didn't say you were wrong,' said Katie. 'Perhaps you are onto something. Maybe he did bury a body there, and maybe there's enough sand in the soil to keep the skeleton intact.'

'It's not much help if we can't prove it, though, is it? Geoff

Wilkins seems a nice enough bloke, but I can't see him agreeing to let me dig up his allotment just because I have this bizarre theory there might be a skeleton down there.'

'Especially if he's so proud of his sweetcorn,' said Katie.

'What about detective sergeant Hard Man? Can't you ask him to help?'

'I'm sorry for what happened yesterday,' said Katie.

'I'm not asking you to apologise for anything,' said Flutter. 'It's not your fault your boyfriend's an arse.'

'Yes, well, it doesn't matter. I can't ask him for help.'

'Why not?'

'After he showed me up with his behaviour yesterday, I told him I don't want to speak to him for 48 hours.'

Flutter couldn't stop a smile creeping onto his face.

'Really? You did that for me?'

'Don't kid yourself, Flutter. I did it for me. No-one tells me who I can or can't have as a friend. And besides, he's only just started at Waterbury and he's trying to fit in. Suggesting they go digging up random allotments for no other reason than our outlandish theory is unlikely to win him any friends.'

'I suppose you're right,' said Flutter gloomily. 'We need some sort of proof, but how are we going to get it thirty-five years after the event?'

'I could always ask Raymond Hammer why he went digging at night,' suggested Katie.

'I don't think he's going to admit he buried a body there, do you?'

'Of course not, but he won't expect me to know about his nocturnal digging. The question will catch him off guard and he might let something slip.'

'Are you sure you want to do that?' asked Flutter. 'Maybe it would be better if I went. He doesn't know me.'

'Actually, I think we should both go. If I go alone and he lets something slip, he can always deny it, and then it would be his word against mine. That can't happen with two of us there.'

'That sounds like a plan,' said Flutter. 'When do you want to do it?'

'There's no time like the present. Will Winston be alright here on his own?'

Flutter pointed to the old dog who had curled up in his bed and was just beginning to snore.

'The poor old thing's walked miles on those little legs this morning, and now he's knackered. I bet he won't even notice we've gone.'

CHAPTER 30

KATIE LED the way to Hammer's front door, rang the doorbell, and waited. A moment later, the door swung open to reveal a beaming Raymond Hammer, but the smile vanished as soon as he saw Katie with Flutter alongside her.

'What the hell do you want?' he snapped.

'I was wondering if you could spare a few more minutes to answer a couple more questions.'

'I told you before; bugger off, and don't come back.'

He went to close the door, but Flutter had been expecting that, and he quickly wedged his foot in place. Hammer took hold of the door and looked meaningfully down at Flutter's foot.

'I've said all I'm going to say, so you're wasting your time,' he snarled, looking up into Flutter's face. 'I don't know who you are, but if you don't take your foot away, I'm going to slam this door on it.'

'We only want to ask a—' began Katie, but an anguished cry from Flutter interrupted her as Hammer made good on his promise.

'Ah, shit! My foot!' he yelled.

Flutter would have removed it from the door, but Hammer had got all his weight against it and it wouldn't budge. Things weren't quite going to plan and Katie realised she had to be quick or they would lose their chance. She began a barrage of questions.

'What about your younger brother, Barry?' she asked. 'He wasn't like you and your other brother, was he?'

For a moment, Hammer looked as if someone had slapped him, but he quickly recovered and continued to crush Flutter's foot.

'I don't know what you're talking about. I don't have a younger brother.'

'Sure you do. He changed his name to Terry Harrison after he got caught with a little boy.'

'I told you before, it was the teacher. I had no doubt about it.'

'You mean Mr Rooke? You ruined that man's life, Mr Hammer, do you realise that? He didn't do it.'

'Of course he did it. I've-'

'Got a nose for these things? Yes, you said. The thing is, your nose was wrong.'

'No!' he cried.

'David Rooke has an alibi. He was with Miss Goodie. You remember her, don't you? Surely you must have interviewed her?'

'She never said!' shouted Hammer.

'You never asked her, did you? David Rooke told her to keep quiet because he didn't want his wife to know he was with her.'

'No!' Hammer was still shouting, his face red and angry. 'If that's true, why didn't she come forward and say so at the time?'

'You could have found all this out if you had tried, but you didn't want to, did you? And why were you digging on your allotment at night? We found a witness who says he couldn't believe how deep you were digging. Why was that? Were you burying something? A body perhaps?'

Suddenly, he stopped shouting and pushing on the door and a look of shocked realisation crossed his face and he ducked back behind the door. Flutter let out a sigh of relief as the pressure was released from his foot.

'Jesus, that bloody hurts,' he muttered, biting at his lip. He rested his left arm against the door frame and took the weight off the damaged foot.

'Flutter, look out!' Katie suddenly yelled from behind him as Hammer re-emerged from behind the front door, clutching a cricket bat, which he raised above his head with both hands.

'If you two don't piss off, right now,' he threatened, 'I'll break your bloody arm.'

Almost too late Flutter realised his left arm was an inviting target and as he tried to get out of the way the bat whooshed down, catching a glancing blow on his wrist.

'You stupid old fool, you could have broken my arm,' he yelled.

'Well, don't say I didn't warn you,' roared Hammer. 'I'm going to call the police about you two. Then we'll see how bloody clever you are.'

'You do that, Mr Hammer,' said Katie, ushering Flutter away from further harm. 'But don't think we're going to stop now. We know what you've done and you will not get away with it.'

Hammer slammed the door so hard there was a noise like a sonic boom, and then suddenly, there was silence.

'I think he might have broken my wrist,' said Flutter, 'and my foot.'

'Come on,' said Katie, putting an arm around him. 'Let's get out of here.'

Flutter leaned against Katie as he hobbled back to the car and climbed gingerly into the passenger seat.

'That didn't exactly go to plan, did it?' he said as she started the car and pulled away.

'Well, at least we got a reaction, but I didn't expect him to assault one of us into the bargain.'

'D'you think he'll call the police?'

'Oh, yes. I have no doubt he'll make a complaint of some sort, and we can probably expect a visit from DI Hammer first thing tomorrow, if not tonight.'

'I think you'll find we've got a few days' grace there,' said Flutter.

'What does that mean?'

'According to Bennet, Hammer the younger is in Portugal on vacation.'

'This is, Bennet, your gangster uncle, right?'

'That's correct.'

'And he knows this how?'

'He knows because he's Bennet, and in his position it pays to know things like that.'

Katie glanced at Flutter.

'My God,' she said derisively. 'You look up to him, don't you?'

'No, Katie, I don't look up to him, but he is my uncle, and if people like Jimmy Jewle are breathing down my neck, it might help to have someone on my side who has a handle on what's going on.'

'Perhaps Robbie's right and I am getting involved with gangsters.'

Flutter stared at her in dismay.

'Katie, you know I'm not a gangster.'

'Do I?'

Flutter stewed in silence as he took a few deep breaths to control his anger. He felt Katie was the only real friend he had right now, and he really didn't want to fall out with her, but it seemed even she was now turning against him.

'I tell you what,' he said finally. 'If that's how you feel, why don't you just take me back to the office so I can collect Winston, and then I'll disappear from your life and you'll never see me again.'

'There's no need to be like that.'

'Really? We were getting on fine until detective sergeant jealous boyfriend arrived on the scene and now, suddenly, you see me as public enemy number one. How d'you expect me to feel?'

Katie kept her eyes glued to the road and said nothing, but Flutter wasn't prepared to endure an uncomfortable silence.

'Look,' he said, 'it's not my fault my family are who they are, it's not my fault I went to prison, it's not my fault a guy called Jimmy Jewle turned up on my doorstep, and it's not my fault your boyfriend doesn't like me. But, if you want to let all those things colour your opinion of me, then fine, you do that. Just don't expect me to hang around because, like you, I don't need anyone to tell me who I can, or can't, be friends with.'

They were in the car park behind her office now and Katie kept up her silence as she focused on parking the car.

'We can end this partnership immediately, if that's what you really want,' said Flutter.

Silently, Katie switched off the car and uncoupled her seat belt.

'Well? Is that what you want?' he asked.

'Of course not,' she said at last. 'I actually quite enjoy working with you. I think we make an excellent team.'

She climbed from the car and headed for the office, Flutter following in her wake.

'You're sure about that, are you?' he asked. 'Only DS Hard Case doesn't like me being part of your team, and if he's going to be around all the time there's going to be a lot of friction for you to deal with.'

'Calling him names won't help. His name is Robbie, as you well know, and once he gets to know you, I'm sure he'll like you.'

Flutter laughed.

'Yeah, right,' he said. 'I admire your optimism, Katie, but I think this time it's badly misplaced.'

They were inside the office now.

'Please, let's not fall out over this,' she said. 'I'm sure we're close to solving this case but I don't think either of us could finish it on our own, so, if you leave now the whole thing will have been a waste of time.'

'D'you really think we're close?'

'We must be. You saw Hammer's face when I suggested he was burying a body on his allotment.'

'To be honest, Katie, my attention was more focused on my foot than his face, but if that's what made him go for the cricket bat, then I reckon you must have triggered his panic button.'

'Maybe we can use the cricket bat against him.'

Flutter frowned.

'Sorry, you've lost me. How's the cricket bat going to help us?'

'If you tell the police he assaulted you with an offensive weapon they'll have to interview him and he'll have to tell them why.'

Flutter couldn't hide his smile.

'Since when has a cricket bat been an offensive weapon?'

'Of course it's an offensive weapon when it's used with intent to harm. He threatened you and then nearly broke your arm, for goodness' sake!'

'Yeah, but they won't nick him, will they? He might be retired, but he's still one of their own. He'll probably tell them we were harassing him and they'll come back and nick us. They'll probably do me for trespass because I had my foot in his door.'

'Where's your optimism?'

'It's been overshadowed by my experiences, and they tell me we'll be wasting our time.'

'Well, I think we should try. What else have we got?'

'You'll never find a copper who will be sympathetic towards us, over Hammer.'

'I think I know one and he's new to the area, so he doesn't know Hammer.'

'You mean your friend, Robbie? Ha! He definitely won't want to help.'

'At least let's speak to him,' said Katie. 'He could surprise you.'

'Yeah, and a team of footballing ferrets could win the Premier League,' said Flutter, 'but I wouldn't put my shirt on it.'

'Perhaps you should go home,' said Katie. 'Maybe the walk, and the fresh air, will neutralise your cynicism.'

'D'you know, that's probably a good idea. In fact, I think I might just take a few days to myself until the dust settles.'

'If that's what you want.'

'It's not a question of what I want, I just think it might be a good idea, at least until DS Jealous Boyfriend has calmed down a bit.'

'If you mean Robbie, I'm sure he will do what he can to help.'

'I'm afraid you're being naïve, again,' said Flutter as he clipped Winston's lead onto his collar.

'Perhaps I am, but we'll have no chance with your attitude.'

Flutter nodded.

'I don't doubt for one minute that he'd prefer to speak to you without me around, but I don't think it will make him any more helpful.'

'D'you want to bet on it?' asked Katie.

A wry smile creased Flutter's face as he paused at the door.

'I would, Katie, but if you recall, I'm trying to give up taking advantage of people. Come on Winston, it's time to go home.'

Defiantly, she poked her tongue out at him as he left the room, then reached for the phone.

'I thought you didn't want to speak to me,' said Bright when he answered her call.

'Are you busy?"

'Not really. My boss is on leave and no-one else has anything for me to do, so I'm at a bit of a loose end. It's almost as if they weren't expecting me.'

'Oh good. Something's come up and I need your help.'

'What's up with your friend, Flipper? Why can't he help'

'His name is Flutter and he can't help because someone crushed his foot and tried to break his arm so he's gone home.'

'So there is some good news,' said Bright.

'Please, Robbie, let's not start all that again. Will you help me, or not?'

'Of course I will. What's the problem?'

'Why don't you come round to my house in an hour,' she purred, 'and I'll tell you all about it.'

'Now, that sounds like a plan. I'll be there,' said Bright.

CHAPTER 31

'So let me get this straight,' said Bright doubtfully, after he'd listened to Katie's problem. 'You want me to get a search warrant, so I can dig up an allotment, because you think it's possible a body was buried there thirty-five years ago, but you're not sure. Have I got that right?'

'That's about the sum of it, yes,' said Katie.

'And it's also possible that, if I dug up the allotment, there's a good chance we'll find nothing because the skeleton might actually have totally dissolved by now.'

'Old George told Flutter the soil is quite sandy, so there's a good chance at least some bits will have survived,' said Katie.

'Old George?'

'The old man from the allotments who got talking to Flutter in the cafe.'

'And this man, Old George, is an expert in soil forensics and body decomposition, is he?'

'Don't be silly. He's just a man who keeps an allotment, but he's been doing it for fifty years and he knows his soil.'

'And he told you there's definitely a body buried under this plot.'

'No. He told Flutter that Raymond Hammer used to dig his plot every night after dark.'

'Have you actually seen this man and spoken to him?'

'No, not yet.'

'Ah, I get it. So what you really mean is Flipper would like to think there's a body buried there so he can get one over on the police.'

'His name is Flutter, and we both think it's a possibility. Don't you think digging an allotment at night is suspicious behaviour?'

'Not necessarily,' said Bright. 'Cases like that are very stressful. Maybe he really found it helped him to cope.'

'Or maybe he really was burying a body,' said Katie.

'So, this supposition of yours is all based on the word of an old man called George who claims this happened thirty-five years ago?'

'That's right, when Hammer was leading the case of the missing boy.'

'Why didn't he come forward before if he thought it was so odd?'

'He didn't come forward now, it just came out in conversation. Don't forget the boy was never seen again, and nor was Hammer's younger brother.'

'This is Hammer's younger brother who changed his name, and has never been heard of since?'

'Yes.'

Bright sighed.

'And you think this must mean DCI Hammer buried a body under his allotment.'

'Well, it all adds up, doesn't it?'

'And your soil expert said he thinks the soil is sandy enough to preserve a skeleton for hundreds of years?'

'No, all he said was that the soil is sandy. But I looked it up online; there's a good chance the skeleton won't have decomposed.'

'How good a chance?'

'Well, a possibility at any rate.'

'So it's also possible it would have decomposed.'

'Well, yes, I suppose.'

Bright sighed. His patience was wearing thin, but he was hopeful the evening would improve dramatically if he could just humour her a bit longer.

'Okay,' he said, 'let's move on from the possibility of a non-existent skeleton and on to the suspect. Now you say the person who possibly, but not definitely, may have buried this possibly non-existent body, is a retired DCI who happens to be the father of my new boss.'

'That's right.'

'The new boss I am yet to meet as he's currently on vacation in Portugal.'

'I believe that's the case.'

Bright steepled his fingers thoughtfully.

'And that's it?'

'Don't forget we've got the statements from Miss Goodie and Helen Linden.'

'Right, yes, the statements. Do they incriminate former DCI Hammer?'

'They suggest he didn't do his job properly.'

'Hmm,' said Bright.

'You don't sound convinced,' said Katie.

'What exactly is it I'm supposed to be convinced about?'

'That Hammer perverted the course of justice and buried a body.'

'But whose body?'

'Probably the missing boy, Stephen.'

'You're suggesting Hammer killed the boy?'

'I'm suggesting Hammer's younger brother killed the boy, and they buried the body in the allotment before the younger brother made his getaway.'

'But you have no proof?'

'Not as such, but it all adds up.'

'Katie, what it is you expect me to do?'

'Arrest Raymond Hammer for a start.'

'Arrest my boss's father? Now that sounds like a good way to start my new job. Arrest him on what grounds?'

'Can't you get him on suspicion?'

'Suspicion of what? All you have is supposition. You have no actual evidence.'

'Isn't that a rather pessimistic way of looking at it?'

'It's not pessimistic, Katie, it's realistic.'

'He assaulted Flutter. You could arrest him for that.'

'I think I'd like to congratulate him for that,' muttered Bright.

'I'm sorry? What was that?' asked Katie.

'I said he'd probably argue you two were harassing him and he acted in self defence.'

'You're joking.'

'What would you believe, the word of a retired police officer, with an impeccable record, or the word of a convicted criminal?'

'I'd rather hope you would believe me as I was a witness.'

Bright sighed again.

'I'm sorry, Katie, but it's not going to happen. It would be a waste of our time and resources.'

'Flutter said you'd be like this.'

'Like what?'

'He said wouldn't listen, and you'd stick up for Hammer because he's one of your own.'

'It's not that,' argued Bright. 'You've got no proof!'

Katie picked up a folder and threw it at Bright.

'Here's everything we've got,' she said, 'including the statements from Helen and Miss Goodie. If you ever want to see me again, you'd better at least read it all!'

Bright just about caught the folder before it spilled its contents all over the floor.

'Katie! This is blackmail. I don't know what's come over you recently. You've changed since this guy Flipper arrived on the scene.'

'Look, I'm just asking you to read some notes. If that's too much trouble, then that tells me all I need to know. I think it's time you left, don't you?'

Bright stared at Katie, but he could see he'd be wasting his time arguing. He got to his feet, picked up his coat, and made his way towards the door.

'And just to be clear, his name's Flutter, and there's nothing going on,' she yelled as he let himself out.

Bright stomped his way back to his car, climbed inside, tossed the folder onto the back seat, and threw his coat on top of it. He gripped the steering wheel tightly and counted to ten. This wasn't exactly going to plan. When he'd been told his transfer to Waterbury was going ahead, the plan had been to move into rented accommodation for the first couple of months while he settled into his new surroundings, and then eventually to move in with Katie.

But now this guy called Flipper, or Flutter, or whatever his stupid name was, had appeared on the scene, and suddenly everything seemed to revolve around him. And they expected Bright to take a back seat.

'Well, we'll see about that,' he muttered as he started his car, put it into gear, and roared off down the road.

'If she thinks she can push me away, she's going to find I can play that game, too. Give it a day or two and she'll be the one chasing after me.'

CHAPTER 32

It was 7pm. When Doris walked out, Flutter thought he'd be fine living alone in the big house, as he didn't intend to stay there long. He was usually a pretty happy-go-lucky sort of guy, but with only a snoring dog for company, he was becoming increasingly bored every evening, and he was lonely.

He was enjoying the investigation, especially working with Katie, but now Bright had arrived on the scene with his toxic jealousy the whole dynamic of their relationship had changed. Right now, he thought it highly unlikely they could work together for much longer.

To add to his downbeat mood, he was also starting to believe they were on an impossible mission. Even if Jewle was correct in his assertion that Hammer had deliberately botched the investigation, who was going to believe them if they couldn't come up with concrete proof? No-one, that's who. And, worst of all, whatever Jewle might have promised, he was sure there would be repercussions if they failed.

It was just as he reached this depressing conclusion that his phone rang.

'Hallo.'

'Flutter, it's Katie.'

This was a surprise.

'Oh, hi, Katie. What can I do for you?'

'You could try to cheer me up.'

Flutter thought there was nothing he'd rather do.

'Why? What's up?'

'I've just been speaking to Robbie. You were right; he won't help us.'

'I'm sorry to hear that, but I can't say I'm surprised.'

'I suppose you're going to say, I told you so.'

'I don't think me scoring cheap points at your expense is likely to cheer you up, is it? We could go out for a meal if you like, or a drink.'

'I can't tonight.'

Flutter felt as if he were in a lift which had been blasting upwards, but was now zooming back down to earth with a crash.

'Oh, okay.'

'It's my grandfather's birthday, and I promised I'd visit him this evening.'

'Your grandfather's birthday?'

'Yes. He's in a nursing home, and he doesn't get many visitors, so I can't let him down.'

'Lucky old grandad,' he muttered.

'I'm sorry?'

'I said, never mind, maybe some other time,' said Flutter, sounding far more cheery than he felt. 'Wish your grandad a happy birthday from me.'

'That's sweet of you. He won't know who you are, but I'll tell him. Will I see you in the morning?'

'I don't think so,' he said. 'You and your boyfriend need some space. I enjoy working with you but I think its best if I stay out of the way, at least until things calm down.'

'He's not my boyfr—'

'Well, he seems to think he is, Katie, and he must have a reason for that. Whatever's going on, you two need to sort it out, and I don't want to get dragged into it.'

The disappointment was obvious in her voice.

'Oh, well, if you really think it's the right thing to do.'

'We both know I'm in the way, Katie. Let's give it a few days and see what happens.'

'What about the case?'

'We can still keep working on it, but independently. Anyway, with no proof we don't have a case, do we?'

'You will come back, won't you?'

'Let's see how it goes.'

'Take care.'

'Of course I will,' said Flutter.

With one last 'Bye then,' she ended the call.

'Did you hear that, Winston? For a moment there I thought I was in with a chance, but the reality is she turned me down in favour of a geriatric.'

He looked at the old dog who snored on, blissfully unaware of his master's anguish.

'Oh, great. Even my dog doesn't want to know me,' he muttered. 'Right, that's it, then. I need a drink. I'm going out.'

CHAPTER 33

It didn't take Flutter long to get to Bennet's snooker club. He wasn't really sure why he'd come, but he justified the decision by telling himself that if he went anywhere else, it was almost certain he wouldn't know anyone, whereas here he at least he knew Bennet and a barman called Tony. Of course there was no guarantee Bennet would be around, but the enormous office above the snooker club suggested he spent a lot of time here, so it was a good possibility.

Flutter pushed his way through the door and on into the long room filled with snooker tables. To his surprise, only one table was lit up and in use by two men. The rest of the room was in semi-darkness apart from the brightly illuminated bar at the far end where a solitary man in a suit perched on a stool at the bar, his back to the room.

Flutter made his way down the length of the room and approached the man whom he now recognised as Bennet.

'Fancy some company?'

Bennet looked around in surprise, then his face broke into a smile as he recognised his nephew.

'Tony, can you pull my nephew a pint,' he called to the barman.

He pointed to the nearest bar stool.

'Help yourself,' he told Flutter.

Flutter dragged the stool closer to Bennet and settled at the bar. His pint arrived, and he took a mouthful.

'Nice pint,' he said.

Bennet tilted his head enquiringly.

'Have you come for my help?'

'Don't take it personally,' said Flutter, 'but no, thank you. I'm trying to stand on my own two feet.'

Bennet nodded his approval.

'That's highly commendable, but you know you can always ask, don't you?'

Flutter nodded his thanks. But he had no intention of asking. Ever.

'To tell the truth, I didn't expect to see you back here so soon,' said Bennet. 'Are you sure a potential private detective should mix with someone like me? It'll count as a black mark if the old bill finds out we're related.'

'As if I care,' said Flutter. 'It seems they've already got me marked down as a cert to go back inside, so one more black mark is hardly going to matter.'

'What about your partner? Will she approve? If they mark you down for your choice of company, it will count against her, too.'

'Yeah, that could be an interesting one. She had a big bust-up with her boyfriend this afternoon about not being told who she can and can't like, so it would be hypocritical if she tried to dictate the same thing to me.'

'She's got a boyfriend? Is he going to be a problem?'

'A problem in what way? If you mean is he jealous of me being with Katie, then yes, he is.'

Bennet took a sip of his beer as he considered this news.

'You didn't mention him before,' he said.

'I didn't mention him before because I got the impression he was just a friend and nothing more,' said Flutter. 'But apparently, I got that wrong. He's just arrived in town to take up a new position so he can be closer to her.'

'D'you want me to get one of my lads to have a quiet word in his ear?' said Bennet, taking another sip of his beer.

'That's probably not a good idea,' said Flutter. 'His new position is a detective sergeant at the local nick.'

Bennet almost choked on his beer, and it took a heroic effort to stop him spraying it across the bar.

'He's what?' he asked, when he recovered his poise.

'He's the new DS at Waterbury. Detective Sergeant Robbie Bright.'

'Wait a minute,' said Bennet. 'Are you telling me my nephew is setting up a private detective agency in partnership with a woman whose boyfriend is a police officer? This is outrageous. I can't have the police that close to me!'

'Hang on a minute,' said Flutter. 'You're rather getting ahead of yourself. We haven't actually spoken about setting up an agency yet.'

'But you said—'

'I said I thought starting a business with Katie was something I'd like to do.'

'Oh, I see. You want to start something with Katie, and you think if you set up a business with her it might open a few doors in other directions, so to speak,' said Bennet.

'It's not like that,' said Flutter.

'Of course it's not,' said Bennet knowingly. 'What about this jealous boyfriend? Doesn't he complicate matters?'

'Because he's a police officer, or because he doesn't like me being near Katie?'

'Either way, he's going to be a problem.'

'Yeah, we found that out this afternoon. We think we've worked out where the kid's body is buried, and we also think Hammer probably helped to bury it. Katie thought she could persuade DS Boyfriend to help us prove it. I told her she was wasting her time and his loyalty to his mates would be too strong, but she said I was wrong and that he'd help.'

'And were you wrong?'

'Of course not. He turned her down flat and wouldn't even look at the evidence we have. The thing is, the current DI Hammer is also his new boss, so even if he didn't hate me, there's no way he's going to rock the boat, is there?'

'So where is this body you think you've found?'

'Remember you told me there was a rumour Hammer had gone off his head because he went digging every night?'

'That's right, but it was only a rumour.'

'It was actually a fact. He might not have gone off his head, but he was digging the nights away,' said Flutter.

Bennet turned to face Flutter and gave him his full attention.

'And how do you know this?'

'I accidentally stumbled across someone who used to run the local allotment association. He remembers Hammer digging his plot every night. He says Hammer claimed it was the only way he could deal with the stress of running the missing boy case, but we think it was something quite different.'

'Such as?'

'Hammer had a younger brother who was a problem, right? Well, we think he was a problem because he liked little boys and girls. We think he took the little boy and murdered him.'

'Something like that could ruin a career like Hammer's,' said Bennet.

'Exactly. We think Hammer knew what his brother had done, but he didn't want anyone else to know. So, he buried the body under his allotment, sent his brother on the run, and created a diversion by focusing the investigation on an innocent teacher.'

'And you can prove this?'

'That's the problem,' said Flutter.

'So it's a hunch, then?'

'I'm sure we'll prove it if we dig up the allotment. I even know which plot was his. It's owned by a guy called Geoff Wilkins.'

'Dig up the allotment? And how are you going to do that? I have a limited knowledge of the sort of people who keep allotments, but I would imagine they take a lot of pride in their plots and wouldn't take kindly to some bloke digging them up on a hunch.'

'Katie was hoping Bright would get a search warrant.'

'And she actually thought he would?'

'She was hoping, but there's no way he's going to risk upsetting the applecart.'

'I'm not the biggest fan of the police, but I think I can understand why he might be reluctant, especially as he's the new kid in town,' said Bennet. 'It's not exactly a dead cert, is it?'

Flutter's shoulders slumped.

'I suppose not,' he said. 'I don't suppose you've got any suggestions, have you?'

'Me? I thought you didn't want my help.'

'I don't mean I want you to send troops or anything like that, but if you've got any ideas...'

'You could always hire a digger,' suggested Bennet with a grin.

Flutter gave him a dirty look.

'Ha, ha, very funny.'

'Getting involved in old police investigations, or new ones, is not something I care to do,' said Bennet. 'I don't want to solve one, and I don't want to become the subject of one. If you'd come to me in the first place, I would have told you to walk away and leave well alone. You could still do that now. You'd have to keep out of Hammer's way for a while but the dust will settle, eventually.'

Flutter finished his pint, sighed contentedly, and placed the glass on the bar.

'There's only one problem with that idea,' he said. 'I don't think Jimmy Jewle would be too impressed if I walked away. He made it quite clear failure wasn't an option.'

'Can I get you another pint?' asked Bennet.

'No thanks. I'd better get going.'

'What already? But you've only just got here.'

Flutter slipped off this stool and patted Bennet's shoulder.

'I know, but I need to think so I'd best keep a clear head. Maybe next time.'

As Flutter made his way back through the snooker tables, towards the exit, Tony the barman came to collect his empty glass.

'Is this Jimmy Jewle as bad as they say he is?' he asked Bennet.

Bennet finished his own beer and placed his glass next to Flutter's.

'No, Tony, he's much worse than that,' he said, slipping from his own stool and heading towards his office. 'And if he comes back down here, we'll have police everywhere. I can't allow that.'

CHAPTER 34

ROBBIE BRIGHT WAS BORED, and he couldn't stop thinking about Katie. It had been two days now, and he'd heard nothing from her. Worse still, no-one seemed to have any work for him to do, and right now he wished he was back in Birmingham. At least if he were there, he would have been much too busy to think about anything other than his job.

His only instructions to date had been to get out and familiarise himself with the area, and that he would be busy enough when DI Hammer returned to duty. But driving around all day wasn't Bright's idea of effective police work.

He was currently driving through the village of Pockton, a few miles east of Waterbury, and his grumbling stomach reminded him he hadn't eaten for several hours. His dashboard clock told him it was coming up to 1pm, and an inviting pub sitting alongside a picturesque village green suggested now would be a good time to stop for lunch. He parked his car and clicked on the radio.

'Hallo, control receiving,' said a bored-sounding male voice.

'This is DS Bright. Just to let you know I'll be off air for an hour while I have some lunch.'

'Sorry, who did you say?'

'DS Bright.'

'Bright? I didn't know we had a DS Bright.'

'I started on Monday.'

'Are you on secondment?'

Bright sighed. He was feeling like he was invisible.

'No, I'm not on secondment,' he replied irritably. 'I'm permanent. I transferred from Birmingham.'

'Oh, I see. Sorry, but no-one told me.'

Bright ground his teeth.

'It seems no-one has told anyone. You're the third person who did not know who I am. Don't you people get memos about staff updates?'

'Memos? No-one reads memos. They're always about safety procedures and boring crap like that so we stick them straight in the bin.'

'Well, can't you stick a bloody post-it note on the screen so everyone can read it?'

'All right, mate, keep your hair on. If you've had a bust-up with your missus, leave it at home. Don't bring it to work and take it out on me.'

'I don't have a missus.'

'Well, whatever your problem is, you want to remember we're trying to do our best here, and it doesn't help when our own people start swearing at us. We're supposed to be on the same side.'

'Well, you'd do the job better if you knew who everyone was, and then maybe your own people wouldn't feel the need to swear at you. I'm beginning to think I don't really exist at all and this is some weird sort of dream.'

'A post-it note on the screen, did you say? Now that's a good idea. In fact, it's such a good idea I'll do it right now so I don't forget. What should it say, d'you think? How about, "Watch out for a new bloke called DS Bright whose a miserable git with a short fuse?" Will that do for you?'

'Oh, put whatever you like,' said Bright wearily. 'I really don't care. Just make a note that I'm off duty for an hour.'

As Bright hung up his radio, he immediately regretted losing his temper, and as he climbed from the car, he made a mental note to apologise to the operator when he reported back for duty.

It had just started raining, so he opened the back door of the car and reached inside for his coat, uncovering the folder Katie had thrown at him as he did so. He stared at the folder as he slipped on his coat, finally deciding to take it with him. It would give him something to read as he ate his lunch.

An hour later Bright climbed back into his car, clicked on the radio, reported back for duty, and apologised to the operator. Apparently, his services were still unwanted, but this time he didn't mind. He had something he'd like to check out for himself, and it would be much easier to do it under the radar.

He found the phone number he wanted, tapped it into his mobile phone, and waited while it rang.

'Good afternoon. Is that Miss Goodie? My name's DS Bright...'

CHAPTER 35

DURING HIS TIME inside Flutter had been unceremoniously awakened by 6.00 every day, and now he was free he found it had become a habit he couldn't break. He wasn't one for lying in bed so he was usually showered, dressed and making breakfast for himself and Winston by 6.30 every morning.

This morning was no different, and he settled to eat his breakfast at 6.35 precisely. At 6.37, his mobile phone rang. He'd only had the phone a few days and hardly anyone knew his number, so he thought it was probably someone selling insurance or something similar. In the past he had always dealt with such calls by ignoring them, knowing the person on the other end would eventually hang up, but it soon became apparent whoever was on the other end had no intention of hanging up. He hadn't seen Katie for a couple of days, so, hoping it might be her, he picked it up.

'Hallo?'

'Is that Harvey Gamble?'

'Speaking.'

'This is Geoff Wilkins from the allotments.'

'It's a bit early to be calling to offer me a plot.'

'I'm not calling to offer you anything. This is more of a courtesy call. Someone dug up my plot last night, and I've called the police. The thing is, I'm going to have to mention your name as you came up here asking questions about it, and before that you were asking my dad questions.'

'Hang on a minute,' said Flutter. 'Enquiring about an allotment doesn't make me a vandal who goes around digging up vegetables.'

'I'm not saying you did it, but look at it from my point of view. You're not like the usual people who ask about joining and you were asking a lot of questions. Last night someone took a digger to my plot and all that's left is a damned great hole. Now I'm letting you know that, when I tell the police about it, they might come calling.'

Flutter thought it was unlikely the police would waste much time on what was probably a piece of mindless vandalism, but right now he was more concerned with what Geoff was implying.

'And you think you can do their job for them and frighten me into a confession, is that it?'

'Of course that's not what I mean.'

'Are you sure about that?'

There was a brief silence, followed by a long sigh.

'I'm sorry,' said Geoff wearily. 'To be honest, I don't know what I'm trying to do. I'm just so disappointed I guess I need someone to blame. I've put years into this plot and now it's ruined and I'm going to have to start over.'

For a few seconds, Flutter wondered about his future. If he was going to be suspect number one every time something happened around here, did he really want to be here? Then he glimpsed Winston's big sad eyes staring up at him, and his resolve stiffened.

'There's no need to send the police here,' he said. 'Ill come up there now and speak to them. I've got nothing to hide.'

He slammed the phone down.

'Come on Winston. It looks as though I need to clear my name for something else I didn't do.'

. . .

Flutter was disappointed to see a police car parked among the allotment holders' cars in the car park. He had been hoping to arrive first so he could see the damage for himself and at least try to convince Geoff Wilkins he had nothing to do with it. Now he was going to have to tread a little more carefully.

He could see an enormous pile of soil from the centre of Geoff's plot had been dumped alongside the small shed. Two figures were surveying the damage. They had their backs to Flutter as he approached, but he soon recognised one as the rounded figure of Geoff Wilkins. The other was a uniformed police constable.

As he got closer, Flutter slowed to a stop, and his heart sank, as he realised he knew who the police officer was from a previous encounter.

'PC Blackwell. Great. That's all I need,' he muttered.

Part of him wanted to be somewhere else as quickly as possible, but the more sensible part of him knew running wasn't an option. It would only make him look guilty and give Blackwell a ready-made excuse to arrest him. And he'd already decided they were not going to arrest him for something he hadn't done. He'd been down that route before.

He took a deep breath and strode towards the two men, Winston reluctantly in tow. As he neared them, they turned, and PC Black-well's face creased into a cruel smile.

'Well, well, well,' he said happily. 'Here's the culprit come to give himself up.'

'In your dreams, Blackwell. Why would I dig up an allotment in the middle of the night?'

'Now, there's a question,' said Blackwell. 'And I have to confess I don't know the answer yet. Maybe you had some loot stashed from a previous job.'

'Oh yeah, like what?'

'Perhaps the last few diamonds from that heist you got sent down for?'

'You read too many comic books,' said Flutter. 'I was never involved in a diamond heist.'

'No, of course you weren't, that's why you got sent down,' said Blackwell with a smug grin. Then he turned to Geoff Wilkins.

'I bet Mr Gamble didn't tell you he was the mastermind behind a jewel robbery, did he?'

'Don't show everyone what a moron you are, Blackwell,' said Flutter.

'What's that supposed to mean?'

'Work it out, man. I was seventeen, going on eighteen, when that happened. Do you really think a team of hardened crooks would let a kid mastermind a sophisticated crime like that?'

'Ah, yes,' said Blackwell. 'Good argument. But you're assuming hardened crooks think like normal people and we know that's not the case. Who knows what really drives the criminal mind?' He pointed towards the mess that was Geoff Wilkins' allotment. 'I mean, why do people carry out these acts of mindless vandalism? There must be something about your lot, because normal people don't do these things, do they?'

'My lot? What d'you mean, my lot?'

'The criminal fraternity.'

'I'm not a criminal.'

'Yes, you are. Don't you remember showing me the paperwork that proves it?'

Geoff Wilkins had been watching in bemusement, but now he felt he had to speak.

'Whatever Mr Gamble might, or might not, have done in the past,' he said. 'I don't think he had anything to do with this.'

'I beg to differ,' said Blackwell. 'Experience tells me he's exactly the sort of person we should be questioning. In fact, I think I'm going to take him in, right now.'

'On what grounds?' demanded Flutter.

'Yes, on what grounds?' echoed Wilkins.

'On the grounds he's a suspect. Just a couple of days ago he was asking questions, and now your plot has been vandalised. It's obvious there's a connection.'

He took a step towards Flutter and reached for his handcuffs.

'Don't you touch me,' said Flutter. 'You've got no right.'

'I've got every right,' said Blackwell, lunging forward.

'Step back, constable,' said a voice. 'I'll handle this. You interview the other allotment holders.'

Unseen, a detective in plain clothes had arrived on the scene, and now he assumed control.

'Bright?' said Blackwell. 'What are you doing here? This isn't a CID case.'

'I think you'll find it's Detective Sergeant Bright to you, Constable. Now, if you'd like to do as I ask.'

Blackwell glared at the newcomer.

'Yes, but—'

'If you want to argue, I can easily make that an order,' said Bright.

Muttering darkly under his breath, Blackwell slunk away.

'I'm DS Bright,' he explained to Geoff Wilkins, offering his hand. Wilkins shook hands.

'Geoff Wilkins.'

'This is your allotment, is it?' asked Bright.

'Well, it was my allotment. As you can see, now it's just a damned great hole in the ground.'

For the first time, Bright acknowledged Flutter's presence.

'Do you know this man?' he asked Wilkins.

'Mr Gamble was here a couple of days ago, enquiring about having a plot of his own. He's come here this morning to help me sort out this mess.'

Bright turned to Flutter, who was doing his best to hide his surprise.

'Is that right?' asked Bright.

'Er, yeah. I was out walking the dog when I saw the enormous pile of soil, and the police car, so I came up to see if I could help.'

Bright stared doubtfully at Flutter.

'Now there's a lucky coincidence,' he said.

'Yeah, isn't it?' said Flutter, holding Bright's gaze.

'I wonder if you'd mind giving us a minute, Mr Wilkins,' said Bright.

'What?'

'I'd like a word with Mr Gamble.'

'Yes, of course. I've got a flask in the car. I'll get it.'

Bright waited until Wilkins was out of earshot and then rounded on Flutter.

'You bloody idiot, Flipper.'

'As you know, my name's Flutter, not Flipper, and I've no idea what you're talking about.'

'Flipper, Flutter, what does it matter? It's a stupid name for a stupid person. You couldn't wait, could you?'

Flutter wasn't sure what this was about.

'I really don't know what you're on about. Wait for what?'

'A few more days and I might have been able to find a good enough reason to get a search warrant to dig this place up, but now it's probably going to be a waste of time.'

'A search warrant? Katie told me you weren't interested.'

'I wasn't at first. But after I read the statements, and had an informal chat with Miss Goodie, I approached my Superintendent. Now we've looked at the old files he's considering re-opening the case.'

'Have you told Katie?'

'Of course I haven't. It's police business.'

'Are you saying you don't trust her to keep quiet about it?'

'It's not that.'

'Having done all the donkey-work for you, don't you think she deserves to know?'

'Well, yes, but not yet. I was hoping to surprise her.'

'Oh, I think you'll do that,' said Flutter. 'Anyway, if you haven't even told her, how was I supposed to know?'

Bright was struggling to find an answer.

'Don't worry about it,' said Flutter. 'It doesn't matter. The investigation is bound to turn into a cover-up. Old Hammer has too many mates in high places to come to any harm. I expect your Superintendent is one of his best mates.'

'On the contrary. He's young, and newly appointed to the area. A new broom ready to sweep the place clean, and he doesn't care who he upsets. It's one reason I was happy to transfer down here.'

'That's fine, but you're going to be working for DI Hammer, aren't you? I don't think he's going to be impressed when he comes back home and finds out you're trying to put his dad behind bars.'

'Yes, that's one thing you probably are right about. I had planned to cross that bridge when I get to it, but it won't be a problem if you've contaminated the crime scene.'

'This has got nothing to do with me,' said Flutter.

'But of course you're bound to say that, aren't you?'

'I'm bound to say it because it's true. Besides, where would I get hold of a digger in the middle of the night?'

'A digger?'

Flutter pointed at the surrounding ground.

'You don't seriously think this has been dug by hand, do you? Open your eyes. There are wheel marks all over the place. Whoever did this used a digger, not a spade!'

Bright considered the wheel marks for a moment. He was so keen to get the better of Flutter he'd blundered in without looking, or thinking, and now he was in grave danger of being made to look a fool.

'Katie says I should trust you, but how do I know you're for real?'

'I can't help you there,' said Flutter. 'I mean, I'm bound to say I'm trustworthy, aren't I?'

'But if you didn't do this, who did?' asked Bright.

'Aren't you supposed to start with an open mind, or is there a new policy that says you have to make every crime fit me?'

'Okay, Mr Super Detective, if you didn't do it, who did?'

'How am I supposed to know? Maybe someone fancied sweetcorn for dinner last night and the shops were closed.'

'That's not funny,' said Bright.

'And I'm not laughing,' said Flutter, 'but I am getting fed up with everybody assuming everything is my fault.'

Waiting patiently by Flutter's side, Winston was becoming increasingly bored listening to these people droning on and on. Everyone seemed to have forgotten about him, and he badly needed something to sniff, just to break the boredom. He was on an extending lead which allowed him to edge, unnoticed, towards the vast pile of soil.

There was no denying he was getting slower as he grew older, but his nose was as good as ever. He soon found something suitably smelly to focus his attention upon and carefully followed the growing scent until he found the source. It was just below the surface, so he used a paw to scrape at the soil.

'Winston, what are you doing? Stop that and come here,' said Flutter, reeling in the lead.

Bright turned to where the dog had been pawing at the soil.

'What's that he's found?' he asked.

He bent down to look where the dog had been digging, then reached in his pocket for a latex glove. He slipped the glove on, reached down and gently eased an object from the soil.

'What is it?' asked Flutter.

Bright held the object up for him to see.

'I'd say it's a kid's shoe, and it looks as if it's been there for a long, long time.'

'How long?'

'That's not my field of expertise,' said Bright, 'but I reckon we're talking years, not weeks.'

Flutter moved towards the heap of soil.

'Perhaps we can find another one,' he said.

'No,' said Bright. 'Stay back! This is just the excuse I need to get permission for a search, but if we're going to do it we need to do it properly. I'll have to call in a forensic team.'

'How long will that take?'

'How long is a piece of string? Once the wheels are in motion, it will take as long as it takes, but I guarantee they'll do a much more thorough job than you or I can do. They'll turn every inch of this place over and go through it with a fine-toothed comb. If there's anything to find, they'll find it.'

'What can I do?'

'I'd go home if I were you,' said Bright.

'Oh, I see. So me and Katie do all the legwork, and now you swan in and take all the credit. What a great bloke you are.'

'This is a police case now, and we can't have civilians involved. You should know that. If you want to help, you can make a statement about what you know. Besides, if you went through this soil grain by grain would you know what you were looking for?'

'But this is our case!'

'Don't be an idiot. You have no authority, so how can it be your case? If you found a body down there, could you identify it? Do you have the weight of the law behind you to make sure the family gets justice?'

Bright's words stung Flutter, but he knew he was right

'Katie won't like this. I bet she won't be any happier than I am.'

'So you think you know her better than me, do you?'

'I know how much work she's put into this, and when she finds out—'

'I'll tell her when she needs to know,' said Bright. 'And you need to stay away from her, and keep your gangster friend Jimmy Jewle away from her, too.'

'Jewle is not my friend any more than you are, and we've already explained how he came on the scene out of nowhere. Anyway, from what I understand, it doesn't matter what you want. Katie doesn't take orders from anyone. She has her own mind.'

Bright was running out of patience. He needed Flutter out of the way so he could get on with his job. He thought perhaps a threat might have the desired effect.

'I could call Blackwell over and have him arrest you on suspicion of vandalism.'

'Ah, yes,' sneered Flutter. 'PC Blackwell, the Waterbury police bulldog. Go on, call the bullying thug over and set him on me, and then we'll have the proof that you're no better than him. That should finish your relationship with Katie.'

Bright wasn't sure what Flutter was getting at.

'What d'you mean, "no better than him"?'

'Haven't you heard? Blackwell is just a thug in uniform. He's also bent. If you don't believe me, Katie can tell you all about him.'

'How does she know what Blackwell's like?'

'He's Katie's older brother.'

'She's never mentioned an older brother.'

'He's not the sort of brother you'd want to boast about, is he? She doesn't talk about him because she finds him an embarrassment. You don't want her to think you're like him, do you?'

'You're lying.'

'About Blackwell and Katie? Why don't you ask her?'

'I will, don't you worry.'

'I'm not worried,' said Flutter. 'Katie will back me up.'

'I haven't got time for this now,' said Bright. 'I don't know about you, but I want to know if there's a body buried under here.'

'I hate to admit it, but you've finally said something we can agree on,' said Flutter. 'Because I want to know, too.'

'In that case you need to go away, and let me do my job. D'you think you can do that?'

'And there won't be a coverup?'

'Not if I have anything to do with it.'

'And you'll keep us informed?'

'I'll keep Katie informed as, and when, I can. I will not call you both.'

Flutter thought for a moment.

'I suppose that's fair enough,' he said. 'Come on, Winston, let's get out of here.'

CHAPTER 36

IT WAS two weeks since Flutter had spoken to Bright at the allotments. The first week of which had been rather like a holiday. He and Winston had spent the mornings exploring every inch of countryside within walking distance of the house, and then spent the afternoons chilling out and enjoying the garden.

He spent some time pondering the apparently fortunate timing of the attack upon Geoff Wilkins allotment. It seemed too good to be true that someone should take a digger to it, just as they were struggling to make progress and persuade Robbie Bright to get involved with the case. Obviously someone in the know had to be responsible, but who?

Flutter became convinced Bennet was involved, but when the question was put to him, he would only agree that 'yes, it was an amazing coincidence' and 'wasn't it wonderful how fate sometimes intervenes at the most opportune moment.'

In an attempt to catch him unawares, Flutter had challenged him on a second occasion. This time his response had been to deny owning a digger, or knowing how to drive one, and did Flutter seriously think someone with this much style would risk getting one of his suits muddy?

During that peaceful week Flutter had also had plenty of time to consider the house, and the offer Jewle had made, and what he was going to do about it. Having thought long and hard, he finally decided that once the month was up, he would tell Jewle he really didn't want it. Yes, it was worth a fortune, but they had purchased it through dubious means and he was sure keeping it would make Jewle an ever-present thorn in his side, whatever he might have promised.

Having come to this momentous decision, Flutter set about enjoying what time he had left at the big house, soaking up the peace he found in the enormous garden. But as the second week wore on he soon began to realise there was only so much peace he could take, and that he wasn't best suited to life as a solitary animal. He needed company, and he needed a purpose, and he badly missed working with Katie. On several occasions he had thought about calling her and then allowed stubbornness to persuade him she was the one who should call him.

So, for two weeks, he'd heard nothing about what was going on at the allotments, but just this morning an angry Jimmy Jewle had called and his peace had been rudely shattered. The month was nearly up and Jewle wanted news. He particularly wanted to know why police officers had visited his sister-in-law, when he'd specifically said the police couldn't be trusted and shouldn't be involved.

So now Flutter had no choice but to call Katie and find out what was going on.

'Katie Donald.'

'Hello, Katie. It's Flutter.'

'Oh, hello.'

'I thought you might have called.'

'Why would I? Robbie told me you said you were going to go away and let us get on with our lives.'

Flutter sighed.

'I should have known he'd twist my words. What actually happened was he said I should go away and let the police get on with their jobs, which is what I did. I said nothing about going away, I just went home as he asked, and that's where I've been for the past two weeks.'

'You could have called me,' said Katie.

'I thought about it a few times, but I said I was going to give you some space to allow you could sort things out with Robbie.'

'It's not like you to call him by his proper name.'

'Yeah, well, what's the good of calling people names? It's childish, isn't it?'

'Do I detect a hint of maturity there?'

'I can be grown up when I want to be.'

'You should do it more often, you might find people like it.'

'So, have you and Robbie sorted things out?'

'Yes, we have.'

'So what does that mean, exactly?'

'Does it matter?'

'It might, if we're going to work together again.'

'Robbie and I are friends, but that's all.'

'I thought he transferred down here so he could move in with you.'

'Yes, he thought so, too. I don't know where he got that idea from.'

'But you're still speaking?'

'Oh yes. He's got to speak to me to let me know what's happening with the case.'

'Ah, yeah, about that. Jewle has called. He's heard about the police digging up the allotment, and he wants to know what's going on.'

'Did he know about it because one of his guys drove the digger?'

'He knows because the police went to see his sister-in-law and told her they were re-opening the case.'

'So who drove the digger? It wasn't you, was it?'

'Not guilty,' said Flutter. 'My money's on Bennet. I remember telling him about it. He didn't drive the digger himself, but I'm sure he arranged it.'

'Why would he do that? Did you ask him?'

'No, I didn't ask. It's because we're family. He feels obliged to help me when he can.'

'Are you happy about that?'

'No, not really. I told him I wanted to stand on my own two feet. I think he respects that, but he's trying to keep Jewle as far away as possible.'

'Coming back to Jewle, what did you tell him?'

'What could I tell him? I had to admit the police had taken over.'

'What did he say about that?'

'He's not happy. I've told him it's going to be okay, and they want to solve it as much as we do, but he's convinced it'll just be a coverup. I was hoping you might know something so I can update him.'

'You were there when the shoe was found, weren't you?'

'Yeah, Winston found it.'

'Well, they now have a pair of boy's shoes, which they think are a match for the pair Stephen was wearing the day he disappeared. They've also found a man's shoe—'

'A man's? Blimey, who owns that?'

'Hang on, there's more. Unfortunately, we were wrong about skeletons being preserved intact, but they have found what they believe are human bone fragments.'

'Can they get DNA from them?'

'Possibly, but it doesn't really matter because they've also found teeth.'

'Teeth?'

'Apparently teeth are more resilient than bones, and the good news is they can extract DNA from teeth.'

'So they should be able to tell if it's Stephen.'

'It's not just Stephen. Apparently there are adult teeth as well. They're waiting on test results to confirm it, but the working theory is that they could have belonged to Terry Harrison.'

'Does that mean he didn't escape and old man Hammer murdered him too?'

'That's what they think. The old man's been arrested and they're pretty sure they'll get a confession if his DNA matches the DNA from the teeth.'

'So, did the brother kill Stephen, or did Hammer?'

'Ah, now that's the question, and the only person who knows the answer is old man Hammer.'

'But he can say whatever he wants. No-one can prove otherwise, can they?'

'Yes, we might never know what really happened to Stephen, but at least now his mother will get some sort of closure.'

'So, we were on the right track,' said Flutter.

'You really didn't know any of this?'

'I'm an ex-con, Katie, they're hardly going to share stuff with me, are they?'

'No, I suppose not. I don't see you that way so I hadn't thought of it like that.'

'That's nice to know,' he said. 'How do you see me?'

'I see you as a trusted friend.'

'Really? I don't think anyone's called me a trusted friend before.'

'And a colleague I enjoyed working with.'

'It doesn't have to be in the past, you know.'

'I'm sorry?'

'We could always do some more work together,' said Flutter. 'If you wanted to.'

'It is something I've always wanted to do,' said Katie 'And it was fun.'

'I miss working with you.'

'You do?'

'Yeah. It's the best job I've ever had.'

'Is it actually called a job if you don't get paid for doing it?'

'But it won't always be like that,' he said. 'Anyway, I don't think I'm the right person to answer that question. It's the only proper job I've had in over ten years, but I mean it when I say I've enjoyed it.'

'But what if we get no more work?'

'Yeah, that could happen but, on the other hand, we might get loads. Come on, Katie, where's that optimism you told me I needed to have? We'll never know if we don't try.'

'I suppose it wouldn't hurt to have a go.'

'Great! I can start on Monday.'

EPILOGUE

FORENSIC EXAMINATION and DNA testing subsequently proved the teeth found were those of Stephen Bowles and Terry Harrison.

Faced with a growing mountain of evidence against him, Raymond Hammer agreed to co-operate in exchange for a reduced sentence. Subsequently, he was charged with the murder of Terry Harrison. His story that Harrison had murdered Stephen Bowles and that he, Raymond, had only hidden the boy's body was accepted, and no further charges were made.

Geoff Wilkins has now restored his allotment to its former glory, and he and his father now have an incredible story to share with anyone who is prepared to listen.

DI Sebastian "Sledge" Hammer returned from vacation just in time to see his father charged with murder. He now holds the unfortunate DS Robbie Bright, a man called Harvey Gamble (aka Flutter), and a local journalist called Katie Donald responsible for the destruction of his father's once unsullied reputation.

Katie and Flutter have now begun working together as Donald & Gamble, private investigators.

The story will continue...

NEXT BOOK IN THIS SERIES

If you don't know how things are supposed to be, how can you know when they're not?

Katie Donald formed an unlikely partnership with Flutter Gamble after he was released from prison. Now they would love the chance to prove themselves as private investigators so, when an old friend asks for help, Flutter thinks this could be the case they've been waiting for. But solving a mystery which occurred over 60 years ago takes more than simple enthusiasm and its only Katie's training as a journalist that might enable them to find an answer, (even if it's not the one they were expecting!)

Meanwhile, Flutter finds he now has a probation supervisor. This is a shock as he's sure probation was never mentioned when he was released from prison. But then paying attention to rules has never been his strong point so it's quite possible they told him, but he missed that bit.

Any lingering doubts Flutter might have soon become irrelevant when he finds out who has been appointed to supervise him. The chance to rekindle an old romance is something he just can't resist. Katie has her suspicions about the unusual probation set-up, but even with a crystal ball she could never have predicted what was about to happen next.

The problem is, if you don't listen when things are explained to you, you won't know how things are supposed to be. And then it's easy to find yourself at cross purposes, as Flutter discovers when the police come hammering on his door with a search warrant.

It seems, not for the first time in his life, Flutter is being framed for a crime he didn't commit.

Click here to learn more

DID YOU ENJOY THIS BOOK?

You can make a big difference

I hope you have enjoyed reading this book. Reviews are one of the most powerful tools in any authors arsenal when it comes to getting attention for books, and I'm no different. A full page ad in a daily newspaper would be great, but that's just a tad beyond my budget!

But I do have something equally powerful (probably more so), and that's a growing bunch of loyal readers.

Honest reviews of my books help to bring them to the attention of new readers who will, hopefully, go on to join this growing band.

If you've enjoyed this book and you can spare a few minutes, why not leave a review? It doesn't have to be War and Peace, just a few words will do!

Click here if you'd like to help

ABOUT THE AUTHOR

Having spent most of his life trying to be the person everyone else wanted him to be, P.F. (Peter) Ford was a late starter when it came to writing. Having tried many years ago (before the advent of self-published ebooks) and been turned down by every publisher he approached, it was a case of being told 'now will you accept you can't write and get back to work'.

But then a few years ago, having been unhappy for over 50 years of his life, Peter decided he had no intention of carrying on that way. Fast forward a few years and you find a man transformed. Having found a partner (now wife) who believes dreamers should be encouraged and not denied, he first wrote (under the name Peter Ford) and published some short reports and a couple of books about the life changing benefits of positive thinking.

Now, happily settled in Wales, and no longer constrained by the idea of having to keep everyone else happy, Peter is blissfully happy being himself, sharing his life with wife Mary and their three dogs, and living his dream writing fiction.

You can follow P.F. Ford here:
https://www.pfford.com

Printed in Great Britain
by Amazon